The female statue, no more
than 20 inches high, held a stillness about
Her. This female was standing her ground. *What have
you seen?* I wanted to ask her. *Do you stand for all the women
whose voices have been silenced?* I wondered what would happen
if I stayed behind through the dark night with Her, if a veil
would be lifted between the known world and the unknown.
On this day that began with giddy lightness between me
and my dear friend, the tides of mystery rushed in to fill
me with questions. More than ever before, the Black
Madonna made her way into my soul—like a long
curling root seeking nourishment and
water from the soil.

Miriam's Dive

DEBORAH E. BOYLE

Debsriverbooks:
Gaithersburg, Maryland
Cape Elizabeth, Maine

Miriam's Dive

First Printing, 2020
ISBN-978-0-578-73830-7

Cover and Chapter Design by MarkGelotte.com

PROLOGUE

Miriam: Veneux D'Eau, France

AUGUST 2001

I awakened as the sky was beginning to lighten. It filtered through the sheer curtains that billowed like sails in front of the open windows. *Something is wrong,* I thought, wincing as the aftermath of last night's alcohol hammered through my head. I squeezed my eyes shut tight as I knew by the slant of light that it was too early to be up. But my sense that something was wrong was growing. My heart pounded in rhythm with my head as my thoughts circulated: *Had I heard a noise? Or was I still dreaming? There.* I heard it again and this time I was sure; someone was stirring and had just closed the side door to the house.

Odile! The thought came to me, unbidden. Odile, the daughter of my childhood friend Bernadette, had joined us on a picnic near the river last summer. She'd remained on the blanket in her bathing suit as Dette and I swam blissfully in the deep water. "She refused to learn to swim after that time she almost drowned when she was three years old," Dette said, rolling her eyes. It was not the first time I'd recognized my friend's disappointment in her daughter. But for me, Odile was a rare muse. Yesterday she'd left her school in Paris and had unexpectedly shown up at her mother's country home in Veneux D'Eaux.

Now, shifting slowly between sleep and wakefulness, I frowned as I tried to discern whether I really had heard soft sobbing during the night or if it had been part of my overwrought imagination. My childhood dream about the foggy shape that seemed to be a woman crying had plagued me again last night. Odile's room was next to mine in Dette's house; had she been crying? A mixture of fear and guilt pressed me to move. Rising out of bed, I quickly pulled on shorts, a faded blue tee shirt and sneakers. I walked by the tiny statue of a Black Madonna on the nightstand and tiptoed over to Odile's door. Her room was empty, the bedcovers thrown carelessly aside. I moved through the dark hall to the door with the quiet stealth of a panther so as not to awaken Dette.

Odile is still a child. This thought came to me as I opened the side door and slid out into the street. The early morning air was full of pearly moisture that clung to the fine strands of my hair, lifting it en masse as I trotted through the village. I barely noticed the scent of freshly baked bread and buttery croissants coming from the bakery because in the distance I could see the running figure of Odile. What chilled me was that she was still in her pale nightgown. I offered up a silent prayer of thanks for the many hours of indoor swimming I'd done through the long New England winters that gave me the endurance to keep her in sight. We were now well beyond the outskirts of the village and beginning the long incline into the woods and up to the hills beyond. Was she running to her beloved waterfall? It had rained heavily during the night and the mossy ground near it would be soaked. And slick. If she slipped and tumbled into the churning water – my heart clutched – Odile did not know how to swim.

CHAPTER 1

Miriam: Washington, D.C.

MARCH 2001

I've always walked straight into the ocean. No stepping in tentatively inch by inch for me. This may not seem remarkable, except that it's not in my nature to be bold. Also, I grew up in Maine. The water is icy cold there even in high summer. Every year as soon as school was out my Granny Meg and I drove from our paper mill town in the deep woods all the way to the Maine coast to our beloved Down East. There, I'd walk straight into the water until it reached my shoulders giving myself a delicious, icy shock. Then I'd swim. Not for long; a little goes a long way in water that cold.

I've loved to swim ever since I was a little girl. Maybe this was because neither of my parents nor any of my close relatives had ever learned to swim. They hunted, gardened, split wood, and sewed their own clothes, but swimming was a joy that was mine alone and I reveled in it.

But now I lived and worked in Washington, D. C. That March night moonlight poured through my bedroom window and onto my face. One of the truths of my life is that for a long time moonlight has felt like the sister I never had. There's a quality of her milky light that soothes something in me. So, when her light awakened me that night I smiled and moved deeper under the covers, drifting back to sleep. Perhaps it was the moon's silken whisper that called to me as I dreamt yet again of a shadowy figure moving toward me. It was a powerful image and it filled me with confusion. A woman – wearing a flowing skirt of black silk so fine the light glancing off it reflected a spectrum of flame, cobalt, and emerald – danced nearby as if her feet were wings. The foggy shadow reached forward and seemed to beckon to me. Just as I took a tentative step toward the dark shape, a sword thrust out. The light glinting off the silver blade blinded me, causing me to stumble and lose my sense of direction...

I awakened with a start. *Stop it!* I chided myself as I rubbed sleep from my eyes and arose from my bed. *Dreams don't portend anything!* I was glad there was no one there to notice me tossing my head to dispel the sense of unease I felt.

I was perplexed at the dichotomy between this recurrent childhood dream and my pragmatic New England self. I dimly realized that to follow the compelling figure in the dream meant upending my life. But that meant risk and that was anathema to me. As a scientist trained in botany I'd worked hard to suppress the fanciful vein of my nature. I disliked dwelling in the land of possibility; I much preferred the solidity of order and hard evidence.

And yet, something had called me to complete a second Master's degree, this one in the visual arts. My thesis had centered on the golden illuminations found in art throughout the ages. I combined my knowledge of golden illuminations with the use of copper plates to create my own unique designs. Hadn't I done that precisely because there was a longing in me that hard science couldn't fill?

I opened the tall windows to let in the sweet air with its scent of cherry blossoms. For a moment I leaned against the window frame as I thought about my partner Seth. A few nights ago we'd been seated across from one another in Zaytinya, our favorite D. C. restaurant, and had come to an impasse: I wanted a child and he did not. He had two children from a previous marriage and didn't want another.

Seth had said, "Please, Miriam, let's not disrupt what we have."

"But giving birth to a child will bring me, I mean bring us" – I amended quickly – "such *happiness*." This longing for a child was as close to desperation as I ever wanted to feel.

He waited a beat before asking me, "Aren't we happy?"

The question lingered in the air around us. I knew we wouldn't talk about it again unless I brought it up. Seth hated conflict unless it was in a courtroom where he was in control. He rarely displayed raw emotion; it's what made him a good lawyer. It had taken him years to cry out openly when we made love. Lately those cries had died down again.

He was right, of course, that with our common interest in art, music, and history, all so readily available near our condo in Washington, D. C., we shared a lot. More than some couples had, I knew that. Part of me said I should be content; but another part that I was secretly ashamed of, wanted more.

I shoved these thoughts aside, glancing at the mirror's reflection of my light gray eyes and curly chestnut hair as I moved to my closet and pulled out khaki pants and a green top. Busy with 10-hour work-days containing a full docket of teaching as well as trying to cram in time to work on my own art, I had arranged my life in an orderly fashion and found comfort in its predictability. Granny Meg had taught me that. She would be proud of me, for now, some 15 years since I left her home to be the first woman in the family to attend college, this is still how I lived. No-nonsense Granny who had raised me in her home in Maine after my parents were gone. She lived now only in my memories.

That morning the kitchen was alive with sunlight; it backlit a giant spiderweb clinging to the window. *Oh my, spider, you've had a busy night*, I murmured softly. I was still aware of the quiver of possibility that had tickled me earlier but chose to focus instead on the welcome smell of Seth's specialty coffee. Steady as a rock, he held a solid place in my life. It's just – here, my thoughts stumbled. I sighed and moved toward the coffee he always made before leaving for work.

I snapped on the tiny kitchen television and picked up a mug, smiling at the words of Alice Longworth Roosevelt scripted there in dark letters: *If you haven't got anything nice to say about anybody, come and sit by me.* I giggled, thinking of Bernadette who'd given me the mug. My childhood friendship with Dette had been a private joy, the two of us always prancing around together, oblivious to the woes of the adult world. The sound of my own voice raised in laughter startled me. I could not remember the last time I had laughed out loud.

Dette would have left Seth long ago I thought with unhappy recognition. Then another thought, this one causing my heart to leap, followed closely behind. *Why not visit her this summer?* She'd been begging me to visit for ages. Dette – now a vivacious, wildly successful designer of boldly printed fabrics in France – with her flawless skin, huge brown eyes, and petite stature. Visiting Dette and her daughter, Odile, in northern France seemed like the best idea I'd had in a long time.

Suddenly, the keening wail of music caused me to move toward the television as images of snow-covered mountains and the words 'Bamiyan, Afghanistan' scrolled across the bottom of the screen. Slowly I took in what the news report was about. *Holy Mary, Mother of God. They've blown up the two ancient Buddhas of Bamiyan.* Dismayed, I slumped in my chair. *Sacred treasures of art even to the nonreligious. Deliberately blown them up.*

Stealth, our Maine Coon cat, always attuned to me, poked her face into my lap. "Oh kitty," I said as I lifted her up and rubbed her silky fur, "the world can be a grave and terrible place." Stealth yawned widely as I held her close. I glanced at the clock and realized I didn't have time to call Dette and if I didn't hurry I'd be late for work. That would be a big mistake on the very day my boss planned to announce who would be the artist to compete in the prestigious international art competition, the *Opus Magnum.*

"It will probably be Harriet," I murmured to myself as I rushed out the door. "She wins goddamn everything."

CHAPTER 2

Miriam: Washington, D. C.

MARCH 2001

I'm an artist who works in metals. Sounds simple, but it's not. That year far too much of my energy had gone to my teaching job at the D. C. Art Academy. I taught *Techniques of Light and Shading, Introduction to Sketching, and Finding Place: Romanticism to Utopic Abstraction.* I loved my students and watching them develop their latent talent always made me smile. But the pull to spend more time creating my own art was clawing at me even before I heard about the destruction of the Buddhas. Ancient art, huge and powerful – what was the point of blasting it to smithereens? It both saddened me and pissed me off. More than that, it pulled from me an ineffable longing that let me know I needed to return to my own work, bills be damned.

Seth was also on my mind as I drove to work that day. We'd met when he'd given a lecture at the Academy on the legal rights of artists and their work. Tall and thin, I liked the unassuming way he presented himself. We grew closer each time we shared in the musical, theater and museum offerings of Washington. Later, when he took me to Missouri to meet his family, I knew instantly his mother didn't think I was good enough for him. She'd looked me up and down and turned away. But I'd touched her shoulder and stuck my hand out. Her hand in mine was cool and limp. I repressed the urge to wipe my hands on my chinos. Seth thought I was plenty good enough for him, who cared what she thought?

I shuddered at the memory of her and moved quickly into the Academy. As soon as I entered the hallway of my office, I saw my colleague Rafe. All six feet three inches of lean muscle stood waiting by the locked door. Dressed in wrinkled cotton trousers, his neon yellow silk shirt was sliced by the macramé belt some pretty student had no doubt crafted for him.

"What?" he shrugged, understanding my critique of his shirt without my saying a word. "Silk breathes."

"Ok, Rafe-e-o, if you say so," I said. He laughed.

He's not just any colleague. Back in my younger and less wise days when I was new to the job, Rafe took me in. Another one on his charm bracelet, but I only realized that after he'd tossed me out when his eye fell on someone younger and prettier. I nodded at him as I unlocked the door. I knew he was waiting for my undivided attention. As soon as I'd deposited my leather catchall of students' work on the wooden slab of my desk and looked up at him, he began.

"Miriam," I heard the usual self-assurance in his voice but something else, too. I glanced at his face noticing his cleft chin, though it no longer drew me. He was surprisingly nonchalant about his looks, though he was fully aware of his charms, knew just how to fine-tune them when he wanted to. Certainly, the coeds followed him around like drooling puppies. I felt a moment's regret that I'd once done the same. Pushing away that thought, I crossed my arms and lifted one eyebrow. He took the cue.

"Miriam," he began again, and this time I clearly heard it: hesitation.

Curious, I waited.

"I have news for you: the Academy's entrant for the *Opus Magnum* has been chosen."

Huh? I thought. Since when is Rafe handing out news of the entrant? Normally that's done by the department chair and Rafe lost that title long ago courtesy of one too many affairs with a married professor's wife. Could it be one of the puppies?

"I think it's something you'll like." I looked across the narrow room at him.

"Hit me," I said, pushing books and papers aside as I lifted myself up onto the top of my desk.

"You know the copper work you did in graduate school?"

"I do." My mind flitted to copper sheets of pressed shapes and swirling paint colors. Animal figures erupting from the hammered copper in spirals of color and motion. How could I not remember that time when joy was mine in every minute? When creating art had seemed like me making magic happen? When I'd fallen in love with a much older man? Or tumbled deeply inside love's mirage, more likely. He leaned close, put one hand on my wrist. "Careful there, Rafe," I said shooting him a look and briefly recalling Dette's lack of surprise when I'd tearfully confided Rafe's betrayal. Like me, Rafe was an artist; unlike me, he was famous. Mostly, though not always, for his art. I pushed myself back further on my desk, flitted away his hand.

"Just be straight, got it?" I said.

He looked at me. "Got it. What a fool I was."

I laughed. "Oh, Rafe, stop," I said dismissing him with a wave of my hand. "What's the news?"

He waited a beat then said, "I know who will be the Academy's entrant in the *Opus Magnum*. It will be announced at the faculty meeting later today." Briefly, I was annoyed that Thom Sessman, the chair of our department, would confide in Rafe, even though he was the most senior staff member after Thom. I stuffed my pique deep inside and kept my face neutral as I asked, "Why are you the one telling me?" A titch of embarrassment flitted across his face and then I understood. Thom hadn't planned on Rafe's spilling the beans; he'd gone ahead and told me despite protocol. I'd bet my last dollar that Rafe, a powerful figure in the art world, had made a recommendation to Thom. Politics being what they are, his nod toward me would hold weight.

He ignored my question and continued, "*You* have been chosen to be the entrant representing the D. C. Art Academy in the *Opus Magnum*! Because this year guess what the focus of the grand art competition is?" He was tantalizing me, and he knew it as he flashed his megawatt smile.

I kept my face a mask. I'd earned the poise I now commanded and refused to relinquish it to him.

Overlooking my silence, he said, "This year the medium is – drumroll please – work in metals: silver, gold, and copper." I heard my intake of breath. "They want a new, original piece. And the focus is – another drumroll please – female icons!" he finished in triumph as my mouth opened in surprise.

"Silver-eyed enchantress, I believe this one is yours to claim."

"Rafe," I said, "I asked you to be straight with me."

"Christ, Miriam, I *am* being serious," he said. "It's positively uncanny how this is tailored to you! You are incredibly talented. Do you know the only one who doesn't fully believe it?"

"Me."

"Bingo."

I knew this was the break I needed, but I struggled to believe it. My disbelief mingled with the detritus of our failed relationship. *Is he telling me the truth or setting me up for another fall? Why would he recommend me?*

I sighed, "Come on, Rafe, why me, really? You have your puppies; surely you recommended one of them."

A muscle tightened in his face. "Miriam," he said, his voice tense,

"They don't have one-one thousandth of the talent you have. You piss me off, you know that?" I crossed my arms against my chest willing myself not to look at him.

"I thought that with this news your face would finally show emotion. But no, same old Miriam." He let the taunt hang in the air where it banged around inside me. He knew more about my inner life than a lot of people, knew about my Catholic upbringing, the loss of my parents at a young age. He'd helped me begin to understand how Catholicism had shaped me as a child. He'd studied the art of the Church and as I'd listened to him, a seed was planted: art could open up the world to me. I was hooked.

After we broke up, I was glad that I'd never confided in him about the Black Madonna figure on my mother's nightstand that I'd looked at so longingly on the day she died. In truth, that I'd grabbed before Granny could toss it or pack it away. I don't remember much about that eviscerating day, except that as my world disintegrated I held that little statue in my hand so tightly all my fingers turned white. No one could uncurl my fingers and take it from me.

During the months I was with Rafe he took care to breathe on the embers of art within me. Unfortunately, if you're not careful, fire burns. And for the first time in my life I wasn't careful. I swam headlong into the joy of his attentions. We managed to work together collegially now, but I was always on my guard around him.

"I'm interested," I said coolly. "But now I'll be straight. Does Thom require that you work on the project with me?"

I frowned when I heard him laugh before he answered, "No. But I'd be glad to offer any support you need." *Lord of condescension, here you are.* I hesitated before I spoke. He was talented and well known. The *Opus Magnum* was a very big deal; a win could set in motion huge opportunities for me. For one thing, I needed to secure tenure. And I needed the prize money. I could barely let myself imagine the thrill of how my world would change if I gained financial security.

The *Opus Magnum* competition was international and the rivalry was fierce. I could use Rafe's professional connections and support, and we both knew it. "Perhaps," I said coolly. "I'll let you know once the entrant is actually announced." If I were to be the Academy's entrant, perhaps I'd give him a call when my perpetual self-doubt raised its ugly head, but I determined then and there that I would not give him any details of the art piece itself.

"Understood," he said curtly. I refused to let the note of disappointment I heard in his voice sway me. "The saintly Miriam doesn't need assistance."

"I'm no saint, Rafe. Just one very human woman."

"One very lovely woman," he murmured.

"Rafe, stop!" I said, shaking my head at his irrepressible flirtatiousness. "As you know I'm quite settled with Seth," I said, recognizing in that moment that it might no longer be true. Not so long ago, Seth had provided welcome, cooling relief after the heat of my time with Rafe. But things had changed. "Not to mention," I rushed ahead, "that you're with..." I waved one hand in the air, unable to come up with the name of his latest conquest. "What's-her-name."

"We broke up."

"Ah," I said sending her a silent message of sympathy. "Thus, the offering to me."

"Oh, for Chrissakes, Miriam! It's not like that. Honest to God you can be such a tight-ass. Look, it's simple; the competition is now. Thom and I believe you are the one to win it for the Academy. We sorely need a success to keep the Academy funded. And I'm guessing you could use the half-million-dollar prize money, right?"

I flushed. He had no business bringing that up. Then his voice softened. "Besides, you bring such transcendence to your work." My breath caught in my throat as I heard his words. I looked at him and for just a second our eyes sealed in a remembered place.

When I dropped my gaze he continued, his voice sharp again. “Miriam! What the hell is there to think about?”

CHAPTER 3

Miriam: Washington, D.C.

MARCH 2001

For the first time ever, I left work early that day. I was thrilled when Thom confirmed in the afternoon staff meeting that I was, indeed, the Academy's entrant in the *Opus Magnum*. As I drove home, I was struck by the synchronicity of my becoming the art entrant on the very day I'd been dreaming about visiting Dette, the childhood friend with whom I'd made mud pies, chased lightning bugs, and slept in a pup tent. Now I had a sabbatical to work on a major art work to be entered in an international art competition. I could do this in Europe where Dette now lived! I dashed into the house to call her.

"Woman, how the hell are you?" Dette's strong, husky voice rushed out over the airwaves from France and into my ear.

"Oh, Dette." Hearing her voice made me realize how much I'd missed her. "Just this morning I was thinking about you when I picked up that blue mug you made me."

"That old thing? I can't believe you still have it. Lord, girl, I need to make you another one! What color would you like?"

Laughing, I said, "No, that's alright. I'd rather spend time with you than having you make me a new one. Besides, you've probably lost the sculptor's touch with all the men you've been running ragged."

"Ha! François just left me." Dette's voice wavered, quickly rebounded. "Entirely his loss, I might add!"

"You've got that right! And the timing is fortuitous. I've decided to accept your invitation. I am coming to see you. Soon!" In fact, I hadn't quite decided whether I should go, but hearing Dette's voice settled something in my mind, like a drawer sliding into place.

"Hold on there, girl, what's this? You're really coming to France?"

"Yes, yes," I said, my words now tumbling over themselves. "I've just won a scholarship, no, wait, not a scholarship, it's a competition and I'll have to work really hard –"

"Damn! It's about time!"

"I know, I'm sorry, it's just –"

"Oh, stop apologizing for Chrissake! You're coming, that's all that matters. Today?" Dette asked, laughing, hopeful.

"Well, *ma très bonne amie*, I do need to buy a ticket."

"So, buy it already! What on earth is stopping you?"

"Well, only a thousand things. But not anymore. I'll leave in early June after the end of the semester here, how does that sound?"

"*Fantastique!* Ooh, I'd better go buy some new shoes to wear when you arrive. Can't have you thinking I've become your slovenly friend."

"I hardly think that will be an issue. In fact, the other way around seems more likely."

"Nonsense, *chérie*. You just wait until you get to *La Belle France*. Ooh, and I have some vintage shoes that will fit you. We'll have you dressed so chic no one will recognize you back in the U.S.A. If you do go back, that is. Ha!"

"Oh, Dette, I've missed you." I thought back to the last time I was in Paris, nearly six years ago. Dette and I had joined a group of her friends one evening. As we entered the dark smoky bar, I squirmed.

Women chatted together, flirted, and tossed their hair, each one dressed in a tight skirt or jeans and a shimmering top. I was a drab wren compared to these iridescent peacocks; Parisian women are so effortlessly elegant. Two days later I saw Marianne, to whom I'd been introduced in the bar, on the street. She glided by me without a word.

"Listen, Dette, I got some amazing news today," I said.

"*Vraiment?* Something to do with the rave reviews you got on your copper wall art?"

"Yes. Well, and no," I said. I twirled a strand of hair around my finger, then bit the inside of my cheek, a habit I've been half-seriously trying to break for decades. "My boss – unbelievably – has nominated me to be the Academy's artist entry in this year's *Opus Magnum.*

"*C'est formidable!* Tell me more!"

"Well, you know it's the international *art* competition, yes? You need to be nominated by a juried school of art. The entrants must create at least one completely new art piece. It's a huge honor to be nominated."

"*C'est fantastique,*" she said with growing excitement in her voice. "Your boss must be a damn smart guy."

"Thanks. He is. It doesn't seem real yet. But you're right; I'm pretty sure my metals work in my Master's in Fine Arts program must be why he thought of me now."

"A smart man," she mused. She paused a beat. "Is he married?"

"You haven't changed," I said, laughing again. "And yes, he is."

"Happily? I bet I've conquered lesser foes."

"Stop!" We were yin and yang. She, fearless; me, anxiety enthroned. I've often wondered if that was the cement of our bond.

"And, uh, Miriam..."

"Yes?" I noticed the hesitation in her voice and I stopped pacing.

"When you get here, there's something I need to talk with you about. I've been meaning to do it for quite some time."

I briefly wondered if it was about Odile, her spirited teenage daughter, but I didn't want to press her. Time for that after I arrived in France. I've known Odile since she was born; Dette had honored me by asking me to be her godmother. She and Dette visited me in the States every year or two, but it had been years since I'd seen Dette in the country she's made her own.

"Well, how about a clue, huh?"

"We'll talk when you get here, ok? Call me with your flight infomation. I'll be waiting with basted breath."

"With bated breath, I think you mean," I said, giggling.

"Garlic breath, whatever."

"See you soon!"

Over the next few weeks, I swam between excitement and anxiety. I wrestled with what to tell Seth, chewing on the tip of one finger then another, before reminding myself to stop. I wrapped up my courses, I packed. I was not unflappable, I knew that. Between the time I called Dette and the moment I boarded the plane I imagined every calamity that could befall a traveler - from missing my flight, to the plane crashing, to being the victim of a crime on the side streets of Paris. And yet, in between and around these fears, I was relieved to feel so deeply about something. I felt excitement sparkling through me - a new art project! And seeing Dette! And Odile!

I tried to ignore the threads of worry about my friendship with Dette that also wound their way inside me – in France would we be able to recreate the closeness we'd felt in the past? Would she like my fuller, un-straightened hair? I relaxed into a giggle when I thought about how she would frown at my bland clothes and take such matters into her own hands. I could see us strolling down the wide boulevards of Paris, laughing, but me knowing the men's glances were for her, the impossibly chic one. I imagined quiet chats over a glass of red. I probably wouldn't order the 'correct' wine and Dette would wink and wave her hand at the waiter and presto! he'd arrive with just the right bottle. I pushed these fears aside because, really, what was the point in wasting the energy? And I knew that with Dette even things I normally dislike, such as shopping, would take on a sense of fun.

Early one morning I called Odile. Despite the physical distance, we were tight. The past couple of years she'd visited me in Washington without her mother and we'd become even closer. But I'd sensed something unsettled about her during our last phone call, a wince in her voice that she repeatedly denied. And she was unusually curt with me when I called to tell her I was coming to Paris. I let it ride; I would spend time with her in Paris and hear what was troubling her.

Finally, the day of my evening flight to Paris arrived. Seth sat on our bed as I was packing, surveying me with his cool blue eyes. He took my hand and slipped a green slag perfume bottle into my hand saying, "Here you are, Babe. A matched set." I saw at once that it was the same vintage as the miniature glass vial I'd inherited from my mother. The only difference was the design on the tiny brass twist on the top. I opened it and breathed in its scent, shutting my eyes as memories closed my throat. She'd left me so long ago when I was still finding my way through childhood.

"Where –" I began.

Seth said, "I saw it in the window the other day when I was walking by that antique store you can't resist." He rubbed his forehead, and I knew he was embarrassed to be caught being sentimental. I leaned toward him resting my head against his chest as he folded his arms around me. He pulled me close in a movement that let me know more clearly than any words that he knew how much was at risk in my leaving for France.

CHAPTER 4

Miriam: Flight to France

JUNE 2001

The first person you know from the inside out is your mother. And yet, because my mother passed when I was only eleven years old, I knew her only as a child knows the person who feeds her, scolds her, helps her with homework, and puts her to bed. I have never known the woman she was apart from me. What were her dreams? Her joys and sorrows? I'd caught a glimpse from time to time but that was all. And there was no one alive now who could fill in the painting of my early life.

As I flew to Paris I was thinking about my Granny, several years gone, and her best friend, Gert, who'd died a year ago. Margaret, known only to me as 'Granny Meg', had been my lifeline after Rose, my Mumma, died and Ed, my daddy, ran who knows where. Rumor has it he hightailed it to the wilds of Canada and died in an ice fishing accident, but I've never searched to confirm or deny this. I've no interest in finding a man who deserted his child when she needed him most. Some wounds are best buried.

Bits of conversations overheard when Granny and Gert were talking came back to me as I sat, sleepless, on the plane. I recalled their happy voices when Mumma was still alive as they swatted flies and shelled peas on the front porch of Granny's house.

"That Rose," Gert would begin. The sound of the peas hitting the tin pail with small thuds carried like raindrops falling from a roof after a storm. "Ah-yuh, she's a talented one alright. Makes the best damn strawberry-rhubarb pie this side of the Mississippi. Can sew up a fine dress from a scrap o' potato sack."

"She can," Margaret agreed, waiting for the next salvo from Gert.

"Too bad what happened, she might've –" Gert wiped her brow and stopped.

"Stop that nonsense. No use going backwards," I was surprised to hear Granny snap at Gert. I snuck closer to the porch from my hiding place under the lilac shrubs that were tickling my nose.

"All I'm saying is she was damn talented," Gert defended herself.

"You hush now, little pitchers have big ears," Margaret snapped again.

"Oh, heavens, Margaret, she's outside playing with her dolls," Gert replied. "And it'd be a damn sight better if Rose was out there with her instead of staying in bed."

"It's only 7 in the morning, Gert." Margaret stopped shelling for a minute. I knew this because the shell-shaped back of the aluminum chair she was sitting on stopped squeaking. "And we shoulda done these peas yesterday." Squeak, squeak. Margaret was back at shelling.

"Oh, it don't matter. They'll make a fine salad. And like I was saying. She needs to stop worrying about losing that baby. Sheesh, you'd a thought it was the first one ever lost the way she carries on. It's not like she didn't get to keep the first one."

"Shut your mouth!" I'd never heard Granny so angry. She stopped shelling and repeated, "Shut your damn mouth, Gert!"

"Sorry, my dear, sorry," Gert mumbled.

"Don't you ever forget again, you hear me?"

"Course I do, Margaret, I'd have to be deaf as a fence post not to hear ya."

"Anyways, why you pickin' on Rose? It'd help if *he* was around more - if you catch my drift," Margaret continued.

"You mean Eddie, Rose's lawfully married husband. Claim they was married smack dab in the Church, no less!" Gert said. "Not that we saw it," she added softly.

Margaret's peas were hitting the pail faster and faster. Gert's voice rose again, "Anyways, he done a lot for your girl, Margaret, and you know it."

"Well, he ain't payin' the bills."

"Oh, I know. Damn foolishness that man is capable of. Paintin' pitchers and such, as if that'd ever pay them bills. Oughtta keep hauling more lumber, that's what I think. 'Fore ya know it, Rose'll have to take that job over to Milly's grocery."

"Over my dead body. She needs to be with Miriam. If he ain't gonna do lumbering no more, he'll just have to be the one to take the grocery job, not my Rose. That's the end of it, no more talkin' nonsense now." For once Margaret was firm with her friend.

"She ain't with Miriam if she's in bed all day," Gert said under her breath. Margaret, if she heard it, ignored her.

"Well, they gotta do something," Gert sailed on. "I heard the post-master tell his wife that the bills keep comin' in and he don't see no envelopes being posted back."

"It really ain't our business, now, is it, Gert?" Margaret was really put out now.

I wondered whose bills they were talking about. And whose baby got lost? How'd a baby get lost, anyway? But what really took my breath away was the criticism of my daddy. No one looked at me with such warm eyes like he always did, every single time he saw me. And he was the only one, the *only* one who liked my drawings. I mean *really* liked them. Mumma always praised them but there was a faraway look in her eyes. Why, daddy even bought me a Crayola box of sixty-four coloring crayons. Sixty-four – I was in heaven! And colored paper; that was a surprise – colored paper! And every time, I mean, *every* time he came home, he asked me, "What did ya make today, little gal?" I took his hand and walked with him into my bedroom and opened the closet where I hid my drawings. Cause Mumma got irritated with me if I made a mess in my room. But not daddy. His big paws held each paper so gently. And sometimes his eyes would shine and he'd say, "You've got it, alright, little gal. You sure do have it." Then he'd cocoon me in the big bear hug that told me I was safe.

That day, listening under the porch I pinched my nose to try and stop a sneeze but it was no use. "Ker-CHOO!"

"Holy Mary, Jesus and Joseph!" Gert jumped up and nearly knocked over the tin pail of peas. She peered down the three cement steps at me. "Whatcha' sneakin' around like that for, child?"

"Leave her be," Margaret said. "Come help me, Miriam. There's plenty of room for your skinny little bottom on this here chair." She moved her plump haunches over a good half an inch and I squeezed in beside her. I was never so content as shelling peas with Granny. Fresh peas are still my favorite food.

The day I left for college Gert rode along with Granny and me but found some errand to do in Bangor while we drove on to the bus station. Granny slowed the car and slipped something into my hand. It was a tiny, two-inch perfume bottle of slag green with a brass screw-on cap. "This was your mother's" she said, her voice as gruff as I'd ever heard it, "Been keeping it for you. Be sure you don't lose it now." She turned away abruptly as I got out of the car and searched my bag for the bus ticket. She tooted the horn once and roared off without looking back. I keep the cap tightly closed for there is still a faint scent of her. The marking on the bottom of the bottle reads: *'Renaud Paris France 1817'*. I have no idea where she would have gotten such a thing. Was it a gift from my father? Dette's mother? No one seems to know.

My mother was there one day, gone the next. I hold close the fragments I have of Rose with my ache to know her, to believe we were close. Her silver hair brush with one or two of her hairs still clinging to the bristles. The memory of her lemony scent. Her voice, softened by time and by my calling it forth like a well-worn love letter, calling me 'Sweet Pea'.

In Maine sweet peas bloom in early June. I learned in my botany classes in college that they look delicate but are far sturdier than they look. They belong to the pea family but are not edible. They entice with their fragrance yet their seeds are highly toxic.

She called me Sweet Pea, I thought as the plane's engines eventually lulled me to sleep. *She loved me, she did...I'm pretty sure she did. But why did she seem so far away sometimes?*

I startled awake when the plane landed with a thump and the brakes roared as they slowed the 747 safely down the tarmac. Paris!

CHAPTER 5

Jules: Paris

JUNE 2001

"Christ, Véronique, I've got to meet that woman from America and we're not even half-way done here." Veronique looked up at me from underneath her impossibly long eyelashes and smiled at me, shrugging and blowing smoke from her cigarette through her nose.

"*Merde!* I knew I should've let Christien meet with her."

"You promised the woman's boss..." Véronique began.

"*Oui, je sais.*" I had spoken with Thom, her boss, and with Rafe, her colleague. And I'd promised them both I'd meet with her. But they would've hardly known the difference if Christien had met with her. Okay, Rafe would have known the difference. But *she* certainly wouldn't have noticed the difference. *Merde*, what was her name, Michelle? Marie?"

Véronique said, "Mirielle?

"Well, for godssakes, don't make any coffee, I'm not about to prolong the meeting. *Zut alors!* See if you can find Christien, tell him I can't make it after all."

She nodded and left the room but not before I caught her smirk as she turned away. I slipped into my navy blazer, drummed five fingers on my desk, and reached for a cigarette. Damn, it was hot; I removed my blazer and congratulated myself on the modern refurbishment I'd made to my office in the Louvre museum. I'd paired my glass and steel desk with vintage botanical prints and two Louis XIV chairs, both nods to the museum's history. To allay my annoyance, I returned to my computer and began reading the newest articles from *Architechture: France.*

"He's not answering, *Monsieur*," I heard Véronique say in her glossy voice. Just then I remembered how much Americans hate cigarette smoking. Damnation! My hand hit the desk as I cursed again.

"Fine, fine, make sure you're around, Véronique, when she arrives," I said, muttering under my breath, *These damn Americans, think they're going to reinvent the Mona Lisa by taking a quick trip to Europe to work on their damn art. Fuck-all. I lit up. Damn the Americans and their puritan ways. I'll smoke if I goddamn feel like it.* Minutes later I heard a light tap on my door. Sighing, I crushed out the cigarette and bowed to my fate on this hot June day.

"*Entrez*," I said, making sure my voice conveyed a degree of cool *politesse*. As the door opened the sun fell flush on her, causing every strand of her wildly curly hair – a shining chestnut brown – to be limned in light like a fiery halo against her caramel silk dress. Before I had fully taken in her face, I had the oddest feeling – come and gone in less than a split second – that I'd met this woman before. *Nonsense.* I shook off the feeling as I strode around my desk and extended my hand.

"Jules Poirier," I said.

"Miriam Verger," she replied with a shy smile.

"Ah, a French name," I said, surprised.

"My father was Canadian," she replied. "From Quebec."

Christ, I thought, *even worse than American, a Canadian who speaks bastardized French.*

I motioned toward the two antique chairs facing one another in front of my desk, indicating she should sit in one. "Delighted to meet you. Your boss, Thom, speaks highly of you." This was true; he'd raved about her work, pressing me to meet with her. She inclined her head slightly though her eyes did not leave mine and I admired her for that, for holding her own. Only a slight tapping of one high heeled shoe, a vintage Louboutain, I noted with surprise, betrayed any nervousness on her part. An American woman with good taste; that was a new one. I was immediately curious about her, I'll say that. As we made the requisite small-talk I watched her face. It wasn't until the conversation moved on to her own art that her face came alive.

"The Black Madonna is the impetus for my current art," she said, her leg swinging back and forth.

"*C'est intérressant*, I replied. Briefly I wondered why *la Vièrge Noire* compelled her, but I had meetings to get to and knew it best to focus on art and not get caught up in anything too personal.

"Actually," she said, sitting up straighter, "the Black Madonna will be the theme of my submission for the *Opus Magnum* art competition this year." One of her hands was fingering the carved filigree of her chair, I noted. A true artist.

"A most intriguing idea," I said. I hoped she wasn't one of those hairy-leg feminist types, God help us. We should present ourselves well, period. But even as I had the thought, I dismissed it. For one thing, I could see for myself there was no hair on those long, smooth legs.

"That's why I'm in France," she added. "Most of the Black Madonnas are here."

"*C'est vrai, ça*," I replied. I liked that she knew that. There was something so authentic about her that I sensed immediately she wasn't flailing about trying to save the world with her art. Thanks be to God.

I suspected Véronique was lurking just outside my office door, listening. She confirmed this when I buzzed her, and she appeared immediately before us.

"Deux cafés," I said. When she brought them I ignored her arch look.

As we sipped our café Mademoiselle Verger timidly asked, "Could you direct me to the medieval Madonna paintings?"

"Of course," I replied. Then I made a quick decision. I jumped up, poked my head into Véronique's office and told her to reschedule my next meeting, ignoring the raised eyebrow. When I returned to Miriam I said, "*Puis-je vous faire une visite privée?*" She intrigued me; besides, it was in my own interest to observe her carefully. I knew she sometimes made sculptures – I do my homework before I meet with anyone – and I wanted to show her the sculpture galleries in the *Carrosel du Louvre* as well as the paintings she wanted to see.

"Oh, no," she demurred. "I was certainly not expecting a private tour."

"It's no problem," I replied. "*Venez*, let's not waste time." With that, she relented.

I'd noted her interest in powerful mother images so I decided to first take her to the antique steatite and enamel statuette of Queen Tiye of Egypt. I felt rather than saw the shine come to her eyes when her eyes took it in. I stepped back to give her some privacy. I have great respect for those who are moved by extraordinary works of art.

In silence we moved down the hall and over to the grand marble staircase, my favorite one in all the Louvre. Just before we stepped onto the wide gleaming steps, I took her arm lightly. "Look!" I said, pointing at the dragon sculptures that curved around the balustrades at the entry point to the stairs. I was rewarded by the delighted look on her face.

"I would never have noticed that," she said with the first smile that reached her intelliget gray eyes.

"Yes," I agreed. "Few do." I paused. "But it's good to notice dragons, *Mademoiselle*, because they live for centuries, just waiting for the opportune time to roar." I expected her to laugh, but she did not.

"Yes," she agreed somberly.

Again, she'd surprised me. I took the stairs quickly and she gamely came along with me. One point for her. Not touching her arm but leading her with one hand at the small of her back, we entered the hushed corridor where a number of resplendent Madonna masterpieces hung. First among them was Da Vinci's *Madonna of the Rocks*. When we stood before the massive painting, she put her hand straight up in front of her, palm out, indicating a pause and I heard her long intake of breath. She took her time gazing at each sculpture when we crossed to the Medieval Gallery. I could see her estimating dimensions of Watteau's exquisite *Nymph et Satyr* and watched with curiosity as she sketched Canova's *Psyche et Eros*. At times I made comments, adding details when she asked a question. Otherwise, we let the art speak for itself. When I came back to myself, that is, when I checked my watch, I saw that I barely had time to circle back to the paintings to show her my personal favorite Madonna. In fact, *merde!* I didn't have time, was already late to the meeting Véronique had just rescheduled. I stopped short and she nearly bumped into me. I said, smiling, for she looked embarrassed, "I beg your pardon, but I must be off, I'm late for a meeting. This way, I'll show you to the exit."

"Oh, no," she said quickly, her words stumbling over themselves. "I mean, that is, I'd like to stay here a while longer on my own. I need to see, I mean, I really want to see, Boticelli's *Madonna of the Sea*."

"Why, yes, of course." This time I was the one nearly tripping over my words because this was my own favorite of the Madonnas. "Wait, let me see if I can change my meeting time again," I said.

Oh, no!" she said more forcefully than I'd heard her speak thus far. When her hand touched my arm, I stepped back as if burned. She added, "I mean, please don't delay yourself any longer. This one I want to see on my own."

I wondered at the fervency in her voice. Most interesting woman. "Certainly, *Mademoiselle*," I agreed, bowing over her hand. I left her there, already contemplating how I could maneuver another rendezvous with her.

CHAPTER 6

Miriam: Paris

JUNE 2001

From the beginning I thought he was beautiful. Around forty, younger than I'd expected, of average height with broad build, he walked briskly around the desk in his office inside the inner sanctum of the *Musée du Louvre* to greet me.

At a glance I took in the dark trousers that fit close across his slim hips and the expensive shirt, a pale lavender one of fine linen, the sleeves rolled up, revealing deeply tanned arms. The confidence and energy he exuded spun across the space between us and triggered a frisson in me that was unfamiliar. I struggled to maintain a cool composure as he approached me and stuck out his hand.

"Jules Poirier."

"Miriam Verger," I replied, hoping that my trembling hand would not betray me. Thom, my boss in Washington had arranged for me to meet Monsieur Poirier in Paris but had not told me much about him. I remember the slight start of surprise as I felt something kinetic sing from my hand to his when our hands touched for the first time. I was relieved when he immediately indicated the chair where I should sit. It would not do to begin by sitting in the wrong place.

He was every bit the polite Frenchman when he asked me about my art and capably guided the conversation. To my embarrassment, at this point some of the papers in my portfolio that I'd been looking at while I'd waited for him slipped onto the floor and our heads bumped lightly as we both bent to retrieve them.

"We have to stop meeting like this," he said in perfect English with only the barest trace of an accent. Our faces were close together and I took in the faint scent of his cologne – damp tree bark and a whiff of citrus peel – and saw the faint shadow of his dark beard as that first smile opened across his face. I am not certain if I laughed, but I know I felt unusually flustered.

It seemed to me that he took this in for he stood and said, "I'll have Véronique bring us a café."

"*Merci bien*," I managed, feeling a knot of tension twist at the back of my neck. I wished that I had had a better night's sleep, could wipe away the dark smudges under my eyes. Even in my Sonia Rykiel dress borrowed from Dette expressly for this meeting, I felt inadequate. "The time change between Washington and Paris has set my circadian rhythms adrift, so coffee would be wonderful," I added lamely.

"Yes, it's difficult," he responded, once again in English. Our first understanding: his English was better than my very good but not quite native-level French. Our eyes met and held as we took in the measure of one another before the moment slipped away. We moved to sit in the gray velvet chairs with elaborate gold-leaf designs scrolled along their arms. The chairs faced one another, and I reminded myself to sit up straighter. I crossed my legs carefully and cleared my throat to distract myself from the tiny spider crawling up the leg of his chair. I tried to recall what Granny had said about spiders as Jules picked up his lighter and tapped a cigarette from a silver case. I was aware of the bead of sweat running down the slopes of my back and hoped that it wouldn't show through the silk of my dress. I rubbed my damp palms together then leaned forward. I reached for my portfolio which I'd placed on the ebony and steel table beside me. As I opened it, some of my work again spilled out.

"Your work seems to have a mind of its own," he said.

"Yes," I answered, laughing, glad to feel my muscles relaxing.

Smoke curling out of his mouth, his head leaning back he asked, "*Eh bien*, tell me more about your work. I understand you are a botany illustrator." His eyes did not flicker over me as men's sometimes do and I was glad of that. He gazed steadily at me as I spoke.

"Well...the work that interests me now, I mean my own work, rather, er, what I am here to do..." I hesitated to see if he was following me, and when I saw him nod, I continued, "is done with copper".

"*Formidable*," he said. That spurred my confidence. He brought the front legs of his chair to the ground and I said, "I've been nominated to create a work for the *Opus Magnum*."

"Ah, *oui*," he said. "The international art competition. Metals and females this year, right?" Of course he knew the details; he worked in the Louvre. And Thom would have informed him I was the entrant for the Academy. "Quite a nice reward for top winners. A few hundred thousand Euros or so, *n'est-ce pas?*"

"Yes." I didn't tell him it was also about me keeping my job. Maintaining independence. "But it's about the art," I said, reminding myself as well as Monsieur Poirier.

"Ah, *oui, oui, oui, bien sûr*," he agreed. "Competitions can bring out the best in us."

I nodded, resisting the temptation to chew on my inner cheek.

He added "Also, I suppose, the beast in us."

I frowned. "Well, for me, hopefully not the worst, anyway," I managed.

"*D'accord*," he smiled. "*Un moment*," he said, then he called out, "*Véronique!*" and a woman with spiky black hair dressed in a tiny mini skirt that barely covered her *derrière* appeared. She murmured agreement to his request to bring us two cafés and withdrew. I was only dimly aware of her shadow lingering behind his office door.

"What will your focus be?" he asked.

"The Madonna icon." My foot continued its tapping against the floor. I wasn't ready to say the Black Madonna but before I knew it, the words escaped my lips, "Actually, the Black Madonna."

His eyes widened briefly as he flicked ash from his cigarette into a small onyx ashtray. "Evocative," he said slowly, looking at me straight on, "and that could go so many ways."

That was exactly my fear: that I would become overwhelmed by the options.

"*Non, non, non*, options are widening!" he said with emphasis.

What!? He'd read my mind? More likely, my face, I decided.

"Of course," I said with more confidence than I felt.

As we continued our discussion about art our heads were moving closer together. At one point they touched. I immediately sprang back which made him smile. We were both surprised when the mini skirt gal chose this moment to appear with our cafés. It had been a long while since he'd requested them. I caught the look between them, but I couldn't read it.

The coffee, brought in two tiny demitasse cups, was luxurious with taste.

"Ah...I have missed this rich flavor," I said taking my second sip.

"You've been here before?" His brows were raised in surprise.

"Oh yes," I said. "I have friends here whom I've visited in the past."

"I see," he replied. "And I agree. It's hard to get this taste in America." I smiled when he said, "But let's continue with art."

I nodded and we tossed ideas back and forth. I experienced a mixture of relief and pleasure in the careful attention he paid me. After a while he said, "What do you need from me?" It was not asked unkindly, but there was a distance now in his voice as the professional man replaced the earlier, warmer one. I was taken aback by this shift but I was glad, too, for it brought me back down to earth. I uncrossed my legs and tucked one foot behind the other.

"I'd like to know if there's a tour specially directed to the medieval illuminations section of the museum," I said. "I'd love to experience once again how they convey light."

"I can do that," he said and crushed out the dying embers of his cigarette.

"Oh, my goodness, I didn't mean you," I said. "I would never presume that!"

"I know," he said easily, "but it would be my pleasure. Give me a minute to ask Véronique, my assistant, to change my schedule."

"No," I began. But he was already standing in the door of Véronique's tiny office and giving her instructions.

"*On y va*," he said turning back to me. I stood. I was hesitant, it's true. But I did not have it in me to refuse his offer.

Oh! The paintings he showed me that day, what they meant to me! Lavish, drenched with color, exploding with graphic scenes of light and darkness, of terror and joy, of birth and death and dying – even these words do not contain the majesty and fire that opened within me as we took in the opulent art.

"Ah, the lights pick up the sheen of copper in your hair," he said at one point. I didn't have a clue what the right response would be so I simply nodded my head.

And so, I walked with Jules Poirier to the glorious first-floor sculpture gallery where we paused before an ancient statuette of a woman I didn't know: Queen Tiye of Egypt, grandmother of Pharaoh Tutankhamun. Her figure was uniquely compelling but I couldn't put my finger on exactly why. I wondered about Her, but Monsieur Poirier was already moving toward the grand salons of the Louvre's medieval art collections. He was completely at home here, I saw that immediately.

And me? I felt like a tiny snail curled within deep layers of sand as the stirring power of the ocean's waves hit the shore again and again. As we moved, my muscles unclenched further, and words freely flowed to my tongue. Even if I didn't understand or particularly like a piece of art, I felt intrigued by the conversation each artist initiated. And I loved watching animation send varying stories across Jules Poirier's face as he spoke about one painting and the next. Even Rafe, for all his talent and charm, did not exude such powerful aliveness in the midst of spectacular art. How fully this man conveyed – with his erect posture, his steadfast gaze on my face, his active silence – his respect for what I was experiencing in those moments. It made me realize what I had been missing.

After an hour or so he glanced at his watch and said, "I'm sorry, I need to go."

"Of course, Monsieur Poirier."

He smiled. "You can call me Jules."

I nodded, ready to thank him when he added, "Listen, I'm going to Rouen. It's a town just north of Paris that has a good example of a medieval cathedral."

I hesitated. I was eager to see Dette. We'd planned that she would pick me up at my Paris hotel and drive us to her country home in Normandy. We wanted to spend time together before I headed off to visit the cathedrals that I hoped would inspire my art.

"Yes, I know, I plan to go there myself," I answered. "The first time I saw Monet's beautiful paintings of Rouen Cathedral I knew I had to see their source. Two of them hang in the Smithsonian museum in Washington, D.C." The words had spilled out of me, but I stopped abruptly when I saw his bemused smile. Of course, he knew that; there probably wasn't much about French art he didn't know. "Well, anyway, Rouen is on my itinerary," I finished lamely, "but not until after I visit a friend for a couple of days."

I didn't tell him my primary reason for wanting to visit Rouen. The

Cathedral there is dedicated to the Virgin Mary. Though I felt certain it was the Black Madonna who was calling me, I wanted to begin with the Holy Mother my mother and grandmother had loved. It felt right to start my journey in a place that combined a connection to Mary as well as to my home in Washington. I had grown away from my Catholic faith, submerged as I was in the worlds of science, art, and academics. But when Granny had died, and I'd returned to my childhood home in Maine something called to me as I stood at her grave next to Mumma's. *What is Mary's hold on so many across the world?* Then my mind floated to the immediate tug I'd felt in the back of my throat when my artist friend Nicole had first mentioned the Black Madonna. I didn't know exactly what Black Madonnas represented, but I was intrigued enough to want to know more.

"*Bon*," Mr. Poirier was saying as we exited the galleries. "No problem," he smiled, "I'm not going there until next Monday." he said. "I have a work meeting there so I'm taking the TGV – the train. You could come along and then take the return train to Paris any time that suits you." I hesitated. I did not want to impose on this man who had already given me so much of his time.

"It's no problem," he said as if reading my thoughts. "Let's meet at the train station at 1100. Call Véronique if it doesn't work out for you. Here's her number."

On the walk back to my hotel I remembered what Granny had said: *When a spider appears in your life it carries a message to be mindful of the choices you're making.*

CHAPTER 7

Miriam: Veneux d'Eau

JUNE 2001

I left the Louvre overwhelmed with its treasures and full of conflicting emotions about Jules Poirier: attraction and hesitation battled within me. I was ready to be in the let-your-hair-down company of my best friend. She picked me up at my hotel with a huge smile on her face.

"At last!" she shouted into my ear.

"Yes." I said with more restraint but holding her close.

Dette's country home in the village of Veneux D'Eau in the northern province of Normandy reflected her beautifully: it was elegant, sensuous, vibrant. The furniture was an eclectic combination of mid-century modern and antiques, and the intoxicating scent of spices and roses drifted through the rooms. Much as I wanted to chat with Dette well into the night, I was so tired and soothed by the spa-like atmosphere of her home that I fell asleep around midnight.

I awakened early the next morning with a renewed sense of energy that left me eager to rise and start the day. Peeking through the drapes at the tall, narrow windows it struck me that this view of the emerald cross-hatched fields that stretched to the horizon was the same one that Odile had grown up seeing. Here, her innocence had been shattered by the cruelty of other children mocking her stutter. From the moment I'd first touched her tiny silken face I'd felt a deep connection to Odile. She'd shown me with her love of all things feline, her curiosity about my botany paintings and her delight in dancing to all types of music that she was a girl far more attuned to me than to her mother. Whatever was troubling her, I would be her compassionate ear.

I pulled open the levers of the windows that opened inward and leaned out to throw open the old wooden shutters breathing in the scent of lavender and wild thyme. *Lavender for grace and thyme for courage*: I'd learned these associations early on in my botany classes. Just then the bedroom door flew open and Dette bounced over to the bed and pulled me down next to her.

"Come on, girl let's get going! Time to stroll through Veneux D'Eau!"

"Hey, I've seen your town; I thought we were going to Mount St. Michel," I half-protested, giggling.

"*Non*, we're going to take our time and be *les flaneures*."

"Ok," I smiled and squeezed her arm. "Sounds perfect." I love, absolutely love, how the French delight in the tiniest details of life. Sipping a strong, dark coffee – the scent filling the nose – is as appreciated as the aroma of a fine cabernet. Slathering cheese, creamy yellow and moist, onto steaming hot bread just out of the oven. Gathering full armfuls of purple iris, deep pink roses, tangerine poppies and placing them carefully, one by one, into a crystal vase that has been in the family for generations. Here, with Dette, every daily act was taken in, noticed, appreciated.

We dressed quickly. I tugged on my trusty khaki slacks and a sleeveless cotton shirt. I pulled my puffy hair back in a loose ponytail in an attempt to tame it, but I didn't bother with makeup. I raised my eyebrows in admiration – or was it envy? – when Dette appeared in a short emerald dress that captured her curves and contrasted perfectly with her bright red lipstick. It didn't matter; we were best friends. And so, we linked arms and walked to the village. I was filled with a deep sense of contentment to be in this old stone village with my friend from childhood. I breathed in deeply and cherished the moment. Dette's tenderness as she took my arm unexpectedly brought to mind a remembrance of my daddy's gentleness towards me.

"Something's up with Odile," Dette said, abruptly ending my reminiscence.

I made a mental note to call Odile again and said, "I agree. But what?"

"Not sure. She's not herself. She cuts me off when I try to get her to talk about what's going on with her."

Unkindly, I thought, *That's a new one, you, trying to explore her feelings*. What I said was, "Hmmmm. That's troubling." Odile trusted me more than she did her mother; that was a path they'd built themselves.

As we neared the village's tiny café Dette put a finger to her lips. I understood: this was a small town and both Dette and Odile are well known here. Best to keep our worries about her to ourselves. "Mum's the word," I whispered and she squeezed my hand in thanks. Together we stepped beneath the wooden sign that proclaimed: *Le Chat Qui Bavarder*. She glanced at me, "Do you know what the name means, *chérie?*"

"*Mais oui*," I replied. "It means, 'The cat who chats.'"

"I see you've brushed up on your French."

"Hey," I said in mock indignation, "I got all A's in my college French classes."

"Yes, I know," she said. "Course you did. Just checking. Can't have you not understanding the sweet words that the French men will be saying once they successfully pick up *La très jolie américaine*."

"Dette, stop!" I said, smiling. "You are too much." I felt warmth bloom on my cheeks as I thought of Jules Poirier, how friendly he'd been, how he'd looked straight into my eyes. Was this just the French way? Was there nothing special in our connection?

"Miriam, attends!" Dette clapped her hands, bringing me back to the present. *"Un crème? Un noisette?"* I hesitated before I replied," I'll have *café crème."* Might as well treat myself and stop imagining there's anything special with me and the handsome Frenchman I'd met in the Louvre. I admired the authoritative way Dette signaled the waiter for two coffees. I don't understand how such a small movement can be so effective, but Dette has it down.

"*Et deux croissants au chocolât,*" she added briskly to the waiter who nodded and scurried away from us. Chocolate croissants, oh well. When it's time to splurge, you splurge. "We'll get some fruit later at the market," Dette said with a wink at me as if reading my thoughts. That was the moment I felt our old connection rekindling.

"Dette," I said a little too loudly and a few customers looked our way. I wanted to share with her my meeting with Jules.

"Oui?"

"Oh nothing" I said with a dismissive little laugh for suddenly I'd changed my mind and decided not to tell her about meeting him. "It's just...just... I'm really glad I came."

"*Ma foi, chérie,* I thought you'd just spotted Nicolas Duvauchelle in his altogether."

"If only!" We dissolved into laughter. And just like that, any awkwardness between us dissolved and Dette and I were back at it, just like old times.

I leaned toward Dette, both my elbows resting on the table. I saw the flick of her eyes and straightened up immediately. The French are exact about proper comportment. I asked her, wondering if she would meet me on this, "Do you remember when Granny Meg gave me that book about roses? I wrote to you about it – it seemed so strange to me at the time, like there was a part of me that my little-girl-self thought I'd hidden away but that she saw anyway."

"I remember," she replied, curling cigarette smoke out through her mouth as she watched me. Her frame was petite, but her presence filled the room. How I envied her that!

Choosing my words carefully I said, "Well, I think that book was one thread that led me to become interested in botany and science. That little book has a remarkable mix of simplicity and scientific accuracy. How did she already *know* me so well?"

"Don't know," she replied flicking ash into the ashtray. "But the old lady should've given you a saw, a hammer, and a shovel, to help put some oomph into you. Honestly, Miriam, sometimes I think you are too dreamy for this world." Dette stopped when she saw the stricken look on my face.

"Sorry, *chérie*."

I flicked away her apology away said with some urgency, "This is important, Dette!"

She sighed. "Alright, then, go on." Later I would wonder if she had deliberately steered me away from revelations about my mother. I decided to keep talking no matter what Dette said or what expression crossed her face. It felt so important and if I couldn't tell her who could I tell? Any time I attempted to talk about the losses of my childhood Seth said: "Don't waste your energy rehashing old stuff, Miriam. Move on."

Now, in the café, I looked straight at Dette and said, "The name of the book is: *The Science of a Rose*. It goes into detail about the parts of a rose and describes the functioning of each part and how they work individually and together. I paused then asked, "Do you think Granny meant something more than flowers? I mean, something beyond botany? My mother's name is Rose. Was she trying to tell me something she couldn't quite put into words about her daughter?" *Don't shrug, Dette*, I was pleading silently.

A series of expressions flickered across my friend's face - tenderness, bemusement, and, surprisingly, something like fear. But the last expression was gone almost before I took it in and experienced a twitch of unease. She sighed and stubbed out her cigarette with more force than necessary. "Well, there may be some connection there," she said slowly, "though I wouldn't be surprised if it was unconscious on Margaret's part."

"Listen to you, the psychoanalyst," I teased. "But you may be right. I just don't know. Mumma so often seemed....in her own world, you know?"

"Hmmm, I suppose so."

I caught from the vagueness of her response what had been true: whenever Mumma was with folks outside the family she sparkled. The times I'd observed her behind the curtains of her private self had all occurred in the privacy of our home.

But Dette's words were rolling on. "Margaret certainly knew how you and your mother both loved flowers," she said carefully as if walking on slippery stones. "Though perhaps she wanted you to know—" here Dette stumbled. "What I mean is, your Granny might have wanted you to understand more about your mother but found it difficult to – to tell you." It was the careful way she said it, so unlike Dette, that disturbed me. Dette who charged full steam ahead no matter what, no matter the cost.

"*Dette, écoute.* I am here to visit you. But I'm beginning to think that I'm also here to finally come to terms with the loss of my mother." I leaned toward her and stared at her with an intensity that she must have found unnerving for she looked away. Her hands fiddled with the clasp on her wallet.

"That's right." I added flatly, "I'm on my way to finding something I need and I won't stop until I find it, "

Dette passed a hand over her face and picked up the cigarette she'd just stubbed out scrambling in her purse for a lighter. Seemingly from nowhere a man swooped in and offered her a light. She accepted the light, murmured "*Merci*," then ignored him until he faded away.

"I see that, Miriam. I see that now. And, believe me, I'm glad. I just hope you find what you are looking for. And that the price is not too high."

"Now what in the John B. Hell do you mean by that?" I said.

She hesitated. "There are things about your mother..." She stopped and I saw her shift course. "Well," she started again, "you know your mother had been ill, right?"

"Yes, she'd had a miscarriage."

Dette looked steadily at me.

"I know," I said, "I know she was sad. I think she wanted another baby." I added, "I wasn't enough," with a laugh that sounded fake even to my own ears.

"Oh, you were plenty."

"Maybe. Anyway, she slipped and hit her head on the kitchen counter, got a brain bleed."

"Ah, yes." Dette hesitated, began studying her cigarette lighter like it offered the keys to the universe.

"What is it?" We were getting close to something and I both feared and wanted it.

"Oh nothing, *chérie*," Dette said. I felt disappointment and relief sink through me as I recognized that we were done for now. "Let's leave it that I love this fierceness I see in you right now. It reminds me of the time we played that trick on Mrs. Mallory, remember, our third-grade teacher? The ole bully?" She leaned closer to me, smiling.

Ah, Dette. I loved her offering me this memory of a time when I'd been less fearful. I swallowed the lump in my throat and smiled at her. It was only later that I realized how neatly she'd changed the subject.

"Yes, I remember. That was kind of mean," I said, picking up my warm chocolate croissant and taking a bite, closing my eyes in appreciation. "Mmmmm."

"Mean, nothing," retorted Dette, now relaxing as she smiled at me before taking her own dainty bite. "What I loved about it was your *fervor*, the sheer determination it took for you to pick up that snake from the muddy brook behind our houses. Your fearlessness as you marched it all the way to school. Like a *petite générale*, you were. Carrying it in your pink Barbie backpack, no less."

I smiled as she added, "Oh, the scream of terror she let out!" Dette laughed in remembrance. "Then she sent ME to the principal's office."

"I told her it was me, but she didn't believe me."

"Course she didn't, you were Little Miss Perfect."

"I still feel badly I let you take the rap for that one."

"Get over it," Dette shrugged. "But you know what?"

"What?"

"I think it's exactly that fierceness you may be looking for now."

I was stunned. A moment passed before I said, "Damned if you're not completely right." I kept turning it over in my mind. "Yes. You're on to something, *mon amie*."

She waited a minute before saying softly, "But the trick is to find it."

"Yes, 'there's the rub.' " We both burst out laughing as the words called to mind our disastrous childhood attempt to hold a Shakespeare play in her backyard. How we'd carefully rigged a Mickey Mouse sheet on the clothesline. How we'd practiced our lines over and over. How we'd gone around the neighborhood with our flyers hand-written in primary-colored markers. The day of the show it poured. No one showed up. And the next day school began.

"Those were the good old days, for sure," Dette giggled. Then she stood and said, "Damn, I can't wait a moment longer; I'm off to *la salle de bain*. Then we should be on our way."

While Dette powdered her nose, I found myself thinking about my plan to learn more about the Black Madonna. For the first time I had a sense that my search was about more than my art project. An image of my mother's beautiful face came to me, the same one that sat in its silver frame in Granny Meg's house, her face forever young.

Is there some connection between my mother and the Black Madonna? But how in the world could that be? My mother, the faithful Catholic who prayed fervently to the Blessed Virgin Mary? The Black Madonna image seemed to hold something very different from that of the Virgin Mary. I wasn't sure exactly what the difference might be, but I hoped to find out. Because only then could I create meaningful art about Her.

Dette returned and put her hand on my arm. "Now, *dîtes-moi*, what are you planning, you fierce woman, hmmm?"

I decided the time was right to tell her more about the art ideas I'd brought with me to France. I said, "Well, most assuredly, I want to visit with you. I am so impressed with the woman you have become." She dismissed the compliment with a flick of her hand.

"And I want to spend some time with Odile." A deep frown before she nodded.

I looked away, noticed a tiny bug making its slow way across our table. "And, of course, I have the *Opus Magnum* art project to work on. It's terribly important to the Academy that I do well. Important enough that I'm worried."

Dette observed, "Your middle name is worry. But you'll do fine."

How I envied her confidence! What I said was, "Well, I've agreed to do it. And I plan to do something related to the Black Madonna. I have become interested in the myths surrounding Her. For some reason I am very drawn to them. To Her."

"This is news to me. But I'm interested." She shot me a sardonic glance and said, "Despite what you might assume." I knew what she meant. Dette was not a fan of any organized religion. She lit a cigarette and inhaled. Smoke blew out in perfect curlicues through her nose.

"Dammit, Dette, even your smoking is artistic." She laughed, waved her hand again.

I added, "But, yes, I am a little surprised at your response. I thought you might say I'm talking in mumbo-jumbo."

"Well, I didn't say I'm a believer, for chrissakes." When I frowned, she added, "Look, *chérie*, here's the thing." She leaned toward me. "How do I know? How does any of us know, really? This whole sacred-mother thing has been around for thousands of years and exists in just about every major culture. Who am I to say it's hooey?" Her dark eyes drifted across the room. Quietly she said, "I think we're all broken." Immediately, I thought again of Odile. I wondered if Dette was thinking of her, too, though I was reluctant to ask.

Dette went on, "How do we heal in the broken places? Get stronger? Isn't that what determines who we become?"

"My friend, the wise woman," I said softly.

"I'll give you an Amen for that one." Again, we smiled.

My thoughts drifted again to my mother. Dette picked up the melancholic shadings on my face. "*Ėcoute, chérie*, I want to hear more about this art project."

"And we need to talk more about Odile."

"*Absolument*," she agreed. "But now let's get moving. We must reach the market before they close and head back to their farms. Shall we go?" I nodded and Dette did that twirly hand-in-air motion. Immediately our waiter appeared at her side, bowing. She waved away my offered money, paid the bill and stood. We locked arms, my mood lifted and I began to hum. Dette joined in and as we moved grandly out of the café we seemed to tumble backward in time to a place where we were ten years old again, giggling madly, the sun warm on our faces as we dug our fingers in the mud near the brook behind our homes.

We headed into the street towards the market. Hearing our voices, heads turned, and brows either furrowed or eased into delight at the sound. "R-E-S-P-E-C-T, find out what it means to me!" we hollered, really getting into it now. I imagined the waiter we'd left behind was thinking, *Quelles folles*. What crazy ladies. Our rousing rendition of "Respect" completed, we dissolved into laughter and continued strolling arm-in-arm toward the marketplace. Dette said, "So, tell me about your Black Madonna. Who is she? What does she mean to you?

Can I meet her?"

"Sure thing! How about midnight down near the river by your house?" I answered playfully.

"Done!" she replied in kind.

CHAPTER 8

Odile : Paris

MARCH 2001

For a long time, my stutter defined me. Maman wanted a perfect child, but she didn't get one; she got me. Oh, I didn't damage her fine reputation as a fabric designer, *non*, because she hardly let me meet the fine people she surrounded herself with. Only Miriam, her best friend from America, did not seem to see my faults. I was Odile, her beloved goddaughter. She always made me feel beautiful and special. Years ago, she took me to a speech therapist who explained to me that when I relaxed and spoke slowly it would help. Miriam spoke at an easy pace herself and she helped me believe me my stutter wasn't a big deal. Huge.

When I could forget myself, we had a grand time. She took me shopping on Wisconsin Avenue in Washington, D. C. three summers ago. I found cool clothes I liked, unlike when I went shopping with Maman. We had our nails painted turquoise and our hair straightened. I had my hair dyed reddish-brown – like Miriam's – and I asked for a turquoise stripe down the side. Miriam didn't have her hair dyed, but she laughed and hugged me when mine was done.

With her I could be the me I wanted to be.

Three summers ago, when I returned home from the States the very first thing Maman said to me was, how's your stuttering coming along? She was more or less looking out for traffic as we roared down the road, the car bumping up and over sidewalks and out of Paris. She is one hell of a terrible driver. I didn't bother to answer her. With one sentence she had reduced me back to two inches tall. *Merci, Maman. Merci beaucoup.*

I am so much more than my stutter, but it has marked me. The pursed lips of people trying not to laugh. Those who jump in to say the words for me. They can't wait, they think they're the ones suffering. Shitheads. American slang is so cool. My grandmother is French, but I've been told my grandfather is – or was – American. I haven't had the dubious pleasure of meeting him as they split well before I was old enough to miss having a father. I learned English – British English – in school. But talking with Miriam in person and often on the phone helped me speak American English. Slang I learned watching American t.v. shows like *Fresh Prince of Bel-Air* and *Friends*. J'adore *Friends!* I use American slang every chance I get and I don't stutter when I do. Most of the kids here don't really know what I'm saying because they don't understand the American slang and that is awesome.

I grew up gagging on my own speech, the sounds ricocheting off the back of my teeth. But the worst of it was the way other kids reacted to it. Like plump Jacques Giradou. Baby cheeks, bright blue eyes, straight brown hair. One day when I walked into the classroom, I heard him mutter, "O-D-D-D-ILE," and I stumbled over his outstretched foot. Snickers from kids all around me. I asked to be switched out of that class, but I couldn't bring myself to tell Maman why, and she said *Non.*

I've developed a sort of internal barometer to read people and my stutter trots along with me depending on the circumstances. If you are patient and accepting with me like my Uncle Jean, and like Miriam

– she has the world's kindest gray eyes – I'm pretty much fine. But if I get a whiff of aggression or impatience, I'm sunk. That's what sucks: I'm worse with those who are bullies or just plain mean bastards. Sixty percent of folks who stutter (I learned this in speech therapy class, so I guess Bernadette didn't waste all her money) have a family member who also stutters. I'd bet my last francs my real father stuttered, but Maman frowns and says *Non!* Since I don't know him either, I'm stuck taking her word for it.

Every new school year, every new classroom, there was the same derision waiting for me when I opened my mouth. The last English-speaking class I went to – Western European history – I stood up to speak and the K-K-Ks and the C-C-C as I tried to say "King Constantine" kept hammering out of my throat. Kids snickered. I hate them. Fuck-heads. Later the teacher stopped me in the hall and told me how brave I'd been. Thanks for multiplying my humiliation, bitch, by bringing it up. Double-fuckhead.

Relief came when men started looking at my body. Such sweet relief. My woman's body which, thankfully, blossomed nicely when I was only eleven. Not until I developed breasts and my long hair was shiny and straight, did I become other than a freak. And I jumped right into this new self like an Olympic champion taking a dive off the high board. With abandon. Sex, ah, the incredible high of sex. Of course, Maman – ecstatic at my newfound popularity – made sure I was on the pill. I nodded in meek innocence when again she gave me the old lecturoo-crap on sex, diseases, drugs, birth control, the whole nine yards. By then I told her little about my life so what did she know? Only what she wanted to know, that's what.

If the boy agreed, fine; if not, we rolled right ahead. When my Uncle Jean found this out, he was so mad, I mean, really hollering mad, he took my arm – and none too gently, either – and put me in his car and drove me to his place. When I sobered up, he looked straight into my eyes and talked to me for a long time. So almost always I use protection.

I've got enough specialties in bed that the guy usually agrees without a problem. Of course, that's not what I tell Jean. But I'm mostly honest when I tell him that, yes, the man in my life uses a condom. And besides I use birth control pills. Alcohol helps relax me, and sometimes drugs, but I don't much do the hard stuff. Sex and booze can release me, make me high. Mostly I insist on condoms, but you know how it goes when the hormones heat a body up. You just gotta go with it, there's no stopping that freight train. Whenever Maman asks, I nod in meek innocence – she should know right there that the gig is up, but does she ever slow down to notice? She does not. Sometimes I wish so bad that she would listen to me, I mean really hear me. But we talk right past each other. Sometimes I get so sad – which I absolutely hate 'cause I know I could drown there – that I go out and drink my favorite drink and next thing you know I'm with a man. For a little while, the world goes away and I float free.

But, like I said, I have Uncle Jean. He's the only cool one in my whole family. Of course, he's not really my blood family, he's an old friend of Maman's, but we're close enough that I call him Uncle Jean. He says he will be in my life as long as I want him to be. Forever! I say, and I mean it. He laughs and says, "*C'est super.*" He is so rad! I haven't seen him much lately, he's often away from Paris. But when he's here, or sometimes when I'm at Maman's, he visits. He takes me to dinner at *les plus chic* places in Paris. Why his ex-girlfriend took off with someone else, I cannot comprehend. I think she's in Tahiti or someplace like that. Thinks she's living the dream, I guess. Truth is, she is the biggest fool on the planet to leave Jean. It's a fucking tragedy about his wife, she's a vegetable after the car accident they had. Oof, I don't want to think about that. I hope in some small way I've cheered him up from all that. Because Jean is like the father I never had. He even took me to Euro Disney; I was just a kid and I loved it – the shiny rides, the high screeching noises, the laughter! – even though I could tell it wasn't really his thing. But he screamed with me on all the rides and put his arm around me when we walked out, both of us laughing our heads off. And when I wanted to go to a Springsteen concert for my fifteenth birthday, he took me, no questions asked.

CHAPTER 9

Miriam: Paris to Rouen

JUNE 2001

Paris on a drizzly gray day remains gorgeous even as the splendors of its architecture and gardens are shrouded in fog; I love this city and always will. I was happy to return there after my brief visit with Dette; we'd made plans to spend more time together after I'd completed following the path of the Black Madonna. To be honest, I wasn't yet sure what that even meant, but I hoped to find out because my intuition told me it would inform my art. I sat in a taxi breathing in the magnificence of Paris as we sped down the broad avenues to the train station where I would meet Mr. Poirier.

The station itself was hot, a maw of cacophonous sound and an unappetizing smell of diesel fuel meets the grease of fried potatoes. Amongst the press of sweat-slicked bodies, hearing the unfamiliar French, I felt the swell of outsider-ness. All the moving masses, so intent on their destinations. But me – where did I fit in? As I approached the *billets* counter, I was surprised to see Mr. Poirier had already arrived. He stood ramrod-straight smoking a cigarette which he flicked now and then onto the ground. As the line to the ticket counter moved, he turned slightly in my direction and caught me looking at him. I glanced away but not before I caught his barely perceptible wink. I nodded briefly, embarrassed to be caught staring.

I bent to retrieve my wallet from my handbag that held the francs I'd purchased in advance back at Dulles Airport. I concentrated on figuring out how much the round-trip ticket was going to cost so I'd be prepared when it was my turn to purchase a ticket. I certainly didn't want the Parisians in line behind me to have to wait for me. I made a mental note to ask Dette if there was any new complication with using my credit card here. Just then I heard a deep voice behind me say, "*C'est Jules.*"

I whirled around and tried to keep the fluster off my face. "Yes, I remember," I said. "It being only a few days since we met."

"Is that all?" he asked.

"Yes," I smiled. "And I really do appreciate your time."

He performed that nearly imperceptible shrug that's quintessentially French and said, "*Le plaisir était pour moi.*"

I swallowed and turned back to the counter to purchase a round-trip ticket. An alertness on Jules's face told me that he'd heard our train to Rouen being announced. "This direction," he said, pointing the way. Given the crush of bodies, the squawks of vendors and the screeching of trains I was glad of his hand on my elbow propelling me through the crowd. It made me aware of my own physicality just to move next to him. I gripped my handbag and gave myself a stern reminder: *Miriam, stay true to yourself, focus on what you need to do here.* We wrestled our way toward track 12 where the train – a sleek, shining bullet – stood silently waiting it's turn to roar.

"Care to read a section?" he asked as we seated ourselves, pointing to the *Le Monde* newspaper. I was struck again by his easy self-assurance; I wondered with an inward giggle if he could I.V. that quality into my veins. Though I was certain that I hadn't laughed out loud, Jules looked up from his paper and smiled.

As the soot-stained buildings on the outskirts of Paris whizzed by, I recalled with a twitch of annoyance that I'd had that childhood dream yet again last night. The dark shape was less cloudy so for the first time it was clear to me it was a woman's shape. In her arms she held something limned in a coppery golden light. As I moved toward her the light wavered and prevented me from seeing what she held. It seemed I was moving closer to her, while at the same time she receded. I tried to shout, to say I needed to speak with her but no sound came from my mouth.

"*Billets! Billets!*" This time the strident voice of the conductor cut short my thoughts. The train rounded a bend and blasted its warning bellow before multi-jerking to a stop. The long mournful sound of its horn called to something deep in me, the memory of Granny Meg and her 3-bedroom house in Maine. Her home sat on a hill high above the train tracks and I awoke each morning to the sound of the five-thirty-nine train announcing its arrival. I closed my eyes to savor the memory for a moment. I was aware of the lingering sense of unease that curled around me from my dream-remnants about the woman, but I ignored it and pulled my body more fully upright, causing my sandaled left foot to strike the hard side of the coach wall. A flash of pain shot up my ankle and as I winced, I become aware that Mr. Poirier was watching me.

"*Monsieur Poirier*," I said, flustered to be caught woolgathering by a near-stranger. And an important professional contact at that.

"*Mademoiselle Verger*," he replied. "Call me Jules."

"Ok." I reached both arms high above my head and executed a long stretch that even as I performed it, reminded me of Stealth, my sleek, lazy cat. With a pang I wondered if Seth had remembered to give him his special cream. And I flashed to my surprise that Seth hadn't returned my call letting him know I'd arrived. I blinked and was back in the present looking at Jules Poirier. I wondered what he was seeing as I returned his gaze. The moment lingered between us like the thin vibrations of a violin when the last note is drawn. Slowly, my sense of unease dissipated and I relaxed. I was aware of an unfamiliar emotion that grew until I recognized that what I was feeling was simple, quiet joy. I returned my hands to my lap and said softly, "Sorry to have drifted off like that."

He shrugged and said, "*Pas de problem.*" For the first time I noticed the dusting of silver among the dark strands of his hair. He grinned as he asked, "Have a nice daydream?"

I sat up straighter, aware that my beige linen dress was wrinkled and slightly damp with perspiration from my time in the over-heated station. Worse, the skirt had ridden up my thighs as my mind had wandered. "I did," I replied and asked, "Anything interesting there?" pointing to the newspaper. I eased the skirt of the dress further down my thighs hoping he wouldn't notice.

"*Plusieurs choses,*" he replied, "but nothing that can't wait." He studied my face and asked, "*Enfin*, why France?"

For a moment I was lost in the timbre of his voice with the same breathless flutter that, annoyingly, filled me when he smiled. *Dammit, Miriam, stop it!* I told myself. I would not be discombobulated by him, I simply would not. So I said in a neutral voice, "I think I mentioned when we met in your office that I'm following the path of the Black Madonna." I was about to add that my best friend Bernadette lived in a village nearby and I would also be visiting her when he chuckled and said, "Ah yes, I do remember. *Les Vièrges Noires*. Most interesting."

I must admit, I was ridiculously pleased that he found the topic engrossing. I keenly recalled the day back in Washington when Thom, my boss, had told me he'd nominated me for the *Opus Magnum*. I'd feigned surprise – thinking: *Rafe, you owe me!* – as Thom proceeded to ask about my thoughts on the art I planned to create. I'd told him that I was drawn to the Black Madonna statues – here a frown had crossed Thom's face – and that I believed going to see some of them in France would inform my work. When I'd finished speaking, I waited, palms sweating, while he stood up and walked to the window turning his back to me. My stomach had plummeted.

"Well," he'd said turning back around to face me. "If that's what you're thinking. It's your call." I was relieved almost to tears. Thom's continued approval was critical.

So now, on the TGV to Rouen, the interest of my newest contact was all the more welcome. He said, "Tell me more."

"I know very little about what the Black Madonna means myself. I've heard that some people go on a type of trek they call 'following the path of the Black Madonna' as they visit various sites that hold them. I intend to visit some of them in order to get inspiration for my art project."

"Fascinating," he said.

"I think the pull for me might have a connection to my childhood in New England." I asked, "Do you know this place?"

He nodded and said, "I've been to the Rhode Island School of Design, so yes."

I added quietly, "I took a little black statue of a woman from my mother's drawer. After she died."

"I see," he said. A beat and then he added, "And I'm sorry."

"Thank you," I said. I wasn't up for telling him more about my past. I continued, "And later, during a previous trip to France I visited Notre Dame Cathedral in Paris. Something happened to me there as I stared at the statue of the Virgin Mary, the one you know here as '*Notre Dame*'.

"So, there's already a connection there for you."

I was startled. It was as though he could read my thoughts before they'd formed in my head. Something about this gave me pause. My old need for control. *Don't get too close too fast.* But he was somberly regarding my face so I went on.

"When I was younger, I felt this affinity for the Virgin Mary. To me She represented such"– here I searched for words –"distilled purity.

Ineffable beauty." I drew the palms of my hands up near my face and said, "When I thought of her it was as if I were holding light in the palms of my hands." Somewhere inside I was astonished at myself; who was this woman letting down her guard?

He replied, "And something tells me you needed that light." I looked down at my hands, pushed back my hair.

"Yes," I said. I stopped speaking.

He took one finger and placed it under my chin, lifting it up slightly and said, "Please, go on."

I took in a breath. "She seemed so *divinely* alone. Something about Her is so remote. Unreachable. But at the same time, She is also so *present*. How can She be both at once? It's a mystery to me." My hands were in my lap and I stared down at them as though they had revealed a part of myself that I hadn't known existed. I glanced at him and gave him a slightly embarrassed smile. He waited.

I went on. "A few years ago, a colleague mentioned the Black Madonna. That piqued my interest. I wondered then and I wonder still if there is some meaning in Her that helps to explain the mystery. I'm not sure why, but I feel compelled to visit places that have Black Madonna figures to see if I can discern what meaning they hold. To follow Her path as it were." I wondered briefly if this sounded ridiculous to him, but I didn't ask as I could tell from the intent look on his face that he was still interested in what I was saying.

He said, "Setting out without knowing the exact path, simply following your question. How few of us actually do that."

I felt quiet pleasure. I would later take this memory out like a precious jewel from a velvet-lined box and hold it close. What I said was, "Well, I have this opening in my life right now that allows me to follow this inclination and I decided follow it."

"It takes courage to leave the beaten path and go where one is called."

"It also takes a certain kind of privilege, I'm aware. I have a stipend to be here to work on an art project. Most people can't just pick up and leave, they have to sow the fields, pay the bills, care for the young, et cetera."

"True enough," he acknowledged. "But if you are lucky enough to be able to follow your question, yet you don't dare let go of routine and security, it can become a kind of dimming of the light. If you know what I mean."

I felt something clutch in my throat. I did know. It was beginning to alarm me how closely connected to him I felt. I heard the barely perceptible click of a door closing as I changed the subject, asking him, "And you? What takes you to Rouen?"

He raised one eyebrow in recognition of the shift in topic, but he let it go. With a sigh he said, "Well, partly work, partly family."

"Could you be more vague?"

He threw his head back and laughed out loud, and I felt my own face open with delight. He said, "I'm an architect. My primary work these days centers on medieval art and architecture in France. I spent many years traveling to different countries to examine different architectural feats across many cultures. But," he shrugged, "I'm French. This is where I want to be. Hence, today I'm working in Rouen." He added, "I serve on a national committee concerned with the extensive restoration projects that have been ongoing at various gothic cathedrals across France."

"Impressive," I replied. I noticed that he hadn't mentioned the "partly family" half of his response and tucked this away. I crossed my legs at the ankles noticing how small my feet looked next to his. "Anything particular about medieval architecture?"

Here he leaned forward with an eagerness that surprised me. "Well, cathedrals to be exact. Why they came into being? Who built them? What materials did they use? Why did they design the shapes the way they did? How did they know so much about geometry?"

"Pardon my ignorance but don't we know all that already?"

Again, he threw back his head and laughed. Again, I felt a pulse of joy rushing through me. He said, "Well, we know a lot, but there are many questions that remain. For one thing, medieval architects generally did not leave behind drafts of their plans. Most unfortunately."

I was intrigued and eager to ask more questions, but just then a voice announced, "Rouen!"

"Shall we grab a coffee? Or would you prefer a mandarin Napoléon, perhaps?" He smiled when he saw the confusion on my face.

"It's a sublime drink. You'll like it."

I hesitated, torn between the desire to spend more time with him and my need to get on with gathering inspiration for my art. "I'm sorry," I said coolly as we stepped off the train "I appreciate the invitation, but I need to attend to my work."

"Oh, come now, the work will wait. One quick drink won't make any difference," he argued.

"Alright," I agreed. But he was wrong. It made all the difference.

CHAPTER 10

Miriam: Rouen

JUNE 2001

I needed to be more decisive. On the one hand, I was here to work, not to meet men, despite what Dette might wish. On the other hand, my boss had recommended I meet with Mr. Poirier and had assured me he would be a good contact to have as I pursued my art.

"Take a moment, it's alright," Jules reassured me again.

"What about your work?" I asked. He'd mentioned he was here to discuss historic restorations with some of his staff. I imagined that with the cultural weight of France's architectural treasures it must be extremely demanding work.

He shrugged, "Why don't you let me worry about that?"

I clutched my bag before I acquiesced. I was an old hand at rationalization: it was hot and a cool drink certainly would be refreshing before I went into the Cathedral.

"Alright," I said. "Thank you for the invitation."

"*Allons-y*. There's a café-bar just up the street." He was already striding ahead.

Turning back to me, he said, "Some of my family lives in a village nearby. If I called them to say I'm coming for a visit they'd probably send a horse and cart to meet me."

"Wouldn't that be lovely?" I said dreamily. He smiled.

Then I said, "Maybe I'll rent a Vespa when I to go to Chartres Cathedral. There's a Black Madonna there." *Me ride a motorcycle? Where had that impulse come from?*

"I'll be sure to warn the natives."

"Ha! They won't even see me. I'll be speeding by so fast. All they'll see will be a flash of light." Who *was* this woman who spoke so brazenly? I'd better put a lid on it.

As we approached the café, I was enchanted with the charm of the street. The walls of what were likely eighteenth-century buildings were made of thick limestone that proclaimed sturdiness. Doors were painted in shades of butterscotch, salmon, and pistachio. All were faded, the paint peeling in places. "It's so lovely," I said.

"Hmmm, yes, I suppose it is."

"You're jaded." I said. "And you, an architect!"

He laughed. "Point taken."

As we walked, I was increasingly aware of his physicality, the jaunty grace with which he moved. *Stop it*, I told myself, swatting at a fly. When we'd reached the café-bar I was surprised to see a colorful bird sitting in a cage overhead.

"A café with its own parrot. I love it."

"*Oui*, that's *'Fou Rouge'*."

"Red Fool?" I translated.

"*Oui*. A bird unique to this café. Good thing you don't have red hair," he said with a wink. Two black wrought-iron tables embraced by two chairs sat under the dark blue awning of the café. A long tear in the awning sent an oblong slice of sunlight onto the table. Jules pulled out a chair for me and signaled a waiter before relaxing his body into a chair and leaning back with the front two legs completely off the ground.

"Careful!" I said.

He frowned. "What?" He clearly had no idea what I was worried about.

I was trying to stabilize the wobbly imbalance of my own chair on the uneven cobblestones. I noticed the amused look on Jules's face as I struggled and felt my face grow warm with embarrassment.

"*Monsieur, Mademoiselle, bonne après-midi,*" the waiter appeared bowing formally.

"Two glasses of white wine, *s'il vous plâit,*" Jules said, tapping his fingers on the table. My face tightened slightly as I heard him order.

"Actually, I'd prefer a *citron-pressé*." I said. "I need to drink lemonade; a glass of wine would ruin any chance of serious study within the Cathedral." But I was surprised to find that I enjoyed his take-charge attitude because it had annoyed me when Seth did it. But my inner voice was now saying, "*Kiss off, critic!*"

"*Une bonne idée, une bonne idée*." A good idea, the parrot blurted out.

"Hear that? He does have a way of reading thoughts." Jules smiled.

Goodness, I sure hope not. I glanced away and noticed a little boy with a shaft of black hair watching us from the café door, leaning half-in, half-out. I caught his eye and smiled at him. He didn't respond in kind but continued gazing somberly at me. Something twisted inside me as I recognized the longing in his dark eyes. Just then I heard a woman's voice call out from the interior of the café, "*Viens, mon fils!*" The boy turned and darted back into the café.

I grasped the puffy fronds of my thick hair that was curling wildly in the humidity in a feeble attempt to push it out of my face and behind my ears. As I did so, I looked up to find Jules staring at me. I had a moment of quiet pleasure but then I saw a look of such intensity that I was startled.

"A penny for your thoughts," I said, achieving, I hoped, a neutral tone.

He turned away and was silent a moment. Then he tapped his cigarette on the glass ashtray and returned his gaze to mine. "I'd like to hear more about you, Miriam." I sensed somehow that this wasn't what he'd been thinking about, but I let it go.

He gave a brief wave of dismissal to the waiter who arrived with two icy cold glasses of white wine; apparently my request for lemonade had been ignored in the way that French waiters sometimes pretend they can't understand an American's French.

A glimmer of amusement and something else flickered in Jules's eyes before he said, "Begin wherever you like."

I made an effort to resist the comparison with Seth but couldn't help my pleasure in being asked to talk about myself. Had Seth and I lost interest in one another? Did we know everything about one another and have nothing left to learn? Even admitting the questions gave me a pang of sadness.

"Talking about yourself makes you sad?" I heard Jules's voice. *Damn, how does he sense this?* I pushed the thought away, looked once more into his face. Ebullience is the word that came to mind as I stared at him. A simple delight in being alive. *I must remember this,* I thought. *I wish I could capture it in a jar and drink it in every morning when I awaken.*

"Ah, now you relax," he smiled with approval.

"I been told I have an expressive face, but really, you read me like the artist you are," I replied, aware at the edges of my consciousness of the little inner voice that warned: *Beware, woman, beware. Go slowly here.* Immediately following, as if in mocking repartée, came the thought: *Dive into the fire, woman!*

"*Une bonne idée, une bonne idée,*' the parrot bleated again. Jules laughed at the bird, though I did not.

"Ok," I said. "I told you while we were at the Louvre that I work in copper. I'm a metallurgist by training." I looked at Jules, taking in the quizzical look on his face.

"Do you know what that is?" I asked, laughing. The waiter brought the chilled bottle of wine to the table, set it down and departed without a word.

"*Non*, not specifically. But it sounds interesting." He took a sip of his wine.

"Well, basically, it's the study of metals."

I was feeling more relaxed as the wine began to take effect. "I learned to create pieces of art using metal." And now – as I've said, I'm intrigued with the Black Madonna. I've always had an interest in spirit-women, though it's been in the background of my life. I'm fascinated by witches. Who were they, who are they, really? Hmm, maybe I'll dye my hair midnight black," I giggled. Goodness, how much wine had I had?

"I'm not going to encourage that," he said, "because when the sun lights your hair it appears limned in Titian red." I looked away, fingering a scratch on the table as Jules said, "Go on, tell me more. About these women."

I continued, "I feel this connection that is drawn from the ancient myths – the Celtic goddess, Danu; Shekhina, the divine feminine aspect of God; the Hindu goddess, Lakshmi, and of course, from my birth culture, the Virgin Mary." I paused and glanced at him. "I'm searching to learn what they mean, how they might interconnect, but without conflating them. It's partly intellectual interest, but I suppose it's also about me, about exploring my own beliefs." I stopped, suddenly aware that I was revealing far more than I'd intended.

He sailed in, "Did you know that the word 'cathedral' comes from the Latin word 'cathedra' which means 'throne'? So, the cathedrals here dedicated to Mary are dedicated to the woman who sits on the throne."

And the throne of woman is her lap and all that lies therein. I caught myself just in time before I said this out loud.

He continued to watch me and indicated with a snap of his fingers, *Continue.*

I said, "There was this old woman in the little town where I grew up. And I thought she was older than time. It's not that she wore black or flew around on a broomstick," I laughed uneasily, "but she seemed a little spooky. Even so, the things she sold my mother fascinated me." He looked steadily at me, nodded. Crushing his cigarette into the ashtray, he waved away the waiter.

I wiped my sweaty hands on my lap and continued, "I used to visit her with my mother. Her shop was beyond the edge of town, you had to walk through the village and then follow a dirt path through the pine forest to get to it. I loved the smell of the forest, the softness of the steps we took on the pine-needled floor. The woman sold potions, dried leaves, flower petals, plant oils, that sort of thing. It took me a surprisingly long time to figure out that this is where my interest in botany began." Abruptly, I stopped, recognizing I had stumbled onto a path I was not prepared to take with him. I took a sip of the icy wine and said, "Ok, Jules, your turn." I liked saying his name aloud. So elegant, like him.

"I'd like to hear more," he looked at me, "but, perhaps another time?" I bit my inner cheek but nodded. "*Eh bien*," he said, "You know I have a background in art and architecture, *n'est-ce pas?*" I nodded. "And I'm interested in the many unique elements of the gothic cathedral."

I took another sip of my wine and watched his face as he continued. "For example, I'm captivated by *gargouilles*, medieval gargoyles. *Gargouille* means 'throat' or 'gulley'. I'm here to speak with an expert on the ones on this particular cathedral."

"Gargoyles," I said. "Fascinating."

Jules smiled. The waiter standing nearby discreetly watching us seized the opportunity to approach once again. "Anything else?" he murmured. Jules signaled to me, saw the tiny shake of my head and replied, "*Non, merci*."

"So, about gargoyles," he continued. "I'm exploring how they express the dichotomy between body and soul." He leaned back and stretched both arms wide to the sky. "They are such a marvelous way to express the mixture of the absurd, and the sinfulness in us, as well as the grotesque – comprising a whole that is weirdly delightful."

"Yes," I nodded slowly, "like a matrix."

"*Exatement!*" he said with triumph in his voice.

"Though to be honest, I've always been put off by them," I said. "They're so ugly!"

He smiled widely and nodded, "They are, in a way."

"But probably also because I've really never understood what they are about. I mean, the cathedrals themselves are such a profound amalgamation: the physical structure itself represents incredible imagination and human strength. And I think, too, about those who carried the burden and sometimes died to build them."

He held his silence, still watching me.

"They are at once deeply about divinity *and* humanity. Somehow there emerged this enormous capacity to build a magnificence of structure and form. The grand, sweeping arches, the soaring buttresses. The awe that runs through me when I see the stained-glass windows."

Jules said again, "*Exactement.*"

"And then here and there are these creatures, like pockmarks on a face. Such a juxtaposition. They've always disquieted me." I shuddered.

"Exactly as they were meant to do," he said. "You see, *Mademoiselle*, you understand more than you realize. Even if it makes you uncomfortable. Because they represent the part of life that is not perfect and beautiful. The dark underside – the black feeling of terror. the agony of suffering, the mystery of death."

As he spoke, my thoughts drifted to my parents, the homeless in cities across the world, all those in war-torn countries. The evil that man is capable of.

Jules ran his fingers over the edge of his glass and said, "Remember, they were created in the so-called Age of Faith. The entire building of a cathedral was the economic lifeblood to the lucky town that was chosen, employing thousands during the *century or more* it took to complete one. Imagine: The House of God! In those times they literally believed - in a way I think we cannot fully understand - in the presence of God and the presence of evil. Both of them alive smack in the middle of everyday life. Living, breathing forces."

"I hadn't thought of them that way," I said. "But it's true."

"The gargoyles were meant to serve as protectors; they were created for the specific purpose of shooing off 'evil' spirits." He clapped his hands in the air. "Hence, they must be frightening. Remember, too, most people were illiterate so these figures were a way to illustrate the demons who could devour you if you yielded to the devil's temptation." He opened his mouth wide and roared at me.

It surprised both of us when I roared back.

I saw the waiter standing near us glance at his fellow waiter as he gave him a barely perceptible shrug.

Smiling broadly at me, Jules continued, "Some of the gargoyles were shaped as grotesque animal forms with open mouths caught in the act of snatching a naked human being" – he struck a mock-menacing pose opening his mouth wide and twisting his face into a grotesque mask – 'Beware of me, the demon carrying off a human soul'."

Gazing at him I thought, *I'm beginning to understand both the nature and the force of temptation.* What I said was, "You know, Jules, if you keep this up the waiter is going to cart you off to the loony bin."

He laughed, "Don't worry yourself, *chérie*, he could care less." He continued, "The gargoyles also served a practical function; that is, they actually were spouts through which water flowed to direct water away from the cathedral walls. Hence, the name, "spout" or "throat" as I've said. And the sound of water flowing through them is like a gargle. *Enfin*, a beautiful symmetry, *n'est-ce pas*?"

"Yes." I smiled and added, "I love the sound of water. It's so enlivening."

He inhaled deeply on his cigarette, blew the smoke out the side of his mouth away from me, and continued, "Some of them are simply *grotesques;* that is, they have no open spout but simply are there to ward off bad spirits. Hey", he said, his face lighting up, "You're from

Washington, D.C., right?"

I nodded.

"Did you know that Washington National Cathedral has a gargoyle that is the image of Darth Vader?"

"No," I said quietly as my thoughts turned to Seth.

"Yes, yes, it does!" His face was lit with excitement. "It was added in the 1980s as they were completing the north tower. Thus, the grotesque comes to the twentieth century. *Voilà!*"

He saw the shadow that crossed my face.

"*Qu'est-ce que c'est?*" he asked. And just like that, the spell between us was broken.

It took me a moment to answer, then the words rushed out. "I was thinking about my, er, partner, Seth. He loves Star Wars. He's seen all the movies several times, owns the series. He's a lawyer. A good man." I wiped my brow wishing I could do the same for the sweat sliding down the back of my dress. I reached for my purse. "I think we should – I mean, I should – leave now."

Jules said, "I'm sure he is." He placed his hand briefly on mine. "And you don't need to run. Rest a moment longer. You're in France, the sun is shining. What's the hurry?"

"No, I must leave. I need to see this cathedral, then go back to Paris, to begin my work," I said with a confusing sense of urgency. As he looked at me, I had the disturbing sense that this man could see places within me I wasn't keen to reveal. *Be brave, little gal.* I was jolted to hear my daddy's voice in my ear with his familiar words as he encouraged my drawings.

"No, I can't stay any longer," I said, not fully understanding why my sense of joy had turned resolutely to duty.

"Miriam, I'm not judging you. On the contrary. I see a woman containing something big inside herself. Something threatening to engulf her, yes?"

It was too close to the bone. I remained silent.

Noting my refusal to meet his eyes he added, "*Bon*, I become too serious. *Je suis désolé.* Just one more moment to chat, ok?"

"Are we just 'chatting'?" I challenged him. I wanted to meet his eyes and confirm that I had not imagined what passed between us, but I was more afraid of what I might not see to risk it. I crossed my legs and looked down at my hands now pressed tightly together in my lap. "Fine," I said, taking a deep breath, "tell me something about you."

He laughed and said, "Oh, you are priceless. A woman who really knows how to change the subject."

I wasn't sure it was a compliment, exactly, but making him laugh brought back a sense of ease. I watched his eyes darken slightly as another frown creased the smooth skin between his eyebrows. He said, "Me? It's complicated." This was so close to what I'd been thinking about my relationship with Seth that I had to struggle to keep my voice neutral.

"That I understand," I replied. "But you know what else I'm thinking?"

"Non, why don't you enlighten me," he asked. I was glad to hear the teasing note back in his voice.

"Well, how about this?" I raised my hands up slightly as I spoke, "It's like we all have both angels and grotesques swirling into and out of our relationships all the time. Sometimes things can be gurgling along but at other times the grotesques are sticking out their tongues and lowering their goat horns at us and generally wrecking havoc."

Serious now, he said, "So true." Then a wince before he looked away. I saw for the first time a weight on the planes of his handsome face. I resisted the impulse to smooth it away.

"*Ça suffit, ça suffit.*" That's enough. The parrot was back in action with its uncanny sense of timing.

Jules rose to his feet and said, "*Bon*, I think you're right, time to move on. Do you know where you're going?"

"Yes," I said. "After I spend time in the cathedral, I'll take the train back to Paris." I wanted to reach Odile as soon as possible.

"It's been lovely speaking with you," he said, a reserve now replacing the earlier ease between us. He gave me a light kiss on my cheeks barely touching the skin. "Let me know if there's anything else I can help you with."

"Thank you," I said, "I appreciate the offer." I picked up my pale blue pashmina, slowly folded it and put it into my bag. He reached for his wallet, waved my hand away when I reached for mine.

I took a step back. Lifting his own bag Jules straightened his shoulders, gave a breezy wave, then stopped to say, "I have to drive a colleague back to Paris tomorrow morning. A close friend needs me."

"I appreciate your consideration. But I'm just fine on my own." *Liar, liar, pants on fire.*

"You have a very expressive face, you know."

"Yes, so you've mentioned. More's the pity."

"*Au contraire*; it makes you seem more accessible."

Merde, I thought, *that's the last thing I want to be.*

"Alright, off we go," he said. "But, wait, while we were sitting here talking, I thought of something. When I spoke with Thom, he mentioned you would be looking for somewhere to do your artwork." I nodded. "I know of a place near the ocean you might be able to rent this summer." Although it sounded amazing, I hesitated. I wanted to be close to Dette so I could visit her when I needed a break from the intensity of creating art, always a curious mix of inspiration and painstaking effort.

"Think about it," he said before he grabbed his bag and started walking away. "Thom gave me your contact information. I'll have Veronique send you a description of the place." *Ah yes, the woman in the tiny mini skirt in your Paris office.* He waved and walked towards the alley next to the Cathedral where a man who for a split second I thought was Rafe joined him. I blinked and the figures disappeared into the shadows.

Jules offered me a lot that day. What I couldn't figure out was why. With a sigh I crossed the street and stepped into the darkness of the *Cathédral de Rouen.*

CHAPTER 11

Odile: Lausanne, Switzerland

APRIL 2001

My first reaction when I was accepted into the Ėcole Polytechnique Fédérale de Lausanne (EPFL) was stunned relief. Then unabashed, astonished joy. I'd made it! No one had helped me get here; I'd succeeded entirely on my own.

As a child I hadn't wanted to play *le football* but *Maman* had insisted I try a team sport. Turns out I was good at it. Must be from my father. Whoever the hell he is. It was the first time I felt strong: *this is something I can do as well as anyone. Better than most, even*. Met some good *copines*. Ran like hell, kicked like hell. Gave me confidence in academics, too. Though, to be honest, I've always been smart. Just hadn't cared. But when I got accepted to the *Ėcole Polytechnique*, just about the most prestigious mathematics and engineering school in Europe – something I hadn't even told Maman I'd applied for – because, oh, the enormous pressure I knew I'd feel from her! She who still thought I was doing the history program. But after I'd been accepted at EPFL, the next time she deigned to visit me in Paris I hit her with the news.

"*C'est formidable!*" she shouted, just as I'd known she would. "I'll pay for it, of course!"

I nodded. That had been my intention.

"What will you study, *chérie*?" she asked.

"M-mathematics, engineering," I said, shuffling along beside her, the hedgehog to her swan.

"*Merde!*" she said, even more excited now. "Why, Einstein was educated at a Swiss école polytechnique!"

"As was his wife," I added dryly. I noted her look of surprise. *Ha! You don't know everything, Maman.*

She shouted, "*Incroyable!*" It pained me she thought it was unbelievable.

I hadn't told Maman I was planning a career in engineering, let alone applied to the world-renowned EPFL. But I'd always been good at mathematics and I loved the exactitude that it required.

Students rushing around, accents from around the world, the town nestled in the dusky purple mountains - that first semester I loved it all. The work was challenging, and my confidence wavered, but I plugged away as I always had when success was something I wanted. That's what us misfits do; we plug along. Unnoticed or at least not part of any pack. But here, I inched my way toward friendships with shared love of mathematics and physics. And as time passed, I realized I could do this work. I am really smart. I'm not bragging, just stating a fact. I was even able for a time to resist the pull of, the release of, sex.

Louis, a lecturer, who was older than me by 15 or so years took an interest in me. I liked that he was smart and mature and that we could talk for a long time about computers and mathematics, shooting ideas back and forth like ping pong balls. I enjoyed being with him, but I wasn't attracted to him. This also made me glad. Because I knew this polytechnic program was a way for me to learn to shape my environment rather than have it shape me. The EPFL promotional materials made this clear. I could not only advance my learning in the language of computers, I could build an app! I was happy, thrilled really, with the computer science I was learning. And Louis smiled at my eagerness. *A man likes me for my mind* I thought. *How wonderful is that?* One afternoon he suggested we meet that evening at his place rather than a café. Was it my excitement about my new life at EFPL that blinded me to what I would have easily recognized before?

"Come in, come in, Odile," he smiled at me that night. I noticed right away that his shirt was unbuttoned.

I frowned and said lightly, "Louis, you forgot to button your shirt."

Without replying he grabbed me by the wrists and pushed me onto the couch. My mind reeled in shock while he held my arms and pushed his member inside me.

"*Batarde!*" I yelled, struggling to get free of him.

"*Tu voulais ça*," he snarled. He lied; I did not want this and I was shocked. *What was happening? How had he turned into this monster? What had I done?*

The second he released me I kneed him. Hard. *Looks like the soccer games paid off*. Quick reflexes, strength. While he howled, I fled. *You goddamned bastard! You're not getting away with that, not with Odile, you asshole*. Running, sobbing.

I was humiliated in a new way; for the first time it was due to my own stupidity. I'd been a goddamned fool thinking an older man had sought me out for my brains. *How smoothly he'd played me* I thought as tears of rage blinded me. I told only my roommate Celeste. When I stumbled into our room, she took one look at me and got up from her computer screen to embrace me.

"Tell me," she said quietly. She held me and listened without comment. She let me cry. She let me refuse to go to the police. She repeated over and over that it wasn't my fault. She made me chamomile tea when I had night terrors. Over those few months she taught me the power of friendship. When I fell into the morass of despair and started missing classes, she took my arm and got me to counseling. And the venting and the medication helped, which surprised me. But it was hard to pay attention in class as my hypervigilance made me start with terror at every turn. Friends repeatedly asked why I was "spacing out" so I began to avoid them. I tumbled through humiliation and darkness. By the end of the semester I'd managed to fail two courses. Marijuana became my new drug of choice.

Despondent, I took a train to Paris. That night in a smoke-filled bar I met Alain. With his long black hair and chiseled physique, he was the sexiest man I'd ever laid eyes on. And so, from the moment I responded to his "*Salut*," I ignored the inner voice that said, *This one's trouble*. I drank that whiskey straight and stumbled with him to his dank room. It was a slippery slope that I felt powerless to resist. And it was a surprisingly short fall to the crash at the bottom.

CHAPTER 12

Miriam: Chartres Cathedral

JUNE 2001

Always, I am drawn to color.

But nothing had prepared me for the explosion of cobalt blue and crimson that are the stained-glass windows of the Cathedral of Chartres. I entered the dimness of the church and slowly turned around a full 360 degrees. The ravishing movement of light and color seeped into every fiber of my being. Here was art that torched the soul. I slid into a pew somewhere in the shadowy realm of the nave and knelt in an unconscious bowing to the rhythm of the familiar: kneel, pray, listen. Sometime later - ten minutes? sixty? - I felt sunlight gentle my eyelids and I opened them. The light now exploding through the stained-glass colors was alive with fire and I sat up straighter in amazement. This experience shattered what I'd previously understood about color. How does one take in such a transcendent moment? All I know is that the time I sat there, reveling in the glory of that light and color touched me profoundly and made me feel at once exalted and humbled. What power inspired human beings to take splendor from the imagination and bring it to this incredible fruition?

After a while I moved along the right chancel toward the window known as *Notre Dame de la Belle Verrière* or "Our Lady of the Beautiful Window." I stood transfixed before the exquisite stained-glass noting that the age-darkened masonry heightened the intense colors. The late afternoon sunlight made the cobalt of the medieval glass numinous. I had to lift my chin to look up, up, up to where the figure of Mary glowed high above me. As I gazed at Her, something haunted in Her dark eyes tugged at me. Sable eyes the color of wet, fertile earth. Eyes that knew before knowing that the Child She would bear would be torn from Her, His flesh lashed with whips and chains. Eyes that knew before knowing the children who would grow weak with hunger, their bellies hugely distorted. Eyes that knew before knowing the men who would enact cruelties against one another.

Moving closer not taking my eyes from Hers I felt pulled into blackness until all was silence, opaque, beyond.

Hail Mary.

Mother of God.

The words I'd said a thousand times, yet never heard before. I felt them course *through* my body, viscerally. *All women bleed. Know this.* As I continued to stand there, I felt the thudding of my own heart. And water fell from my eyes and slid down the curve of my cheeks so that my face, like Hers, glistened in the soft glow of the candles flickering nearby. Around me. Around Us. We gathered stillness around us like a cloak.

As I looked more closely, I saw it was Her robes that were made with glass stained a dazzling blue. I knew the historical Mary would not have worn blue drapery because she was a village girl and could not have afforded the indigo dye to make the blue color, but it didn't matter here. For what I saw was how powerfully the blue evoked serenity. And there was something more. Perhaps because sunlight now streamed through the window and made the figure of Mary shimmer with aliveness and because Her eyes regarded me straight on, I felt for the first time the full *power* of Mary. No humble handmaid, this woman. I struggled to integrate this vastly different version of Mary from the mild woman with eyes downcast I had known before.

I was so far inside this thought that I startled when I heard a deep voice say in my ear, "*C'est Jules Poirier*." I had stepped up onto a low stone bench to be nearer the Lady's piercing eyes so when I heard his voice and whirled around it was straight into *his* golden-brown eyes I was staring. I was so startled to be back in this time and place and even more so to see him there that I nearly tumbled off the bench. He caught my arm to steady me.

I think I mumbled, "*Bonjour*," but my thoughts were still far away and I was reluctant to relinquish them to the here and now. I think he was aware of this for he waited a moment before touching his warm hand to mine. It gave me time to recollect myself. Then I said, "I do remember your name. Seeing as how it was only a few days ago that we met."

"Was it so recent?" he asked, moving an inch or so closer to me.

"It was," I said.

"Are we quarks, then?" he asked, a smile in his voice.

"Pardon me?"

"Quantum physics. The more two quarks move away from each other, the more the color force binding them together increases to bring them back together."

"The color force," I repeated. Rarely had I felt stranded on such uncertain shores.

He nodded toward the Blue Virgin and said, "*Elle est belle, n'est-ce pas?*"

I thought this a gross understatement, but I murmured, "Yes."

We stood gazing at the luminous window until I broke the silence by saying, "I have not seen such directness depicted in Mary's gaze before. The picture on the wall above my childhood bed, the plaster statue in the little white Church, the reproduction painting in my Granny's home – in all of them Her eyes are downcast or raised to heaven. They connote grace and humility. But I am struck by *this* Mary – She regards one so solemnly. And so directly. I love that." He took a step closer to the window and gazed at it a moment. As he stood there, I felt again the deep pleasure of him contemplating my comment.

After a while he said, "It's a significant distinction." I looked away.

"No," he said, taking a step back towards me, "That is not a criticism. You have seen something that never occurred to me despite the many times I have been here." He touched my arm, "And," he said with a touch of awe in his voice, "you are exactly right."

He waited a beat before he cleared his throat and added, "She is the only window of medieval stained glass that remains from when the cathedral was built. He paused while I took this in. "The others were destroyed in the great fire here in 1194."

"So, She's a survivor," I said. "And what was asked of Her, She accepted with grace. She raised an extraordinary Child. But I wonder if She knew what Her Baby was in for. If She had known, would She have agreed?" I was stirred to think of Mary as resilient. I tucked the thought into my imaginary 'art inspiration' box recognizing how much it enlivened me when I did this.

"Who among us can know the mysteries of faith?" I heard Jules asking.

"Such mysteries are unfathomable," I heard myself answering smoothly. I caught myself again wanting to touch his face. Instead, I white-knuckled my hands.

He broke the silence by clearing his throat and saying, "Do you know about *La Sancta Camisia?*"

"Yes. The holy veil."

"Yes. It was supposedly worn by the Virgin during childbirth."

"Jesus!"

"I assume you're not being profane?" He lifted one eyebrow.

I swatted him lightly on the arm. He caught my hand, held it as he continued. "Furthermore, it is believed that the Chartres religious folk gave each French queen when she became pregnant a blouse that had touched this relic.

"A lovely recognition of the risks and the enormity of birth."

"*Oui, c'est ça.* And French women through the centuries have honored the veil as protection in childbirth." I had only ever thought of the veil in relationship to brides. And in art school I'd learned the veil was symbolic of the separation of the physical body from the soul. Another item fell into my art box.

"*Merveilleux!*" I said. Then I wondered, "Do you suppose the tradition holds true for the new immigrant women giving birth here?"

"I'm not sure," he replied.

I said, "It's a beautiful story. "It conveys compassion and strength during struggle."

He nodded. Bells were ringing softly in a chapel nearby and the scent of incense hung in the air. Scores, maybe hundreds, of people were moving through the Cathedral, yet due to its huge size it was far from full and there was a lovely sense of lingering in the aisle of the Virgin Window.

I said, "I've long been intrigued by the symbolism in the Catholic Church. The cross, the Pope's red shoes, the incense, the flickering candles, the holy water," I paused. "We have such a deep desire to believe in transcendence."

He nodded, "We do."

Other people were nearing the Blue Virgin window as we spoke, their voices murmuring in Japanese, English, Italian, Danish, Hebrew, and other languages I didn't recognize. We moved away and I continued.

"I've heard it translated both as the 'tunic' of the Blessed Virgin Mary and as the 'veil'. In any case, a cloth covering Her, protecting Her. I love that it's a tangible presence connecting believers in a direct sensate way to Mary."

"Exactly."

"One thing I will say, I learned early on about body and soul – at least in an abstract way – at the Church's knee."

"*Moi aussi*," he replied with a smile.

I knew, of course, that I could not touch the actual holy veil here, protected as it is in a golden reliquary behind glass and key. *Why are men always locking things away?* I thought but did not say.

He picked up the history. "This myth has been carried through the centuries way back to 876, the time when the *Sancta Camisia* is said to first have been held here." He took a breath, "Legend has it the relic was given to the Cathedral by Charlemagne, who received it as a gift during a trip to Jerusalem." He shrugged. "Others say an Empress give it to one of his descendants. Who knows?"

"I think there were too many trips by those with spurious motives taken from Europe to Jerusalem," I said, wondering if he'd be offended.

"*Touché*" he said, answering my unasked question.

I felt my body softening before I said, "But Mary was not a part of those battles." I glanced at him and added, "I imagine She might have disagreed with those who fought."

"Interesting," he said slowly. Then, "What a unique perspective you bring."

"Perhaps because I'm a native of another country, while you are of the ancestral flesh and blood of this soil."

He nodded, "I am."

"I know that Chartres has been the center of Marian reverence for millennium."

"*D'accord*."

"I think there is a palpable feeling of the sacred here. And I wonder what that's about?" An elderly couple dressed in pastel sweats had signaled to us that they would like to move closer to the window where Jules and I were standing. We smiled at them and moved to a pew where we sat together and continued our conversation.

"Before I left Washington, I did some research on Chartres," I said in a low voice. "I became intrigued by other myths that place Chartres at the center of ancient goddess worship well before Christianity." I saw a muscle twitch in his face.

"Am I trespassing?"

"*Non, non, pas de tout.*" He waved his hand dismissing my concern. "The responsible architect respects both the weight and the nuances of different cultures."

"Well said." But I decided to let the topic rest.

"Come," Jules decided as he rose from the pew. "You're interested in the Black Madonna. How about I show you the underground Black Madonna here. You know of Her?"

"Of course," I replied. "Lady Beneath the Earth."

"But you hesitate." It was not a question.

"Yes," I admitted. "For some reason it makes me apprehensive. I mean She's underground in the Crypt; it seems...spooky."

"Ah," he said, "So, the composed Mademoiselle Verger *is* flappable." I tilted my face away from him and said, "That's one way of describing me, yes."

"Not the entire landscape though."

"No."

"I see." He hesitated then said, "The artist uses sensitivity as a strength. And takes care that it not become a weakness."

"Thanks for the lecture," I replied tartly. I stood. "I'll be sure to remember it when I'm working on my art project."

For a moment he looked affronted. He started to speak but I rushed on. "I'm tired of those who criticize passion in art." I stared straight at him. "As I think *that's the point*. The passion of the artist as well as the emotional response of the viewer."

"Bravo," he said quietly. "Though not everyone responds the same way."

"Of course not," I replied, my voice taut.

I knew that millions of folks visited Chartres annually. I had no doubt that some lingered, and others rejoiced, while still others passed through without absorbing the full enormity of the place. But then, that is the nature of art; it invites an interplay between the creator and the witness and that dance is unique to each duet. We stood there for a moment until I recognized in his scrutiny that he understood. That he saw me.

Saw *me*.

I was glad when he moved toward me, he did not touch me. I saw the rise and fall of his breath as we allowed a silence. Then our hands found one another again. I said, "Shall we move on?"

As we stepped out of the cathedral and into the blinding sunlight my unease grew. We had to take quite a few steps to wind around the bulk of the Cathedral and on to the entrance of the Crypt. The distance gave me time to think of excuses not to go. *I needed to call Odile! And my friend Dette!*

I barely heard his voice telling me he had access to a key so we could enter the Crypt without the formal tour guide. The last thing I wanted was for Jules to see me lose control. I was about to inform him that I would stick with my plan to do the group tour tomorrow, when I found myself being drawn forward by the combined force of his presence and his hand at the small of my back.

I began lecturing myself that my fear was irrational. Art came from some impulse deep within me that I intuitively trusted was my path. But this – a mysterious Madonna figure *under the ground.* What would happen to me down there in the darkness?

Jules began to speak, and I believe it was in part to ease my fears. "The efforts here, back in the twelfth century," he said as we walked toward the narrow wooden door that led to the underground chambers, "were totally directed towards building the actual structure, massive as it was. But there is very little documentation of the building process itself – the designs, plans, that sort of thing. For many reasons, the complexities of which I won't bore you with," – he smiled at me – "in time it became the principal sanctuary of the Mother of God in France. The original dedication was to 'the virgin who will give birth'."

"Well, there's a paradox for you." Talking about the history of the Cathedral helped return me to myself.

"I'll say," he said. I found myself wondering where he'd learned his American phrasing.

What I said was, "I get quite stuck on the Virgin part of the Blessed Mother story."

He smiled and said, "Yes. Many of us get stuck on the virgin part."

"I've been thinking," I said, feeling the heat on my cheeks even as hearing my own voice loosened my anxiety, "What if 'virginal' means She is *inviolate*? Totally complete in Herself?" I stopped. He turned to look at me, shading his eyes with his hand. I said, "She grew the divine Child within Her human body. She gave birth on Her own in a barn." I closed my hand around his arm, words now spilling out of me.

"Think about it, there is no midwife in the Nativity story, is there? Only some animals in the stable. And Joseph somewhere nearby, but certainly not attending a woman in childbirth. Nor do I think the three Wise Men were lending a hand, do you?" Jules remained still.

Undeterred, I continued, "So, in a way, 'virgin' recognizes that walking in faith with God She is complete in Herself. She is filled with *Her own strength*."

I saw his eyebrows raise and I waited while he took in my words. "That's very interesting," he said slowly. I felt a cooling stream of relief rush through me though I looked away, then up at the clear blue bowl of the sky.

We'd completed our walk around the Cathedral. "As before," he added, "your thoughts are intriguing." He gestured toward a nearby wooden door with black iron hinges, "*Nous sommes arrivés.* I suggest we go inside now so we have time before the afternoon tour group arrives and it gets busy."

I hesitated one more second before I agreed. "Okay," I said, "let's go."

CHAPTER 13

Miriam: The Crypt of Chartres Cathedral

JUNE 2001

The iron hinges on the wooden door bespoke its ancient vintage.

"Hold on, Monsieur Poirier –"

"Jules," he reminded me. "You have nothing to be afraid of," he added quietly. Nodding at the guard, he took a brass key from his pocket. He fit the key in the lock and turned it. I heard the click and Jules stepped with me across the threshold into black darkness. Dazed, my heart thudding, I was a hair's breadth from full-blown panic when I felt his hand reach for mine and a calm settled over me. Gradually, my eyes grew accustomed to the dim light and I put my hand out to touch the cool stone wall as we stepped down, down, down into the underground chambers. When the stairs ended, we were standing on packed earth. I held onto his hand as he began speaking in a quiet voice. "This vast set of rooms was the only part of the original cathedral that survived the fire in 1194."

I nodded though I wasn't sure how much he could see. "The new Church - the one above we were just in - was built on the foundation of the Crypt. For this reason, Chartres is immense, the largest Gothic church in France. The transept is the largest in France, an astonishing 212 feet!" I could see his face now as he smiled, "You see, I translated the meters into feet for you."

"Much obliged," I whispered.

"The choir, too, is the largest in all of France. What makes this extraordinary?"

"All of it?"

"Yes, good point. But here's what I meant. The construction of this massive building, unlike *Notre Dame Cathedral de Paris*, is not in a major city of France."

"But in a very small town," I realized.

"Right." He squeezed my hand. I squeezed back. I'd been so frightened of coming down here. Now I felt I could stay here for a thousand years.

"Now, being the intelligent woman you are, you might be asking: How did this come about? How could such a small, rural town afford to build this monumental place?" he said.

"I was just wondering that, yes."

He laughed and squeezed my hand again. "Good girl. I knew you would like it here."

"Love it."

He laughed again. "I'll explain how in a moment." We kept walking until we reached the base of several massive stone pillars, in some places crumbling with age. "The Cathedral that most pilgrims and tourists visit is actually the second floor. That entire area was built above and supported by these original pillars. We're standing in the original sacred 'cave' of the structure if you will."

The Crypt was much larger than I'd expected, and the air was even chillier than where we'd entered. The atmosphere seemed to shiver with spirits from times long past.

"We're moving to the deepest part of the cavern."

Uh-oh, my uneasiness spiked. We came to stop before a deep well whose walls were made of stone. No words were necessary to tell me it dated from ancient times as I peered into the dark water impossibly far below. "That water is below the level of the neighboring Eure River," Jules said.

"Go on," I encouraged him. I didn't want to think too long about the depth.

"This well is known as '*Saints Forts*,'" he added. The name is derived from *Locus Fortis* or "Strong Place".

"I can't decide if it's magical. Or terrifying," I said.

He smiled. "Maybe both."

How right he was! I didn't really believe in magic, but if there was magic in the world, this place quivered with it.

He looked down into the water. Maybe he was looking for his own answers down there, who knows? But then he said, "Here's how the village of Chartres afforded the cathedral. When a religious man of the twelfth century, Bernard of Clairvaux, to be exact – who was the force behind the building of Chartres Cathedral – was asked what God was, history has it that he said: "Width. Length. Depth."

I was silent a moment to take in the words. Then I said, "Spoken like a true architect?"

Jules paused before he replied, "I concede the point."

"I'm sorry," I said for I could see my levity had shifted something in him. "That's actually a beautiful description of the divine."

"It is," he agreed.

A single lightbulb that glowed weirdly orange hung from a wire above the center of the well. Several black electric cord extensions hung down the side of the well and snaked to an outlet on a distant wall. Neither before nor since have I witnessed such a juxtaposition of the ancient and the modern.

Other than the dim light shed by this bulb, we were standing in total darkness. Strangely, in this sea of unusual light my earlier fear withdrew.

In a low voice Jules said, "The name, '*Chartres*', comes from a Druid tribe named 'Carnutes'. Some believe that the Druids of Gaul gathered here once a year." Now his voice softened to a whisper, "So pagans may have once worshipped here."

"I believe I mentioned this earlier," I whispered back.

"Oh, right."

I couldn't tell if he was teasing me, but in truth the talk of Druids unsettled me again. In response, my practical self swung into action and I moved a step away from him. "Well," I said, breaking the eerie silence of the place, "a cathedral dedicated to the Virgin Mary has got to have a cave, right?"

"Meaning?"

I peered into the well. "You mentioned that the cathedral was dedicated to 'the virgin who will give birth'. It seems fitting to me that there would be a cave, you know, the idea of the woman going to some private dark place to enter the mystery of giving birth." I stopped. My words had poured out of me without any personal attachment to them until I had said 'giving birth'. All my anguish related to wanting a child now rushed in. I looked away from Jules, but he gently turned my face toward him and asked, "What is it?"

"Nothing. Remember the reason you brought me down here?" I said quickly. "To see the Black Madonna?"

He looked at me, jiggling the keys in his pocket, and seemed to make a decision. He would follow my lead and drop the subject I had painfully stumbled onto. "*Bon*," he said, "As you wish."

We left the strange light behind us and crept deeper into the darkness along a narrow pathway. I heard the echo of ancient footsteps, the rustling of robes, the burbling of water from somewhere nearby. We walked under an stone arch into yet another antechamber that held a small altar. I was not sure why he stopped until I turned around and saw Her.

The instant my eyes fell upon Her I felt an involuntary swell of emotion.

"*Voilà: Notre Dame Sous Terre*," I heard Jules say. I was not prepared for the bolt of raw energy that coursed through me when I first laid eyes on "Our Lady Under the Earth." I was struck by how the ebony wood palpably evoked 'primal matter' – *mater* – *mother* – of dark earth. About three feet in height, Her head was not bowed in gentle submission, nor raised in adoration, it was upright and proud. A tangible sense of strength emanated from Her. She was seated on a throne connoting Her majesty in a way that mere words could not achieve.

Suddenly I realized what historians meant when they distinguished between a 'throne of wisdom Madonna' with the child seated between her legs as this one was, and the later 'Christian' kind with a standing woman holding the child within the curve of her left arm. This woman's hands were markedly large. And Her eyes were closed. I had never seen a Madonna seated in an upright position with Her eyes closed.

"Scholars believe the closed eyes link Her to an earlier vision of pre-Christian cultures. Their feminine divine figures were represented with closed eyes." I heard Jules's voice from a distance.

Closed eyes. This made perfect sense to me. Like a curtain lifted, I understood that if I maintained the courage to be with this seated woman, She might lead me to the strength I needed to complete my art project. Long after I left Her at Chartres, this Black Madonna compelled me to dig into the deepest core of myself. I found myself longing to sit with Her, to hear *Her* story.

What stories of faith help us understand the unknowable? As I heard myself murmur this question I returned as from a great distance and once more felt Jules's presence beside me. This man was a near stranger to me, yet down here in the wintry subterranean air I sensed he fathomed a part of me that no one else did. We did not touch, not then. We stood and let the shivering candles and scent of the old stone be our companions.

After a time - 10 minutes? A month? A century? – we took our quiet leave of the place. We climbed back up to the outer world. While Jules chatted easily to the guard, I sat on a nearby bench collecting my thoughts.

Notre Dame Sous Terre is the figure of a mother holding a child in her lap just as the un-birthed soul is held in the womb. Unlike *Pilar*, Her sister who stands in the aboveground Cathedral under a golden crown and is dressed by religious in elaborate gowns, the woman underground is seated upright on Her throne holding Herself in resolute dignity.

When Jules approached me, I stood and motioned toward the Cathedral. I said, "I'm going to return to the Blue Virgin window."

"*Bien sûr*," he said.

"I'm not expecting you to go with me," I said.

"Your perspective is important to me," he replied evenly.

I hurried back along the length of the Cathedral and re-entered it. In my hurry I nearly downed the old woman holding a brass donations plate at the West entry door. I made an effort to slow down to a church-like pace as I moved to my intended destination. There I stopped, breathless, beneath the window of the Blue Virgin. "*Voilà!*" I said. "I knew it!" Jules regarded me with an expression that wavered between pleasure at my enthusiasm and uncertainty of my sanity.

"Don't you see?" I asked. The Blue Virgin is not standing." When I noticed the twitch of unease on his face, I lowered my voice. "And I thought I was seeing Her so clearly." I took his arm, "Look at Her! She, too, is seated on Her throne of wisdom just like Her great-great-great grandmother in her chamber down below the earth is seated. Holy moly!" The words of my girlhood rolled out of my mouth with an ease that surprised me.

"And the significance is?" Jules said carefully.

"Well," I replied, "my thoughts are a long way from coalescing on this. But the Madonnas seated on a throne are, to me, more evocative. For the longest time I've been upset" –his golden eyes steadily held my own – "that the only image I have of the Divine One is male. The holy trinity, the sign of the cross, The Father, the Son and the Holy Ghost? God dammit! Where is the *mother*? Where is the female? If we are made in the image of God, well, you know, I don't have a *male* body."

The faint smile on Jules's lips was quickly withdrawn as he glanced at my face.

"Why don't I, why don't all women of my faith and all the women of the Abrahamic faiths – have a *female* image of the divine?"

"The Virgin Mary we're looking at –" he began.

"Is not considered to be divine Herself," I finished for him.

"Ah," he said slowly, "you're right. By Catholic doctrine She is holy, but She is not divine."

"The Virgin in this beautiful window and the Black Madonna below ground each sit on their throne of wisdom." I looked at Jules. "But one of them is below the ground. Why is that?"

"I'm not sure," he replied.

"Neither am I." I paused. "But it bears thinking about. Even *Pilar*, the other Black Madonna in this Cathedral, is not on the main altar, but hidden away in an alcove. Why are the Black Madonnas in these less prominent places?"

He crossed his arms against his chest. "An interesting question. You don't stop surprising me," he said. "And I really like that."

"It's who I am," I said. "I'm intrigued by spiritual matters."

"No one's asking you to stop," he said.

"And it's necessary for my current art."

"Yes," he said, shoving his hands in his pockets.

We stood there a moment longer, while once again, strangers moved around us. Then Jules said, "*Je suis désolé*, but I must leave you now. I have some restoration work to supervise here and I'm already late."

"It's no problem," I said. In truth, I was relieved for I needed time to think on my own. I made my way slowly to the ancient stone labyrinth that rests on the ground near the rear of the Cathedral. Before I'd begun my research for this trip, I had not known it existed. Now, I felt eager to walk it.

There were several other people walking the enormous maze, and we all walked according to our own rhythm. To my surprise, it became one of the most purely spiritual experiences of my life. As my body moved, I began to understand that the Black Madonna might offer me a spaciousness that allowed for reflection on both my troubled childhood and the feminine divine.

The guidebook had described the labyrinth as 'a confusing set of tortuous paths winding their way inside a larger circular direction'. *How perfect* I thought *just like my life.*

CHAPTER 14

Odile: Paris

JUNE 2001

When I heard that Miriam, Maman's best friend and my godmother, was coming to Paris the embryo of an idea flashed in my brain. Miriam was besotted with me, always had been. It was like a chess game; put all the pieces in place correctly and presto, checkmate. The night before Miriam was due to arrive, I drank a couple of beers as I sat on the sidewalk waiting for Alain. Waiting again, dammit. The asshole had never bothered to make me a key. I touched my talismans: the tiny diamond earring piercing my nose, the other one winking on my eyebrow. My friends, always there for me. Alain had begged me to pierce my tongue, but I hadn't given in yet. Let him wait for a change, see how he likes it.

I'm beginning to wonder about Alain, though; maybe this would be the night he wouldn't come at all. Just thinking of his muscled body filled me with lust and a longing so deep I doubled over, tucking my chin to my chest and feeling myself beginning to melt into the pavement. Slumping toward the ground I exchanged a look with the dark-haired man cleaning the street, the whirring of the bright-green machine he was steering causing my head to throb. He smiled at me, flashing a gold tooth. *Salut, copain. Take me away, make me forget.* He made an obscene gesture and I laughed. Everyone is my friend tonight. This man, Gabriella, the large girl from Argentina who had seduced me several weeks ago in her bed at the university. Strange to be crushed up against Gabriella's plump, yielding body, but exciting, hot. Friends with everyone, *oui, oui*...but where was Alain? I tasted salt-water on my cheeks. Tears, dammit? He wasn't worth it. Since I'd met him, I'd lost track of time, my new classes, even my pills. My world had become a spinning top that was disappearing me into the misty night. When I felt rather than saw the dark shadow approach, I didn't look up. Instead, I belched.

"*Odile, c'est déguelasse.*" That's disgusting. Alain's voice barked at me. "What is happening with you?" I half-lifted my head and moaned as my stomach clenched. He caught my head between his hands and forced open my mouth, his tongue already thrusting. Though a tiny warning bell clanged inside, I giggled. He pulled me up by my arms and caught me when the world tilted and my body sagged. "Alright, let's go. This is going to be a good night, a very good night..." I heard his voice from far away like in a dream and didn't catch the note of menace.

Dragging me upstairs to his room one heavy step at a time, he became impatient. "Odile, *aides-moi, ton fou.*" Help me, bitch. I began to giggle, helplessly, and once he slapped me, hard. "*Arrêtes-toi!*" He was growing angrier, I knew that, but I couldn't stop; even the pain of his slap made me laugh. He pulled my shirt over my face to muffle the sound of hysteria and turned around to drag rather than carry me up the rest of the stairs. "Bump, bump, bump on my bum!" I giggled as he dragged and cursed me. At last he deposited me with a loud thump onto the stone floor, roaches scurrying as I landed near his door. He searched in the pockets of his worn jeans for the key, swore, searched again. Finally, he located it, and turned it in the lock. I heard the sharp sound of the latch clicking into place and only then did I feel a tremor of uneasiness. He picked me up and threw me down hard onto the middle of the bed used food wraps crackling beneath me. Then he took his clothes off and yanked down my zipper. Climbing on top of me he entered me quickly, roughly, and pinned my arms to the damp mattress, his fingers digging into my skin. I knew better than to scream, for hard-won experience had taught me this would only increase his violence. And so, I did not resist. I floated above the room like a cloud lazily watching the figures writhing on the filthy bed below. Afterwards, I stumbled down the dank hall to the bathroom he shared with the other tenants. I covered my nose against the stench of urine and tossed garbage. I vomited again and again into the toilet.

At last I slid to the floor, leaning my head against the cool gray-green tiles of the walls. To my surprise, I heard a small voice I barely recognized as my own whisper, "*Maman, I need you.*" My mother would be appalled to see me in this place, I knew this, but unexpectedly I wanted her with a fierceness that shook me. Maybe it was the color of the tiles, but something made my mind drift back to a morning years ago, a June morning when *Maman* and I were outside our little house in Veneux D'Eau picking flowers. *Maman* was wearing a turquoise apron over her blouse and shorts so we could fill it up with fresh flowers. When we'd filled the apron, she carefully took it off and laid it on the ground. Then we rolled over and over and over down the incline of the nearby hill laughing at our shared freedom and delight. It was one of the few childhood memories I have of our laughing together.

The scurrying line of roaches brought me quickly out of my reverie back to the present. I walked unsteadily from the bathroom back down the hall to Alain's room. I shook my head slightly, and told myself to toughen up. My mother didn't have a clue that this stench-filled place was where I stayed most nights. My own room, closer to the cité uiversité I now attended, was clogged with a mound of dirty clothes, papers, and school books, but I was seldom there. I wanted to be with Alain; he was my drug. I hadn't been to classes in weeks. I pressed my lips together to strengthen my resolve. I'd get through somehow and if I didn't, if I failed, *tant pis*. I could always go to Uncle Jean's.

In the morning when I awakened, Alain was gone. With a groan I clutched my roiling stomach as my eyes roamed around the room, squinting at the bright, late morning sunlight. For the first time I took in the peeling paint, the torn rags we used to wipe up spills and the piles of discarded trash thrown helter-skelter throughout the space. Half-eaten apples and dozens of liquor bottles. No, *Maman*, I spoke silently to her, I'm not doing drugs; booze is my drug of choice. I saw that Alain had taken his personal belongings, meager though they were. He was gone. Something inside me felt like a rat scratching at walls. Scratching, scratching; the sound of desperation.

I fell to the floor and retched. I wiped my mouth with one corner of the sheets, pulled on the clothes I'd been wearing yesterday and left the room. Once outside, I stumbled along the cobblestone street running, running, until I reached the heavy green door of the clinic. When I rushed, breathless, into the small, cramped room, I ignored the cold looks of others who were already waiting. I soon learned that no doctor was available to see me and I slumped, defeated, into an orange plastic chair. An aide with bright hair and a steel clipboard approached me. I kept my voice flat as I made an appointment for the next day.

On my way back to my building I passed the patissérie where I often stopped for a treat, but today the sweet smells made me nauseous. Arriving at my room, I saw the scrawled note that was slipped half-way under the door. Miriam had called to tell me that she had arrived in Paris this morning. I placed the thin sheet of paper on the desk near my bed and reached for the phone. For a moment I hesitated, my thoughts circling, then the idea became focused: beautiful, simple, perfect. I threw one curled fist straight up into the air. I was seventeen years old and brilliant mistress of the universe.

CHAPTER 15

Miriam: Paris

JUNE 2001

"Odile! I gasped.

She'd finally left me a message to call her, but hadn't answered my calls until now. Dette's friend Jean had heard from Odile and had assured Dette that her daughter was alive. However, Odile had refused to tell him where she was and we were extremely worried. I was so excited and relieved to finally hear her voice in my ear that I think I alarmed her.

"*Oui!*" then more slowly, "Mmmmmiiiiirrrriamm?" Her words were slurred and I had never heard her so *removed.*

"Oh, darling girl. I'm so happy to hear your voice. Where are you?"

"Parrrissss."

Perfect, I thought. I'd taken the train from Chartres back to Paris to meet with another contact Thom had given me. I could meet with Odile today!

"Wonderful, *moi aussi!*" I said. "But you sound sleepy. Let's set a time to rendevous and I'll ring off." I was rushing as I always did when I got rattled.

"Okkkaaaaay." I thought I heard a sniffle but couldn't be sure.

"Listen, Odile, can you meet me at Le Fleurus? At 11 today?"

"*Ce sssssoirrrrrr*?"

She thought it was evening? My concern was increasing by the second. "*Chérie*, it's 9 in the morning."

"Ooooooh."

"Where are you? I'm coming over now."

"Nonnnn I'll be at Le Fleurusssss. Onnzzzze heurrrressss."

"That's right. 11 am. Le Fleurus. You sure?"

"Ssssssurrrrre. Cioa." She hung up.

I walked to the window in my Paris hotel room wondering what I'd say to Odile. I had the distinct feeling that the child needed to be rescued. But rescued from what, I had no idea. I dressed quickly and regarded my hair in the long mirror. I'd let it grow longer, though in the humidity that meant that a multitude of fine strands lifted away from my head and formed a cloud around my face. I moussed quickly and then moved to the door and out into the street.

My hotel was located in the 16th arrondissement so I decided to head out early so I could wander the Galerie-Musée Baccarat with its wonderful neo-rococo design. I wanted to see the marvelous play of light and movement there and hoped it would inspire something in me that I could bring to my own art piece.

I surprised myself by humming as I walked, a sign that France was unleashing something unfamiliar in me: I was slowly becoming more open to what the world had to offer. Excited as always by the anticipation of entering a museum, for the moment I pushed aside my concern for Odile. On impulse, I entered a boutique I'd noticed earlier and bought myself a gorgeous silk top, aubergine dusted with silver. *Ooh la-la*, I whispered to myself, *becoming quite the chic Parisienne, are we?* I giggled at the deliciousness of acting on impulse.

The museum was dazzling as I'd known it would be. But now I was late and had to hurry to be at the Café Fleurus on time. It was quite possible that Odile would simply leave if she did not find me there and that was the last thing I wanted. I seated myself *en plein air* at the last table available outside. I waited ten minutes or so, tapping my fingers on the table and sipping a mineral water as my worry grew. Finally, I saw Odile approaching.

Her bright blonde hair looked like it hadn't been washed in days, the first thing that further spiked my concern. Lavender shadows circled her eyes and her drawn face made her look a decade older than she was. And why was she wearing a loose blue top over her shorts instead of the crop tops she loved? But, still, my heart lifted to the sky; she was my girl and I thrilled to see her. I jumped up and hugged her tightly.

"My goodness it's wonderful to see you!"

"You, too," she mumbled.

"What would you like? Wine? Café?"

"Perrier."

When the waiter returned, I asked for coffee and the quiche Florentine. Odile waved her hand, said, "*Rien pour moi*."

"What? You're not eating?"

"Not hungry."

"Since when?" I couldn't remember a time she hadn't eaten with all the gusto of the young. She looked away and shrugged.

What the hell is going on? I decided to slow down. I would start talking about myself in hopes it would relieve the tension in her enough so she would eventually start talking to me of her own accord.

"So, Odile, you know I'm here to do an art project? About a female icon?"

She looked at me dully and nodded.

"I hope you'll appreciate it."

"I will," she said with the first glimmer of a smile.

"You sure you don't want anything to eat? A chocolate croissant, perhaps?" I ventured.

She burst into tears. I froze in dismay for a split second. This was even more serious than I'd expected. I took her hand and said in a low voice, "Come, let's go inside where we can talk more privately." She wiped her eyes and blew her nose with the tissue I handed her. Then she let me lead her inside the café. I negotiated with the waiter who'd come running in our direction. "Perrier, no food," I commanded. He rushed away without a second glance, returned with two Perriers and withdrew.

Odile and I sat side by side in a booth at the back of the café. "What's going on?" I asked touching her arm. She rubbed her eyes and whispered, "I'm pregnant."

"*Merde*." It slipped out before I could stop it. "Come on, back to my hotel room. This is no place to have a conversation about this." I paid the waiter and took her arm. All the way to my hotel, up to the fourth floor in the elevator, and while I turned the key in the lock, she said not a word.

"Here, sit by me," I said patting the place on the wide bed next to where I'd sat down. I put my arms around her and held her. The moment I did that, she dissolved, sobbing as though the world had ended. When she grew calmer and began to compose herself, I brushed my fingers along her brow and said, "You don't have to explain anything. Just tell me how I can support you." My mind was scrambling to doctors, letters to her university professors excusing her absences, whatever she needed.

She completely surprised me when she looked at me and said, "I'm going to need a place to stay."

"But wait," I said, "you came back to Paris to restart courses here? So you have a room at the university, right?"

She replied immediately. "That's not what I mean." A truculent look had stolen over her face.

I shook my head, confused. She couldn't mean stay with me here in France? She couldn't stay with me in my hotel room which I'd be leaving that evening. What on earth did she mean?

"Well," I tried, "you always have a room at your mother's, right?"

"No!" she spat.

That was foolish of me. Dette had made very clear that Odile was not speaking with her.

"Darling," I tried again, "I'm not sure what you mean."

She moved away from me on the bed. "I want to go back to America with you."

"What?" I burst out. I swallowed and added, "I'm not going back until the fall. Is that what you mean?"

"*Non, pas de tout!* That's not what I mean!" she said fiercely.

I blew my breath out, flummoxed. I looked at her, and in seeing the bedraggled shape she was in, softened my tone, "What do you mean, darling girl?"

"I mean, I want to have this baby in America and stay with you." The words rushed out of her like a roiling river.

I looked at her, my mouth agape, so shocked I was unable to utter a single word. Not just surprised, devastated.

Then she began talking. "My life is so fucked up. I'd finally gotten somewhere. On my own! EPFL. This amazing school – I was *doing it*, Miriam, *succeeding*."

I nodded, not breathing a word.

And out it spilled. The whole sordid story of the repugnant professor who'd attacked her. The chasm she fell into after that trauma. She didn't tell me who the father was, nor did I care. But I figured out it wasn't the asshole teacher who had impregnated her. And she'd received counseling and important support from the school. Plus, tender care by a girlfriend.

Thank God for girlfriends!

As she spat out a relentless stream of consciousness, I realized something. She believed this baby offered a way out of her misery. And she truly was ravaged by pain, I could see that on her face. Like a whirring series of frames, I saw the buildup of the past hurts she'd endured, first believing she was a constant disappointment to her mother, then her low self-worth being hammered in yet more deeply by miserable brats in school. Now the assault. Christ almighty, what an aching world.

She pushed herself up from the chair, crossed back to my bed and said, "Please, Miriam, I'm *begging* you. I *need* this. And," she looked into my face with softness now shimmering on her own, "think how fabulous it will be to share a tiny creature together." Fleetingly I thought of Seth, but honestly, he wasn't my biggest concern at that moment. That this was true, made me realize I'd already given up on that relationship; it was over. I would need to tell him and that made my stomach tighten further. But over and above that realization I was swept up in a turbulence of conflicting emotions – confusion, disbelief, doubt, love, sadness, more love.

"Oh my God, Odile." I lay back on the bed and put one arm over my face. "I'm very sorry I didn't know all this before now." I looked over at her feeling both ancient and sorrowful. "But I don't see how this could possibly work."

"Miriam," she snuggled up next to me just as she'd done as a child.

"A baby. You've always wanted a baby, haven't you?" I was sure I'd never said a word of that to her, yet because she knew me so well, she'd somehow discerned it.

"Just let me think, Odile, let me think." That, I later realized was a mistake. I should have said no immediately. Instead, her words sent my mind tumbling to images of a burbling infant, smiling, gurgling, cooing. Of shopping for tiny baby clothes on Wisconsin Avenue in Georgetown with Odile, my beloved goddaughter. Unexpectedly, scrambling, I thought: *Is this something the Black Madonna has brought to me?* And then, as the first flick of excitement rushed through me, *Is this how I am to have a child?* I rubbed my forehead again and again, thinking how wild this day had become.

Dazed, I carefully said, "It's really not a good idea."

"Miriam! You love me! What have I ever asked of you?"

I needed to stop her overwrought state, that much was clear. "Listen, give me a minute to think," I said again, sitting up.

Odile sat up beside me and hugged me tightly. "*Merci-merci-merci*," she said over and over.

"I haven't agreed to anything yet," I said sharply. But she knew me. And when I hadn't immediately shot the idea down, she knew I would fall. "How far along are you, anyway?" I asked tiredly.

"Maybe a couple-three months," she said. "But we have to make plans now. You have to tell Seth." She stopped when she saw what I'm sure was dismay on my face. "What? Seth won't like it?"

I shook my head, no. I'd been thinking about Jules, not Seth. About leaving a man I realized in that moment I really cared about, leaving him behind. What I said was, "I have to be in France at least another eight weeks, *chérie*, to work on my art." It was the wrong thing to say, for it focused not on her mad plan about me helping her with the baby, but on my art. And she was way ahead of me.

"Yes, I know, but that's ok. Once you're ready, we'll go. I still won't be showing much, I can hide in clothes, *pas de problème*." No problem? I should have laughed out loud at the irony, the absurdity. of that statement.

"Hide?" I asked. "Who exactly would you be hiding from?"

She looked at me incredulously and said, "Why, Maman, of course."

"What?" It had not occurred to me she wouldn't be telling Dette immediately.

"Excuse me a sec," she said, "I have to run to the loo," and she rushed off to the well-appointed but tiny bathroom off the bedroom. While she was gone my hand fell on the silk throw flung across my bed which made me think at once of the impossibly soft skin of an infant. Instantly my mind flew back to images of fat babies with tightly-closed eyes and chubby rolls of fat under their chins and along their thighs, and the fetching baby clothes I'd seen in a store window that had twisted my heart in two as I'd walked to my hotel this morning.

Odile rushed back into the bedroom. "Please, please say yes, Miriam. Imagine – a baby we'd share!" I saw in her eyes how much she wanted this.

"Have you thought about how you'd have to stop drinking and drugging?" For the first time I wondered if she needed a rehab placement.

"*Oui, bien sûr!*" she said. "I'm off drugs."

"Except for alcohol?" I was thinking of our phone conversation earlier in the day.

"No more!" she insisted.

Why was I even asking these questions? This was a no-brainer. Except...I'd always wanted to give this girl the world. I could do this for her, couldn't I? My desire for a child and Seth's unwillingness to agree, wasn't that the first impetus that had propelled me to France? And Jules? Jules was an intermittent reverie. Sure, I hoped to enjoy his company while I was here, but if I imagined him staying with me for the long haul, that was pure fantasy.

"Well, here's the deal," I said as her eyes lit up with adoration like a puppy who's been given her favorite treat. "We call your mother today to discuss this."

"No deal!" she snapped. "She will not allow it."

I knew Odile was right about that. But I couldn't keep this from Dette.

"Fine," Odile snapped, "I do have other options I can p-p-pursue." She had not stammered in my presence for a very long time. That's what caught at my heart. That, plus the plummet my heart had taken when the image of a new baby in my home had melted away. Odile saw the change on my face. She sat up straighter to press her advantage.

"Listen," she offered, "how about if we wait the couple of months you need to be in France to work on your art and tell her when you're ready to return to the States?" I knew what she was getting at: by then, the pregnancy would be far enough along that Dette would not insist on a different plan

I adored this girl. And a tiny baby! Against my better judgment, I agreed. I walked straight into that abyss eyes wide closed.

CHAPTER 16

Miriam: Mont Saint Michel

JUNE 2001

My first sight of it made me gasp. I'd been so intent on practicing the names of the small villages we were passing through that I hadn't realized how close we were to the *Abbaye du Mont St Michel*. When Dette slowed the car, I glanced up and my breath stopped. The massive structure loomed before us, the bulk of it balanced impossibly high on granite boulders that exploded vertically out of the ocean. A gargantuan hulk, it looked like God had reached down and pulled the towering stone structure up out of the water and held it there. I could not begin to comprehend the staggering amount of human brawn, effort, and intelligence required to bring such an enormous creation into being on top of a pile of rocks on an islet that had been accessible only by foot.

I'd vaguely known that the island where Mont St. Michel sits was surrounded by flat marshes and water. But I hadn't realized until Dette drove over the crossing from the mainland to the island that the approach to the Abbey was now over a manmade causeway.

"I see your normal powers of speech have deserted you," Dette said as we climbed out of her car.

"If you hadn't already been here several times before I'm certain that even yours would be, too," I retorted. She laughed.

"It's absolutely *incredible*," I said. We stopped walking so I could take in the vista before me. The contrast between the azure sky and the massive stone structure rising high above the sea was astounding. "That enormous, perpendicular mass of stone," I said slowly. "I am *awed*."

"It does give new meaning to the word magnificent," Dette agreed. She pointed to a group of sheep across the way munching on their morning's feast. "There you see the world's only herd of salt-water plant-eating sheep," she added.

"Also extraordinary," I said.

Dette replied, "Damn right!" in such a strong American accent that I burst out laughing "Ah, Dette," I said, "why did I go so long without seeing you?"

"A damn good question," she said and it was my turn to laugh.

She took my arm as we moved closer to the Abbey. "Let's not do the formal tour, let's go on our own. And remember, if we want to walk around the entire island at the base of the Abbey –"

"Oh, I do!"

"– we need to be mindful of the time. It's only possible to do that at low tide." I raised my eyebrows when she added, "High tide rises up to 45 feet and comes in – whoosh! – as quickly as a galloping horse. I've not seen it myself, but that's what the guidebooks warn."

I tilted my head to see if she was playing with me, and she said, "Not kidding."

"This entire place is *tellement incroyable*."

"I had a feeling you'd adore it."

Ease had settled in around us like a soft shawl. With the sunlight warm on our faces we paused to look up, and up and up at the gargantuan form before us. At the apex a golden figure soared into the blue sky. "That's the archangel, Michael," Dette said, her eyes mischievous. "and legend has it that some bishop back in the eighth century was instructed by said archangel to build a church on the mount. Well, His Holiness the Bishop ignored the saintly summons." She continued, "But woe unto him. Because after several requests went ignored the archangel burned a hole in the Bishop's skull!" I leaned in, fascinated.

"That did the trick," she winked at me.

"That would tend to make an impression on one's decision-making process," I said dryly.

Dette smiled and said, "And at last the church was begun, and later on, the Abbey and – *voilà* – it's still here some *13 centuries* later."

"You know the angel Michael has another significance, right?" I asked as we began walking across the parking lot toward the enclosure of stone walls and bastions surrounding the Abbey.

"No, I don't know," she said. "My art education didn't take in the history of art, just its application onto fabric."

"Right. Anyway, my wider education," I winked at her and she stuck her tongue out at me, "has informed me that his representation in sculpture is of a powerful man slaying a dragon with a silver sword." She nodded. "And my professor of spirituality in art told us that beyond the Christian allegory of man slaying sin is another possible meaning."

"And I'm sure you're about to elucidate me."

"I am. It's the allegory of a man pushing down knowledge that others don't want to be heard."

"Very interesting! No wonder I have you for a friend."

"It's a lot to think about."

"True, but we'd better get walking if we want to see everything before the tide smothers us." I nodded and we walked closer to the structure. It seemed even more massive now that its height of over 300 feet loomed directly in front of us. We stood a moment in respectful appreciation.

"The sheer ambition of man," I said softly.

"Indeed," Dette replied. She added, "And with them bigger is always better." That, of course, got us laughing. We started up the winding street that led through a small village and on up a steep hill that gave onto the Abbey itself.

Dette commented as we ambled through the village, "Any piece of touristy crap you could want you will find here." On both sides of the narrow cobblestone street tourist shops were crammed together chock-a-block, each one crammed with every size, shape, color, taste and texture of souvenirs. Brightly-colored silk scarves with images of the Abbey, plastic fans, balloons, postcards, watercolor posters, linens, fake tapestries, cheap glass reproductions, vinyl pocketbooks in ghastly colors, maps, and even a flock of black and white flyers that invited passersby to a night-time ghost tour of the small museum that was tucked between two shops. We heard tourists speaking in Norwegian, Chinese, Spanish, German, English, and Japanese. "It's like the United Nations on tour in northern France," Dette said.

"Yes," I said, "and one thing I love about France is that no matter where you go there is always a café and patisserie to greet you," as the smell of dark roast coffee and sweet cream pastries filled my nostrils.

"Something for everyone," Dette said, indicating with a toss of her head a bar across the narrow street. "But we mustn't linger if we want to walk the circumference of the island before the tide surges in."

"Let's go!" The steep ascent wound around the hill that eventually gave way to stone stairs that proclaimed the way up and up to the enormous Abbey that crowned its crest. As we moved closer, a palpable sense of the ancient caused our gaiety to dissipate. I could find no words to describe the depth of my astonishment at what God and man had accomplished here. Dette, too, was uncharacteristically quiet as we took our first step up the broad stone steps. It was difficult to take in the fact that these stairs were some fourteen hundred years old. The wide sandstone steps, a dusty reddish hue, dipped slightly in the middle, clearly the imprint of the thousands who had stepped here before us.

We kept climbing, Dette and I chatting amiably as we ascended.

"We've made 450 steps!" she announced as I caught my breath. "And we're only halfway to the top!" We were standing on an enormous stone terrace at the entry to the Abbey itself.

"I understand now why you neglected to tell me just how many steps there are," I grumbled, reaching behind my neck to fan out my damp shirt. "Where's that water we brought?" I asked. "This is the perfect place to stop for a bit."

"*Voilà*," she said, handing the thermos to me. How beautiful she looked in her yellow shorts and top, a contrast to her tanned skin.

I took a huge gulp of water and wiped the sweat off my face, turning to look at the view. Golden sunlight glistened off the azure water that surrounded us on all sides. From somewhere in the inner gardens of the cloister I caught the scent of lavender and the gentle sound of bells.

"This. Is. Divine." I said. There was no other sound except the distant cry of seabirds. We moved as one closer to the edge of the terrace.

"Huh," I said looking at the line of small dark birds I saw wading from the edge of the Abbey over to a speck of island across the marsh flats, "look at those tiny birds lining up."

"Sweetie pie," Dette said, "those aren't birds. Look closer."

"No way," I breathed as I moved nearer the edge of the stone plateau. We were at such a high altitude that my eyes had deceived me: the figures moving below were humans, a row of people in single file splashing their way toward the island we were standing on. As they came into focus, I heard the faint sound of their laughter. I saw that, in fact, they were making their way not *to* the island, but back *from* it – and in good haste.

"A good thing they're hurrying back to the mainland," Dette said, "as a few unwary folks have drowned when they disregarded the tide times."

"Good grief." I shivered despite the warmth of the day. "Alright, onward," I decided. We turned our backs to the water and walked over to the colossal arch of stone that formed the entry into the Abbey itself. I said quietly, "Even if you're not here for religious reasons, there is something powerful here."

"Yes," she whispered as she moved closer to me and took my arm. Her warm touch gladdened me. As we crossed over the threshold and stepped into the Abbey, we moved from bright sunlight into dusk, and a silence fell over us again. The air inside held a definite chill and I reached into my bag.

"Here, let me help you," Dette said quietly. She took my pale blue shawl from me and placed it around my shoulders. Then she pulled a light sweater the color of flame from her bag.

"And I'll help you," I said, smiling as she nodded.

There was a nearly palpable sense of the sacred in this place such that we did not speak again for several minutes. Some places hold a sense of the spiritual regardless of the religious intent imposed upon them; this was one of them. The Greeks have a word for this: *temenos*. I've always thought it a beautiful word and it perfectly suited this singular place.

And so, we wandered around the rooms – dim and vast – where for centuries monks have lived. I thought of Jules as we examined the assemblage of rooms, from the scriptorium where the brothers painted their verses, to the stone-walled kitchens with their enormous black iron stoves where huge fires had roared, to a small side chapel filled with lambent light, and on to an inner cloistered garden. It was still thriving with flowers and lacey herbs. Someone took great care to keep the bloom of nature alive here. We lingered a moment taking in the fragrance before we moved into another huge room. Suddenly I stopped. Gasped. For there, inside the ancient chamber a small Black Madonna stood alone.

She wore a flowing gold gown and held an infant Child high within

Her right arm. Both She and the Child had skin as black as coal. I was struck dumbfounded.

"Where did She come from?" I whispered to Dette.

"No idea."

"Who put Her here like this in the middle of this vast room?"

"No clue."

Coming so unexpectedly upon a Black Madonna in this hallowed space moved me profoundly. I knew that art held meaning to the creator. As a result, my mind filled with more questions. *What was the intent behind placing Her here? Why is She completely alone? Does anyone witness to Her?* A woman leading a tour group of six or seven people arrived and sailed right by the Black Madonna. As the guide gave her spiel, not a word was mentioned about the small black figure.

The female statue, no more than 20 inches high, held a stillness about Her. This female was standing her ground. *What have you seen?* I wanted to ask Her. *Do you stand for all the women whose voices have been silenced?* I wondered what would happen if I stayed behind through the dark night with Her, if a veil would be lifted between the known world and the unknown. On this day that began with giddy lightness between me and my dear friend, the tides of mystery rushed to fill me with questions. More than ever before the Black Madonna crawled her way deeply into my soul, the way a long curling root seeks nourishment and water from the soil. I longed to place my fingers on Her face, but instead, I stood back and lowered my head in prayer: *Woman, heal the woundedness of the world. Woman, shed your light into the shadows.*

I was grateful that Dette made no move to leave as I stood, transfixed, in that room for a long while. Truly, it felt like I was stepping outside of time. Our breaths rose and fell, rose and fell. Then, as if on some silent cue, we moved away together.

Later, we sat in a patch of honeyed sunlight in a small garden where we breathed in the scent of jasmine and rosemary. "Miriam," Dette said, touching my arm lightly, "this seems the right time to ask you to tell me more about the Black Madonnas. I know that most of the statues are here in France, but I've never known much about them."

I told her what little I knew. One of the most intriguing things I'd learned from my research was that the hierarchy of the Catholic Church at the time of the Council of Trent in the 16th century – which would be after the time that most of the original Black Madonnas were already in existence – reviewed all cult images and discarded those which did not meet their criteria of 'piety and beauty'.

"What gave those boys the right to decide piety and beauty?" Dette asked munching on the crusty bread, brie, and greens we'd bought for our picnic.

"Well, my friend, listen to this," I said, warming to my tale. "The Black Madonnas were not discarded."

"*Merde*," Dette said in mock wonder, "sometimes the old boys got it right. Kind of makes a woman believe in miracles."

I smiled and said, "The black color gave weight to the belief that the Black Madonna statues were ancient and from the East – where the Mother of God was historically from – and therefore they were considered 'authentic' and 'holy'." Dette stopped eating and began plucking nearby grasses while she listened.

I went on, "As you know, during the French Revolution the priests were hated." Dette grimaced and nodded while I continued, "In fact, this very Abbey became a prison where clerics were imprisoned. Talk about irony, right?"

"*D'accord*."

"Quite a few of the Black Madonnas were destroyed at that time." Dette ran a long strand of grass through her lips. "But, after the Revolution had come to its violent close, an architectural restorer took it as his mission to restore France's famous Black Madonna of Le Puy."

Dette nodded in recognition.

"He painted the cheeks of the woman and child a rosy color and gave the Madonna and Child blue eyes instead of the black cheeks and dark eyes they'd had in the original figure." I checked to see if Dette was still listening. "When he painted them like that, the faithful protested. And loudly."

Dette asked, "Why?"

"Apparently, the dark color represented the ancient and therefore 'authentic' image. The guy lost no time in painting the faces and hands black as they had been before. As for any revered image, it was *the sacred meaning* that mattered."

Dette said dryly, "Of course, the *historical* Mary would have had skin more of an olive tone than a peaches and cream one."

"True enough," I agreed. "What I hadn't realized until I did my research was that there have been many faithful followers of the Catholic Church who revered the Black Madonna as the Virgin Mary for a long time."

Dette considered my words, a somber look on her face. "*Mais oui,*" she said, "there are some who still continue to revere them."

"Huh." I had not known this.

"Yes, many of them are considered to have miraculous powers even today and pilgrims approach them for healing," she added.

I sighed and said, "This is a real testament to their faith. I'd truly like to believe in a Mary who has healing powers. But I just don't know." I paused, "Then again," I said, glancing at my friend, "who am I to judge one's faith, me with all my questions?"

"Nothing wrong with questions. Seems to me what's wrong are the boys in power who believe they have all the answers. When clearly, they don't," she said.

"That's for sure," I replied, continuing, "Many of the Black Madonnas are located in places where followers of much earlier religions worshipped. I have to wonder if in fact the Church appropriated in the Black Madonna the power of an earlier earth goddess?"

Dette nodded, "It's certainly a possibility." We sat for a while taking in the nearby scent of meat being grilled. In the distance bells chimed softly. "I wonder," I said, "who are the monks who still reside here? And if there are nuns here or ever were?"

"Well, I did see some nuns slip around a corner."

"You didn't tell me!"

"Well, they were gone by the time I looked back at you."

"Damn! They would know how that Black Madonna statue got here and what She means."

"What She means to them, anyway." Dette said. She put our sandwich wrappings into her canvas tote and took out a bunch of grapes, tossing one to me. More bells sounded softly nearby.

"The sound of those bells reminds me of something," I said as I caught the grape and enjoyed its sweetness in my mouth. "A few years ago, they remade the gigantic bells that ring at *Notre Dame de Paris.* All but one of the original ones were melted down to be used for weapons during the French Revolution."

"The ones that Quaismodo rang, you mean?" Dette winked as she spoke.

"The same," I smiled in return. "And guess what?"

"I give up."

"The bells are nearly 80% copper!"

Dette's face was a painting of amazement. "Like you use in your art! Good God, you are a wonder of facts, my friend."

"And so much more," I teased.

"Truer words were never spoken," she agreed easily. She raised the bottle of wine to her lips and I watched the last drops fall into her mouth.

But, Dette, I'm not always truthful I thought uneasily as Odile's face came to me. I cleared my throat and steered away from Odile. I said, "And here's something else." Dette rolled her eyes, but I pressed on. "There's a growing interest in the Black Madonna by non-Catholics. I've been wondering: what's the pull?"

Dette shrugged.

"Today when I entered that gargantuan stone chamber and unexpectedly came upon that small Black Madonna, I felt an immediate tug at the back of my throat."

Dette was squinting at me now, the sun facing her.

"The figure evoked" – I searched for the right words – "an intensity. It was visceral. Strange, right?" I looked down the hill away from the Abbey.

Dette handed me a few more grapes.

"Since I arrived in France, I've done a lot of research on the Black Madonna, but I've seen nothing about the one here. It strikes me as odd. Especially, you know, given that this place became a prison. Wouldn't She have been tossed out then?"

"One would think so," Dette agreed. "Someone must've hidden her and put Her here afterwards."

"Right," I said. "But again, I ask: who? And why?"

Dette stretched out on the blanket on the ground. "I'm guessing you're going to tell me?"

"Only when I know," I said, hitting her playfully. "Most likely She had a Christian meaning to whoever placed Her in that room. But that doesn't mean She originally was a Christian icon."

"How do you figure?"

"I have sifted through the suggestions by feminists and other 'experts' in the field of comparative religion that the Black Madonna represents an African earth goddess.

"That would make sense." she murmured.

"Meaning what?"

"She might actually be a representation of that Egyptian goddess." Dette lay down again.

"The ancient goddess, Isis?"

"*Oui.*"

"I see," I said, thinking hard. "It does seem likely that some of them are very old art pieces done by African artists long ago. The physiognomy conveys that truth."

Dette sat up. "You are onto something here, my friend."

"The differences between the pre-Christian ones and those that came later would be in the *intent* the artist had when creating them. And then how they were witnessed to."

"*D'accord*."

"So," I said, continuing to think out loud, "during the process of acculturation a dark-skinned Virgin Mary and dark-skinned Blessed Child came to connote 'authenticity'. And those became worshipped in the Christian world with miraculous healing attributed to Mary."

I plucked more grass, sucked on a strand. "I do find it interesting that the many of standing Black Madonnas in European churches are dressed in cloth gowns. The clothing covers the fact that many of these are actually seated Madonnas. Why are they covering up the bodies?"

Dette raised herself on one elbow. "*Je ne sais pas.*"

"*Moi non plus,*" I agreed. Looking into the horizon I said, "The dark color is certainly evocative, *n'est-ce pas?*"

Dette nodded, "*D'accord.*"

"It does feel different from the Virgin Mary colors we grew up with back in Maine, right?"

"*D'accord,*" she agreed. "This conversation makes me think of the many immigrants coming from North Africa. Changing the shape of France. I think this is a good thing. The complexity, I mean, not the violence."

"Understood." We let the sun rest on our faces a moment. "What I can't stop thinking about," I said, searching for the words that would convey my thoughts, "is that the racial encoding of dark skin accentuated the belief that somehow human beings with darker color skin are less than. A human being's worth has nothing to do with skin color."

"No," agreed Dette. "But that belief certainly plays out in our institutions."

"Yup. And it has caused untold horrors to occur," I said. "Did you know that *over three million* black people living in the United States were sold in slavery? I mean, in addition to the ones who came across the ocean in chains?" Dette shook her head. We let the grimness of that fact fill the silence between us for a moment.

"Dette," I sighed. "I have so many questions. Somehow this place is adding to them."

"Maybe the *temenos* you mentioned is pulling truth from you?"

"Hey," I said, my eyes widening, "maybe so." Then I sighed again.

"What?" she asked.

"I've set myself a major challenge trying to find my way through these complexities and then shape a coherent art piece that speaks truthfully."

"You're up to it," my friend replied.

"Thanks." I paused. "I am only now beginning to shape my thoughts on what the Black Madonna means to *me*. In the Catholic Church we grew up with the Blessed Virgin Mary represents the most humble and pure of womankind. She embodies faithfulness and devotion to God." Dette waited. "But now I wonder, what is it that this dark woman's figure is pulling from me?"

Dette said softly, "You appear to be figuring that out."

"I am." I looked at her. "I think you know, Dette, that in college I threw away everything to do with Catholicism. Everything else was new, exciting, fresh. That's what I wanted: a new beginning." I looked at her, "But maybe I threw away too much." Dette remained silent.

"The Black Madonna caught my attention as the unknown sometimes does." Dette smiled in agreement. "You know what?" She shook her head, no.

My voice dropped to a whisper, "What if She gives expression to what is hidden inside the sweet and venerated Virgin Mary? I mean, the essential female power of Mary?"

Dette's eyes widened.

"And what if they're not dichotomous?" I asked, my voice increasing in volume. "What if they're two aspects that come together to create a full-bodied ideal of the feminine divine?"

Dette sat up on full alert. I went on, "And why would they be dichotomous? For don't we have both purity *and* gutsiness in us?" I asked. "And don't we have both joy and sorrow, pain and bliss in our lives?"

She regarded me as though spellbound.

"Aren't you, aren't I, aren't all women tame *and* wild, ferocious *and* loving?" And – this is key –" I stopped briefly as I felt the intensity of my thoughts rising – "are *women* not also made in the image of the Divine? And could the Madonna herself not also be seen as both human *and* Divine?"

Dette's mouth dropped open.

"I know," I said, looking up into the expanse of heartbreakingly blue sky above the Abbey, "this is blasphemous." I pulled up more grasses. "And that bothers me. It's very difficult to take the Catholic girl out of the woman." My voice caught as I suddenly was filled with the memory of my mother taking me to our village church in Maine, Granny walking alongside us. I glanced at Dette and looked away from the sympathy in her eyes. I swallowed and added, "One thing I do know."

"What's that?"

I said, "I need to follow these questions."

"You will," she said without hesitation. Then she glanced at her watch and said, "*Tiens!* The hour has passed; we've missed our opportunity to walk around the island for the tide must be in now."

"Dammit! I really wanted to do that."

Disappointed, we looked around our picnic spot to make sure we'd gathered up everything. Litter in this place would be sacrilegious. "Something else about the Madonna and Child tugs at me," I said. "But my brain feels muddled now. I sure hope I figure it out before I start to put my hands on the tools for the *Opus Magnum* project."

"Ok, you've tired me right out, missy. I've no need to hear more today," Dette said with her customary forthrightness. "But I will say that I'm sure you'll figure it out in time."

She'd always believed in me. That was a gift I didn't take lightly. And although I was uneasy at Odile's presence lingering between us, I let the ticking of my father's old wristwatch fill the silence between us instead of the sound of my voice telling Dette what I knew about her daughter.

We walked down the curving road from the Abbey to the village, each step paralleling our return to the twenty-first century. When we neared the parking lot, I looked back at the mammoth Abbey. It appeared eerily medieval as evening began to wrap itself around her. Somewhere in the shadows a child wailed.

CHAPTER 17

Miriam: Veneux D'Eau,

JULY 2001

A darkening apricot and gold sunset swathed the sky as Dette and I settled into her car.

"Hey, Dette," I said looking over at her once we'd crossed back over the causeway.

She startled and said, "You caught me daydreaming."

"That's so unlike you," I joked.

She batted my arm and said, "Hey, I was drinking in your words up there on the mountain."

"Nice metaphor!"

"*Tais-toi, chérie*, I'm *trying* to ask you something.

"I'm listening."

"About time!" We laughed.

Then she said, "So, what I'm wondering is if you've spoken with any women of color about the Black Madonna?"

"Yes, recently."

"And she said?"

"Ok, here's the story. I attended a lecture at the Sorbonne."

"Ooh, the Sorbonne, aren't you the intelligent one?"

I ignored her. "Are you familiar with the work of Dr. Haniah Baldwin?"

"The name sounds familiar."

"You ignoramus," I teased. "She's a renowned Ph.D.-level American scholar on art history with a specialty in religious symbolism." I thought back to my time with Dr. Baldwin. I'd been wondering what thoughts women of color might have concerning the Black Madonna, so when I saw the flyer for her talk, I decided to attend. As the thunderous applause after her talk dwindled and people were filing out, I worked up my courage to go up and speak with her at the lectern.

"That was a provocative talk," I began.

"Thank you," she replied politely.

"My name is Miriam Verger. I'm an artist working on a project for the *Opus Magnum*."

"A pleasure," she said. "Dr. Haniah Baldwin," She stretched her hand out to me. Her handshake was strong, her hand warm, but her eyes surveyed me coolly. She wore a headwrap of gold and green. Her floor-length dress of green, red, and gold set off her dark skin and tall frame.

I took a deep breath and plunged in, "Please, call me Miriam."

She nodded.

"I'm here," I motioned toward the lecture hall, "because I know you're an expert on religion and religious icons."

She nodded again but kept her silence.

"I'm an artist," I started again.

"So you said."

"Do you have a minute to talk?" I asked.

"Yes, but only that."

"Thank you." I said. I plunged ahead, saying, "To get inspiration for my art I've been looking at Black Madonnas. The ones I know, er, that I've visited, well, the truth is, they strike me in a powerful way and... I'm learning, slowly, what they mean to me. What they evoke in me. But I'm searching to understand...what might they mean to a black woman?" I finished in a burst of words.

"I can't speak for all black women." Her resonant voice echoed softly in the nearly empty room.

"Of course not."

Dr. Baldwin moved a step back. In a low, measured voice she said, "As I've presented today, there's a real power in religious symbols – the cross, the prayer shawl, the prayer beads – all are efforts to represent the human relationship to the sacred."

"Yes."

"The richness increases when they have a tactile connection." She held her long-fingered hand out towards me.

"Yes. Like dipping a hand in water." I curled my fingers pointing downward.

"Or a whole body."

"Oh, right, of course." Her hand returned to the lectern, mine to my side.

"These things strongly unite people of the same faith tradition," she went on.

"They do."

"You're interested in the Madonna. She exists in most cultures, this exalted mother."

I felt a curl of energy inside as she moved closer to answering my question.

"You asked me about a black Madonna, what it means to a woman of color?" Her eyes were faraway now. "Let me start with Selu."

"Selu?"

"As you no doubt know," she replied in her professor's voice, "the original people of color in America, are now called 'Native Americans' or 'Indigenous Peoples'. I'm from Georgia, the land of the Cherokee people.

"The people who were brutally sent west by President Jackson on the Trail of Tears."

"The same. Selu is the Cherokee goddess of fecundity. She's also known as the Corn Mother."

"The Corn Mother," I murmured, feeling a twinge of pain at the thought of fertility, though I kept my gaze on her.

Dr. Baldwin said, "Since we don't have a lot of time, perhaps closer to your question is the relationship of the Black Madonna to today's communities of color. In Atlanta, where I live, for example, She represents a reclamation of our strength. Taking back, if you will," – she looked into my eyes – "the power cruelly denied our ancestors... stuffed naked and in chains in the bottom of ships – sweating, starving, sitting in their own feces..."

My stomach curdled. "I'm sorry," I said, crossing my hands over my chest.

"Yes," she replied, "though it's not just sorrow we're after." I uncrossed my arms and slowly lowered them as she continued. "Many people pray to the Black Madonnas. I believe in prayer. But prayer alone does not improve my people's access to more equitable health care, jobs, housing, schools."

"You're right." I stumbled on, "But, but...what if the Black Madonna represents all the colors? What if She is leading the way towards healing for *all* of us?"

"Some folks need more healing than others." I felt slapped as her words rang with a bitter truth.

"But, I mean, on a spiritual level?"

She looked at me for a long time. "Then we are talking about much more than symbols. And symbols alone don't do the job."

"True," I replied.

"I can assure you my personal experience is very different from yours. More than once I've walked into a department store and been followed by security. Many times, in fact, before, and now in 2001.

That ever happen to you?"

"No."

"Ever have to stop and think before an interview that what you're wearing" – she pointed to her headwrap – "might decrease your chances of getting the job?"

I shook my head. "No."

She said, "But, listen, Miss..."

"Miriam."

"Miriam. I hear the hope in your voice. That this Black Madonna you're following might offer hope for all of us." I heard the doubt in her voice. Or maybe it was fatigue. Then she smiled. "Your words remind me of our Congressman John Lewis. He always says people of all faiths and no faiths need to band together to bring justice." I watched her bend to put her papers in her bag of intricately-woven sweetgrass. When she straightened, she said, "All of us do need hope." She took in a long breath and said, "But my people need equity as well."

"Yes." I released a sigh though I hadn't realized I'd been holding my breath.

"Look," she relented. "I belong to a black congregation in Atlanta. Our theology teaches that God supports the freedom of African Americans from all forms of oppression." She looked straight at me again. "I wonder if you can begin to imagine how powerful that is to me."

She was cutting close to the bone now. I replied, "Though I haven't lived in your shoes, I'm trying to understand." I was nervously clasping and unclasping my fingers.

After a brief pause, she said, "Alright." Something seemed to settle inside her and she gave me her first smile. "Trying is a start." She folded her fingers together. "In our congregation we do recognize other images of a dark Madonna that are worshipped across the world."

A tiny window opened in my heart.

"You see, Miriam" – the window opened wider when I heard her voice say my name – "the recognition and prayer to a Black Madonna form a deliberate intention to counter damage done by the trauma of slavery."

"And by the oppressive myth of black inferiority," I added quietly.

Her shoulders relaxed and her voice was quiet but for the first time I felt she truly saw me. "Yes," she said.

"So, the black Madonna in your community reinforces an internal sense of power," I said.

"Yes," she said, "though of course there are black worshippers in other communities who look more to the black goddesses of Africa – to Imoa of West Africa, to Imanje of Afro-Brazil."

It was my turn to wait.

She said, "Back to what you first asked. What the black Madonna means to me personally." She lifted her arms wide and said, "It's like she enhances my original power."

"I noticed that as I was watching you speak." It was true; she'd emanated dignity and strength as she'd delivered her talk.

She nodded. "That sense of efficacy is the foundation on which we are further strengthening our communities."

"I'm glad"

"White people need to be a part of this transformation." Her keen eyes regarded me intently. She seemed to be carefully weighing her next words. "To own your inheritance of the brutal exploitation of black people for profit."

I swallowed and again tasted the bitterness of truth. I was taken aback and would have to search myself on how I had unthinkingly benefitted.

She added in a softer tone, "And then to work together with us as we sculpt forward."

I was at a loss for words.

Looking directly into my face she said, "Where is your power?"

The question centered me. "My art."

She nodded then glanced at her watch. "I don't have more time today. I've got to catch a plane back to Washington."

I retreated at once. "Thank you for speaking with me."

"You're welcome. I trust you'll speak with your art."

"Will you see Dr. Baldwin again?" Dette asked after I'd finished my story. We were driving east toward Dette's house, the sky behind us spreading her robes of orange-gold and easing them into swaths of lavender-gray.

"I plan to, yes," I said. "She gave me her contact information. I plan to call her once I return to the States to continue the conversation. If she's willing."

"She might be interested to see your winning entry for the *Opus Magnum*."

"Ha! That's a big assumption," I said. "But as I was telling you about my experience with her, I was reminded of your words about the immigrants coming here from North Africa. How not everyone welcomes them."

"*Non, pas de tout*."

"There's fear there."

"*D'accord*."

"What do you imagine the Black Madonna might mean to the immigrants themselves? Couldn't Her essential mystery and power hold true for all?"

Dette glanced at me. "I guess it depends on what you imagine the Black Madonna to be: does She represent a black Virgin Mary or a Sacred Woman of another culture and time?"

"I'm beginning to think there may be some of both?"

"For once I'm beginning to think you're right," she smiled at me.

"It's about time," I smiled back. "Seriously, I meant 'Her essential mystery' in a trans-cultural way."

"I'm *trying* to move through these thought thickets with you."

"I know, Dette, and I appreciate your willingness to help me sort this out." She nodded and I wandered on. "The Quron has an entire *chapter* on Mary." I paused. "She's represented as an exalted woman. She's the only woman in the Quron to be called by her name: Maryam. And She's named almost 70 times." I remembered that Granny had once said, "Our names come to our parents for a reason, child." *Miriam*. My parents couldn't have known this journey I would take. Could they? My voice drifted off and we sat in silence for a while. Then I said, "I guess by trans-cultural I actually mean a *universal* divine woman."

"I love that."

I squeezed her hand just as a car came careening around a sharp corner in our lane. We both shouted at the driver and Dette laid on the horn. Before we could fully catch our breath, we were bumping along Dette's narrow street. I felt completely drained after the long day of climbing and intense thinking about the Black Madonna. I would have gladly dropped into bed immediately. But when I mentioned this out loud Dette looked at me in mock horror and said, "Absolutely not! You haven't done that much thinking since the fourth grade. So now you must eat and drink!"

I punched her arm, laughing, and said, "Well, if you put it that way. Lead me to the feast!"

We settled on the patio, nibbling apricots and honey and triple-cream Brie on crusty bread in between sips of a fruity cabernet.

"I've decided to be French in my next life," I said in appreciation.

"Your intelligence never fails to amaze me!" she replied with a wink. Finishing her wine, she stood and took my arm. Together we moved to the kitchen to start making dinner.

"Hey, sous chef, speed it up with the vegetable-chopping or the salmon will hop back in the ocean," Dette teased.

"I'm not perfect, gimme a break."

"Hah! And I thought you were!"

She was only half-kidding. She held me in much higher esteem than I felt I deserved and I felt something clutch deep inside. Before I could dwell on it, Dette called out gaily, "*À table!*" As we seated ourselves across from one another I was struck by the simple beauty of the table; Dette had set it that morning before we'd headed to Mont St. Michel. Candlelight sparkled off the etched crystal goblets, and set off the deep blue and ivory china that was adorned by ornate silverware. These treasures had been in her family for a long, long time. The new bud inside me whispered *Are these the fruits of privilege?* before she flitted away.

"The table looks *magnifique*, the food *divine*. And you, *ma chérie, tu es merveilleuse*." I said.

"I am, indeed," she replied with a smile.

We piled our plates high with a *galette* filled with moist salmon mixed with fresh basil, onion, garlic, and tomato; the latter items were all from her kitchen garden. The vegetables were so fresh the scent of the earth still clung to them. She'd also made *Lapin terrine* – that's rabbit for the uninitiated – which I'd balked at the first time I'd visited France, but now ate with gusto.

"You are a five-star chef!" I exclaimed. I looked over at her, adding, "Ok, maybe four-star." She gave a mock pout before we toasted one another with the best red wine Bordeaux had to offer.

"I see France really agrees with you this time, *chérie*," Dette remarked, taking a sip of her wine. She swirled the wine around her glass, breathed in its scent, and sighed with appreciation.

"Can't deny it!" I responded jubilantly, taking a none-too-dainty gulp of my own. She laughed, her long earrings sparkling and swinging merrily in the candlelight. She got up to check the strawberry-plum tarte in the oven. "All you need is a debonair *amour*," she called over her shoulder. "Someone handsome and sexy and not at all well-behaved."

Beyond the obvious, I knew what her words meant; not Seth. During our drive that morning we'd covered the bases on our love lives – her recently-decamped François, and my well-behaved Seth. I wanted to get her read on Jules, but away from him I was having trouble believing

I truly meant anything to him; after all, he'd given me his assistant's phone number, not his. Furthermore, the pain in Dette's eyes as she'd told me about her breakup with François made me reluctant to broach the subject of the interesting new man I'd met.

"Maybe his loyalty is what's getting in your way," she said challenging me with lifted chin.

"He's loyal?" I asked, thinking of Jules.

"Seth's middle name is loyal," she replied.

"Oh," I said, landing back on the same page with her. "He is. And that's important."

"Come on, Miriam, why are you here?" She looked at me over her wine glass.

"To see you, of course," I said, startled. "And Odile."

"Yes, ok. But there's more to it, isn't there?

"Yes! Adventure, my art, the Black Madonna..." I waved my hand in the air as my voice trailed away.

"Oh, bullshit," she said. When she saw me stiffen slightly, her voice softened. "Miriam, you're too close to the wall to see the writing."

"Excuse me?"

"What I mean is, you said it yourself, you want adventure." Her dark eyes searched mine. "How many joyful couples seek adventure individually?"

"Well, there's..."

"Stop right there!" She sighed with exasperation. "Did you consider even for one second bringing Seth along?"

She had me there. The thought had not crossed my mind. Just thinking of it gave me a twinge of guilt. Unexpectedly, my thoughts flashed to Jules and I giggled. "I think I need some Perrier," I said, giggling again.

"*Bien sûr*," she said, reaching for the mineral water. "What's so funny?" I heard her add under her breath, "God knows, it's not Seth."

"Oh, Dette, I'm just so glad to be here. I feel so...buoyant. I haven't felt this light in a long time. Maybe ever."

"Well, it's certainly good to see you letting your hair down." Dette covered the side of her mouth with one hand and laughed. "Quite literally," she added.

Apparently, I had hadn't noticed my hair spilling out of the pins I'd used to twist it up into a loose chignon. "Quite a fetching look," she said with a wink.

"Merci buttercups," I said, using our childhood phrase and reaching over to pour more wine into our glasses.

"I see the wine agrees with you," she said, standing when she heard the timer's *ping!* go off. Her back was to me as she lifted the strawberry tart out of the oven and said, "You're certainly getting into the French spirit of things." *If you only knew*. She wasn't facing me so she missed the heat that bloomed on my face. By the time she returned to the table, proudly brandishing the steaming *tartine* before her, I had planted a neutral look on my face.

"Why the frown?" Dette asked. "Before you were practically singing. I expected the vibes of Andréa Bocelli to fill the room at any moment."

"If only!" I laughed. "The way you're flaunting that tarte is fascinating; it makes me think of 'the sword of Damocles'."

"Heavens!" she said. "The sword of fleeting happiness?" As she set the pie gently on the table she added, "My dear, here in France you will find much more than momentary joy."

"I already know that," I readily agreed.

"Let's dig in and strategize on how to entice one or more sexy Frenchmen your way. Perhaps Jean, the guy I mentioned to you who's in Paris. Hmm, maybe not him. But I know one or two others who would do in a pinch."

I laughed. "Borrowing a phrase from Granny Meg, eh?"

"Yup. She was a fine lady."

"Quite a saucy chick!" I agreed.

"A pip!" she laughed. We lifted our glasses again, this time in a toast to Granny.

Then I said, "Let's forget about French men for tonight. I'm really happy to be here with you, Dette." That much was true; the dinner and our long day together had strengthened the bond between us.

Dette sighed in exasperation at my once again putting her off her determination to land me a French *amour*, but she laughed when I lifted the knife high in the air and slashed it down into the tarte, whereupon we settled into the serious business of relishing every bite, ignoring the juices dribbling down our chins.

Later, Dette said, "I'm even more worried about Odile since she called me."

"She called you?" My heart pounded. "What did she say?"

"Not much," she said with a note of resignation. "But thanks for asking her to call me."

"She told you about that?" Had she told her mother about our agreement? Was I off the hook?

"Yes. But that's about all she said."

My heart dropped.

She continued sadly, "She only gives me crumbs." Dette looked at me closely. "When she dropped out of school in Lausanne – and she was doing really well! – it was my friend Jean who told me." I was unprepared for the tears in her eyes.

"Oh, Dette, honey, I'm sorry." I spoke from my heart.

"You're the one who's her guiding light."

"Oh stop," I protested. I'd forgotten about Odile during our day at Mt. St. Michel but now my guilt came crashing back.

"To be honest, I'm grateful to you," Dette said, surprising me.

"Meaning?"

"She needs a *confidante*. I'm glad she talks with you." Dette took my hand. "You help her sort out her emotions, something she desperately needs."

That was certainly true. But then this thought struck me like a shovel to the head: *I'm betraying my best friend.* I felt the blood drain from my face. *But how can I break my promise to her daughter?* My head felt like it was filled with stones that clattered against one another.

Dette noticed my pallor and clapped her hands together briskly. "You're drooping like a pricked balloon. Off to bed with you."

I took the escape she offered. When I offered to help her wash up, she said, "*Non, non,* bedtime for you, *chérie.*" We embraced for a long moment before I climbed the polished wooden stairs.

CHAPTER 18

Miriam: Veneux D'eau

JULY 2001

Gratefully, I reached Dette's guest room. As I sank into the feather bed, its linen sheets soft with washings, I thought I heard a bird crowing. *Odd. It's far too late – or is it too early? – for a rooster to be sounding off* was my last thought before I drifted off.

The scent of roses and lemons mingled with the swoosh of luminescent water. A pale face – a young woman with wide eyes and curly auburn hair – swam through the blue waters with me. I recognized my mother's face alive with tenderness as she smiled at me. We swam for a delicious while, our legs brushing fronds of seaweed and our bodies arching up and over phosphorescent fish of all colors and sizes. I was delighted to recognize that one of them – a luminescent turquoise – was Odile. Suddenly a dark spectral shape moved closer and closer. 'Remember that sweet peas are poisonous if eaten,' the ghostly woman's voice whispered. I feared the black shape was going to swallow Mumma whole. But instead, it moved to me. 'Come with me,' she commanded. In my fright, I punched through the water and pushed away from her only to see Mumma disappearing like ether into the black water along with the dark spectral...and then an untethered baby appeared in the water.

I awoke with a start. Clutching the pillow to my breast I felt the thick drumbeat of my heart. I took in several deep breaths to tame my pounding heart and as I did this, I realized that tears dampened my face. I struggled to remember details of the dream – it was fast slipping away from me – but I knew it had involved my mother and that she had been warning me. Of what, I had no idea, but I was filled with uneasiness and dread.

I slipped out of bed and walked slowly down the stairs, skipping the one that squeaked. In doing this I lost my balance and landed hard on my bottom. *Shit and merde*! I muttered under my breath, hoping that my hard landing had not awakened Dette.

"Miriam? I hope that's you and not a ghost," I heard Dette say before her nightgowned form appeared at the bottom of the stairs, a glass of red wine in her hand. Clearly, she had not gone to bed yet.

"It's me," I confirmed. "I'm sorry, I didn't mean to startle you." With a wince of pain, I stood and slowly continued down the stairs. "I woke up and thought I'd get a drink of water."

"*Pas de problème*," she said taking my arm when I arrived on the first floor. "Come, let's sit outside." We walked out to the patio behind her house. A light breeze rustled the emerald leaves of the silver birch trees. The moonlight cast her pale light over our faces as we sat and faced each other. Idly I scratched at a bit of dirt surrounding the round bolt nearest me that held the old wooden table together. Dette waited, relaxing back into her chair. The chittering sound of cicada clicks filled the night. Across the distance the deep bellow of a bullfrog called to its mate.

"I had that disturbing spectral dream," I said in a soft voice.

"Again?" she asked.

"Yes." I rested my elbows on the table. I sighed and said, "I wish I hadn't lost Mumma so early. Because there's so much I don't know about her." Dette looked away and began picking dead leaves off the rosebush near her chair.

"What happened to my mother?" I asked. "Do you know anything more you haven't told me?"

Dette stopped cleaning the roses. She straightened up in her chair. "Oh, Miriam," she sighed. I only know what my own mother told me."

"Anie was Mumma's good friend. Sorry to make you think about her so soon after she passed."

"Stop apologizing."

"Bad habit," I said. "I sometimes get the feeling there's something more." I looked at her, "Something you know," I sighed, "that I don't." Despite our many visits, we'd rarely discussed my parents. Or hers, for that matter. But that vast landscape was always with us. And I'd been wondering who the woman, Rose, had been for a very long time.

"Oh, Miriam," Dette said straightening her shoulders. "*Maman* said there was no autopsy. But it is likely she hit her head hard."

I bit my lip. "Yes. There was blood." I swallowed.

Dette's hand reached for mine. "Oh, *chérie*." Her eyes were far away now. "We stayed with you while the others went to the funeral."

I nodded. "But then you left town so suddenly." I looked across the table at her. "While my life shattered around my feet."

"Oh, Miriam, I –" She stopped and pressed a hand to her lips.

"Dette, I'm not blaming you. You were only twelve years old yourself, for godssakes."

"Yes," she whispered.

"But sometimes I get the oddest feeling you know something more. Maybe something you mother told you? It's funny, I got that feeling this morning while we were at Mt. St. Michel."

Dette gave a deep sigh and looked away again. Finally, she said, "Believe me, I was bewildered, too. I mean, it's not the same as what you were going through, not even close." She glanced at me. "But I was in Maine one day, in France four days later. For a long time, I hated my mother for doing that to me."

Was that the inheritance she'd passed on to her daughter? I pushed the thought away; I didn't want to think about Odile until I'd had more sleep.

Dette sipped her wine slowly. We sat there for a long moment while memories and unseen presences floated in the air around us. Then she said, "One thing I do know."

But are there other things you also know that you're not telling me? Of course, I wasn't exactly clean on that score.

"What's that?" Tiredly I regarded my friend.

"She really loved you. I remember how she looked at you. With such a combination of tenderness and pride. Truly, you were her little flower. And she would be so proud of you now. Especially proud you've been nominated to be an entrant in the *Opus Magnum*."

"Maybe," I said. "It's hard for me to figure out. Because I didn't know her. There was something...detached... about her. If ever I asked about her life, like how she met daddy, she'd snap at me and then get busy making a pie." I added, "Sometimes I'd come home from school and I could tell she'd been crying."

"Oh, Miriam." It was a sigh. Then she said, "Honey, we all cry sometimes, right?"

"When I asked her, what was wrong she'd just dry her eyes with her apron. Remember that red and white checked one she had?"

"Yes."

"Then she'd get out the flour and rolling pin." My soft laugh had a tinge of pain. "She made so damn many pies." Suddenly my mind flicked to the way I cleaned – furiously, repeatedly – when I was upset. The things we inherit without a thought.

"They were delicious. Especially the blueberry-blackberry."

"Not the point. Too damn many. She was hiding something. I just know it!"

"Miriam," Dette said in as soft a voice as I'd ever heard from her, "It was all a long time ago." She took my hand and squeezed it. "I think you really need to move on, not dredge up the past."

"You sound like Seth."

"That has to be a first."

"Do you know something more?"

Finally, Dette relented. "She was taking – herbs of some kind –"

"Yes, I used to go to the woman's cabin with her. Daddy hated her taking those herbs. Called them 'those damn-fool poison weeds'."

"Do you know why she was taking them?"

"No idea. But they worried me. I didn't want her taking poison."

"Anie said they weren't poison; they were beneficial herbs."

"Herbs for what? She grew herbs in our garden. Why did she need extra ones?"

Dette sighed. "She told Anie they were to help her get pregnant again."

I was dumbfounded. "Pregnant again?" I echoed my friend. A million insects buzzed in the air around us. I thought back to the day that shattered my life. "Mama had been washing the kitchen floor and it was still wet. Daddy came inside from his truck. He'd been off painting somewhere. Daddy saw her, saw the 'poison weeds', and went to grab the bowl. Mumma rushed toward him and slipped on the wet floor."

Tears welled in my eyes. "Why did he hate the herbs? Did he hate *her*?"

"Miriam, no," Dette said. "He didn't hate her, not at all."

"How do you know? You were only 12 when all this happened," I pointed out. Then, all at once I was remembering my father, how he tenderly held me in his lap and told me stories. How he alone seemed genuinely excited by my childhood scribbles. *Keep it up, little gal.* He *wanted* me to draw. Suddenly I felt beyond tired. I closed my eyes. When I opened them, I was surprised to see tears in Dette's eyes again.

She looked away from me. "You're right, I wasn't there. But, listen, Miriam, I think we're both too tired to talk more about this tonight."

I was a guest in her home. We were both exhausted. So I agreed, determined to press the point soon.

CHAPTER 19

Miriam: Convent of the Sisters of Grace

JULY 2001

I could not resist him; it's as simple as that. As I'd walked beside Jules at Chartres, I'd felt our connection deepening. I wanted to see where it could go. I wrestled with my conscience about Seth, I did. But I was adept at rationalization: I was in France I and wanted to be open to new possibilities. It would enhance my art! Besides, I did need a studio.

And so, after Dette went back to her job I returned to Paris. I contacted Véronique, Jules's assistant. She was curt, but she gave me his number. Nervous, I called him.

"Um, hello, it's Miriam?"

"Bonjour!"

"I'd like to accept your kind offer to see that north-facing room near the ocean," I said, the words rushing out.

"Ah, *c'est formidable!*" he said immediately, and I felt a rush of happiness.

"I can meet you at the train station. What day and time would work for you?"

"*Non, non*" he said, "There's no train station nearby."

My delight sank to my feet. "Oh, well, I guess it was too good to be true." I gave a little laugh that felt as fake as it sounded.

"Miriam," he said, "not so fast. I'll take you there. I always enjoy seeing my cousin. She's the Abbess there. And it's a lovely drive. It will be fun, *je te le promets*."

It was the first time he'd used the French familiar form of 'you' and my heart leavened again. He picked me up in his Bugatti Veyron coupe a couple of days later. As we sped along, the sweet-smelling fields reminded me of my drive with Dette to Mt. St. Michel. I turned to Jules and asked, "Have you been to *Mont St-Michel*?"

"*Mais oui, bien sûr*," Jules said glancing at me with a smile on his face. "Many times. Why do you ask?"

I rushed to cover my embarrassment. "I went there with Dette, my friend. It's amazing. And though she'd circled it in a boat before and had even walked around it when the tide was low, she'd never walked up into the actual Abbey. I found that incredulous."

"She's not like you, then."

His words surprised me. "I don't follow you."

"Great art, great architecture, these speak to you deeply," Jules said matter-of-factly.

"True. But we are similar in some ways. She's a textile artist and very creative in her use of color. We have so much fun when we're together; she makes sure of that. And each time I see her she brings a piece of my childhood back to me."

"Ah, yes, a childhood friend is special," he agreed. "One I never had, by the way."

"Why ever not?"

He shrugged. "We lived far from town with kilometers of fields around us."

"But surely you had school chums?"

"Not so much. For a long time, I was tutored at home."

My New England 'stay-out-of-other-people's-business' training prevented me from asking why.

"Because my father wanted it that way," he answered the question on my face. "And we lived far from other kids. Except my sister," his laugh was bitter. "Who hated me." He lit a cigarette and blew the smoke out through his nostrils. I made a motion with my hands to brush the smoke away. "I'm not sure why." He inhaled again.

"Would you mind terribly putting that out while we're in the car?" The words shot out of my mouth before I could stop them. The smoke made me feel choked.

"Demanding little bitch, aren't you?" he said. My mouth dropped open. "I'm kidding," he said, laughing as he tossed the cigarette out the window.

"That's a bit risky, isn't it?" I asked.

He shot me a questioning glance.

"It could start a fire. It's been really hot and dry for days."

"Duly noted," he said. He slowed the car and indicated with lifted chin, "Go ahead, stamp it out."

"Alright, I will." I opened my car door and stepped out. I walked to the other side of the road and found the dying embers. I caught a whiff of fragrant roses before I stamped out the embers.

When I folded myself back into the little car I said, "Done." with complete satisfaction in my voice.

He leaned one arm out the window and looked at me. "Not all fires can be stamped out so easily, you know?"

I looked away as my thoughts swirled. "I realize that."

"Besides, I might have just driven off, you know," he said as he put the car back in gear.

I turned my head back to face him and said, "You wouldn't."

"Don't be so sure."

"I'll keep that in mind." I was confused. First the comment about fire which seemed directed at the electricity between us. Now the warning not to be sure of him. I decided he was teasing me.

"Good," he said. We drove on a while in silence before he said, "You speak boldly when it comes to something you care about.

"Perhaps I do," I said, glad for the opened windows. It was hot and I was sweating too much.

"Ah, Miriam," he said. "The complexities of you." I liked that he thought of me that way, and I was relieved he'd let the stamping subject drop. It told me he wasn't a man who held onto minor things. I liked that even as I worried that the man was too quickly scratching through the hard surface of me. We do not know who it is who will touch us, nor in what way, nor how deeply. We go about our daily lives seldom conscious that every minute we are in the company of others there exists this possibility – a lingering glance, a voice on the phone, a citrus scent as a man approaches, an accidental brushing up against an arm as we pass in the street...a connection that may last only an instant...or that may – once in a blue moon – be expanded into something entirely other. Just as a caterpillar is worm-like one moment and then becomes something extraordinarily different the next.

My thoughts were interrupted as we came to a lovely village where some sort of procession was taking place. Jules slowed and stopped to let the joyful marchers cross the dusty road. Men, women, and children, all dressed in bright colors, were walking along to the music of trumpets and drums.

"Now, there's a lighthearted group," Jules said. I smiled at him and nodded, delighted to see such a fun and joyous group parading through the village.

Just then I noticed a woman in the procession dressed in a white dress with large red polka dots. We were close enough that I could see her full lips, sheathed in candy-apple-red lipstick, and her curly russet hair bouncing along with her as she walked. The man beside her took her hand and she twirled in a complete circle, causing her full skirt to rise and fall around her.

As we left the town behind, Jules must have noticed my face had gone pale.

"*Qu'est-ce que ç'est?*" he asked.

"It's nothing," I said.

"Your face says otherwise."

I sighed resting my head against the window.

"I'd like to hear it," he said.

"No, it's alright." I reached for a tissue, wiped my forehead, and crumpled it in in my lap.

Several minutes passed, maybe more, as we rumbled along passing through a field full of sunflowers, their joyful faces to the sun.

"Jules," I asked, "Did you see that woman in the red polka dot dress?

"I did."

"She reminded me of my mother." I kept my head against the partially-opened window.

"And?"

"Thinking of her is always hard." I bit a cuticle on my finger. Had I mentioned my mother to him back in Rouen? I couldn't remember.

He reached across the car to take the finger out of my mouth. "You don't have to tell me anything," he said.

"Thanks." I looked at him and said, "Seeing that woman – her dress, it was very similar to the one my mother wore the day she died."

"*Mon Dieu*! I'm sorry."

"*Merci*," I whispered. "It was a hard time."

"I'll say!" This American expression in his voice unexpectedly lifted my mood. Suddenly, I wanted to tell him more. "Mumma had some greens in a bowl – some herbs an old woman in our town had given her. She had just washed the floor and had changed into her prettiest dress, the one she and I both loved with the bright red polka dots on it. And she was humming. I was humming along with her. I think it was a country love song, I'm not sure. Then daddy came home." I stopped, closed my eyes, remembering. "We heard the door of his truck slam shut. I ran to the dining room, hid behind the curtains. He didn't like her eating those herbs." I rubbed my eyes. "He stomped in with his giant lumberjack boots – he wasn't always a lumber jack, he painted – "

"Ah," Jules said. "An artist."

"Yes. Well, part-time. He also hauled lumber."

Jules waited a moment then said, "What happened?"

"I don't remember exactly, but suddenly he was shouting, 'I asked you never to take that stuff from that witch!' and he lunged toward Mama. She whirled around and around in that beautiful dress and then she slipped and fell. She hit her head on the counter and I saw that she was bleeding." Tears filled my eyes. "I never saw her again after the ambulance took her away."

Jules quietly said, "*Chère* Miriam. I'm so sorry."

I heard the ache in my voice as I said, "Why couldn't I stop him?

Jules said, "*Attends*, how old were you then?"

"Eleven."

"A child. How could you possibly have stopped him? I'm guessing the whole thing happened very quickly."

"Yes."

"And even if you'd been older, it wouldn't have been your fault."

"I know that up here," I pointed to my head. "But I sometimes still have trouble convincing myself in here." My hand covered my heart.

Jules touched my arm. I was glad he didn't do anything more. "Miriam," he said, "I am very sorry this happened to you."

I touched his arm then withdrew it and said, "It was a terrible time." I thought of all that had happened to me so quickly afterwards, like a hurricane that roars through homes, blows trees down, lifts cars and then is over, leaving detritus and scars behind. Our house packed up, Dette and her mother Anie leaving, me moving to Granny's house. The torn hole inside me. Softly I added, "My father left shortly thereafter."

"Christ."

I cleared my throat. "Yes, it was hard," I acknowledged. "But I was lucky as it turned out. My Granny took me in. And in her no-nonsense way she helped me put the pieces of me, of my life, back together. She never said the words. But she loved me."

"I'm glad," he said.

I paused. "And in college, when I struggled, I got counseling." I looked at him and said, "So, I'm ok now. In fact, I'm great. I mean, to have time to work on my art, to be driving in the countryside with you, how fortunate it that?"

"It's lucky enough. Though it doesn't erase everything."

I nodded.

He began, "The red polka dots –"

"Jules, I don't want to dwell on the past anymore. I'm on this trip for *me*."

Gently he said, "Colors enthrall you. Maybe that was your mother's gift to you. That's all I meant."

"Oh." I paused as the silence of unsaid things hung in the air around us.

He reached over to touch my shoulder and said, "That woman opened a profound memory in you. Would you prefer to check out the studio another day?"

"No!" I said. " 'One can only prevail on the kindness of strangers for so long'."

"Alright, Blanche," he laughed. "Atta girl!" The tension in the car eased back.

We continued the rest of the way in companionable silence, passing more fields of sunflowers, grazing cows with their limpid eyes, and the occasional old barn and farmhouse. Once he said softly, "You smell like wildflowers and oranges," as he squeezed my hand. We drove through the tiniest village yet. Then we pulled up to a large building, it's creamy-gray stones worn with age. It was comprised of a huge central house with two arms spread perpendicular to the main building, each one topped with a slate-roofed tower. In front of the building a large courtyard bloomed in a profusion of flowers – orange lilies, purple campanulas, yellow daisies, and a wash of sunflowers.

Jules stopped the car and announced, "We have arrived. *Le Couvent des Soeurs de Grace*. That's 'The Convent of the Sisters of Grace' to you." He winked at me. "And herein lives and works my cousin, Esme. Currently known as Sister Agrippina. Like I said, she has a room available for rent that might work for your artwork. Let's hope it suits."

We stepped out of the car and I heard the ocean's song nearby. *Let's hope, indeed!* The place was astonishingly beautiful. Jules had already moved to what looked to be the main door and was holding it open for me. Together, we stepped into the wide central corridor that joined the wings of the building together. It was festooned with enormous ornately-framed paintings of men and women I took to be saints. I felt disoriented as I blinked at the darkening shift in light, but Jules was already halfway down the corridor and rapping on a door. Feeling tentative, I trotted after him.

"*Entrez*," I heard her voice ring out before I saw her.

Sr. Agrippina was imposing, despite her entire figure being garbed in gray. There was a simmering energy about her that hinted of passion beneath. *I have given my life to God*, I could almost hear her saying. She was not wearing a head covering – they only wear the covering while at prayer, Jules had explained during our drive. Her hair, cut short but thick and lustrous, was pure silver. With the strong bones of her face and her unusual coloring – silver hair, amber eyes like her cousin's, she evoked an ethereal beauty. At her feet a large black Labrador lay softly snoring.

"*Enchantée, Miriam*," she said in a clear voice after Jules had introduced us. "And I like your name," she added. The dog opened one eye and regarded us. Apparently seeing nothing amiss, he closed his eye and resumed his snuffling. Noticing my glance at the dog she said, "This is Coco. Did you know Mademoiselle Chanel first learned to sew in the Abbey at Aubazine, an orphanage quite like our own?" She smiled at my surprise.

"*Enchantée*," I said in response, admiring how quickly she'd put me at ease. "And no, I didn't know that. But I do know she was an expert seamstress. I enjoy sewing myself," I smiled at her, "though I'm not particularly good at it." *Unlike my mother.*

"Interesting," she regarded me a bit less sternly. "We sew garments here. For the children."

"This is an orphanage, Miriam," Jules quickly explained. "Children live in the east wing." That explained the distant sound of high-pitched voices.

"Perhaps I could help. Maybe in the evenings sometimes?" I said.

"*D'accord*." she replied. Then she quickly got to business. "*Bon*. We only have one room available at present. But it does face north."

"That sounds perfect. I'm much obliged," I managed. I glanced at Jules; had I so quickly been approved? He shrugged and winked, signaling that his assumption that I would be accepted had been a correct one. In fact, that very morning we'd loaded my belongings and art supplies into the trunk of his car.

"You may take your meals with us. And, of course, attend Chapel with us." She must have seen a stricken look on my face for she added, "It's not obligatory. We're not here to judge anyone." I smiled with relief. Considering how much I assumed they prayed that would have put a real crimp in my time for art.

"Jules has vouched for you. That's all I need," she said shooting him a fond glance. "Now let me locate the key." She left the room with the dog jumping up to follow her.

Jules showed me around her office pointing out the medieval paintings and speaking with the singular animation that came to his face when talking about art. We didn't hear when she re-entered the room, but at one point in his excitement Jules took hold of my arm. Out of the corner of my eye I saw something flash across her face, a movement no wider than the width of an eyelash. When I turned slightly in her direction, she looked away. The dog returned to her pillow on the floor.

Sr. Agrippina pulled a brass key from her pocket. "This is the only key. Please take care." She seemed to mean more than the key though I couldn't say exactly what it was that told me this. "The room is on the top floor at the end of the hall." She looked at Jules, "It's at the very end of the west wing where you and your sister used to stay.

"*Oui*."

She turned back to me. "I understand you'll be using the room for art?"

"Yes."

"Take care not to spill your paints."

"I will," I promised.

Jules turned to me and smiled. "Ah, perfect. *Je vous en prie, Esme*." She arched one eyebrow, exactly as I'd seen him do.

"Sorry. Sr. Agrippina," he amended. She nodded and sat down at her mahogany desk, reaching for a pen. She did not make eye contact with me again, though she did reach down to pet Coco. Business done, I was dismissed.

Jules and I walked to the west wing of the Abbey. On the way he told me more about this particular order of nuns. They worked with children, orphans from many places. It was noble work, I thought, and I understood more about the strong sense of presence Sr. Agrippina possessed. I admired the Sisters' connection to something greater than themselves, this despite the isolated feel of the place.

I was eager to see more of my new surroundings, but I struggled to keep up with Jules's rapid pace as he led the way to a distant wing of the old building. Not slowing down, he sprinted up the narrow stone stairs to a second floor. I followed at a slower pace. I was realizing with each step gained that my dream to create a major new art piece was coming true. The enormity of this flooded me.

"Miriam!?" I heard his voice calling from the top.

"Coming," I called. Once I reached the second floor, I stopped. This was to be my work space for the next couple of months at least. I slid my hand along the wall. In places parts of the wall had crumbled and I pressed my fingers there to feel the textures: the smooth places were intermixed with expanses of crumbled roughness. Life and loss in stone.

I walked slowly to the door where he was standing, took the key from him, inserted it, and pushed the door open.

CHAPTER 20

Miriam: Convent of the Sisters of Grace

JULY 2001

I'd now been at the Convent for more than a week. I sank down to the stone floor of my room one morning, feeling rested after a deep sleep without any shadows haunting me. I moved over to the Persian carpet, a large one knotted entirely by hand. Dette had once told me you could tell whether a rug was real if you turned it over and could see the tiny knots. I loved the ornate design on this one with its colors of faded maroons, inky blues, and moss greens. I trailed my fingers along its silky threads and let my thoughts drift back to the summer when my passion for art had begun.

I had just turned fifteen and Granny Meg was taking me to a special exhibit of botanical art at the Portland Society of Art. Even now, so many years later, I remembered her high spirits that day and how infectious her happiness was. My eyes filled as it hit me how rarely such unfettered joy had been part of my life after my parents left. Or, for that matter, had been part of Granny's. I was riding shotgun in the front seat with my long, sun-splattered chestnut hair flying out the open window. I remember a few strands caught in my mouth and tasted faintly of my Breck shampoo. Granny's pin curls, rinsed blue for this special occasion and shellacked with Helene Curtis Spray Net, were bouncing in unison as the breeze captured and lifted them up and down, up and down. My beloved Granny was unusually effervescent and both of us were singing "*I Wanna Hold Your Ha-aa-aa-nnd!*" at the top of our lungs. Honestly, I was thrilled because Granny never sang along with me. Certainly not to the Beatles! I was wearing my favorite lime green and turquoise striped dress and my new sandals with the silver buckles. I felt so grown-up! Granny had frowned, but refrained from commenting when she noticed my painted toenails, 'sassy pink', a jazzy color that filled me with delight.

At fifteen I was too old for hand-holding, but Granny took my freckled arm and walked with me toward the large airy space of the botanical arts exhibit. As we crossed the threshold into the exhibit, I felt for the first time the hush of a museum envelop me. Working our way slowly through the room, I became absorbed with the precise details of the plants, as intricate as a spider's web. That day I learned much about how the detail expresses the whole. I stood motionless for a long time before each one, longing to reach out and touch the leaves. I lost myself that day and Granny, bless her, let me. At some point she moved to the back of the room and sat on a low bench clutching her faux-leather handbag. I don't know how much time passed before I realized she was no longer standing beside me. When I turned to seek her out, I found her watching me with a smile on her powdered face. It was dusk when we made our way outside to her black and white DeSoto station wagon. I traced one finger in the dust on the side of the car longing to hug her, though I didn't. That wasn't our way.

Going to the art museum became one of the special things Granny and I did together. The next year's outing was even better. We went to the same Portland museum, this time to an exhibit on copper works.

Even before we set out it was special, for Granny had allowed me to wear my pink-flowered hip huggers, a huge concession on her part. Ladies wore dresses, not pants. Once inside the museum she was, once more, unusually animated. "Art made by smelting copper, an actual element of the earth," she said, "it's quite something." For her, that was effusive. That Granny "got" art made me inordinately happy. When I laid my eyes on that first copper plate hanging on the wall, something twisted in my heart. At that moment a knowing in me took wing, for I had an unformed sense even then – If I could do this! If I could! – that art could make me whole.

Now, on the stone floor in France, I smiled. At my first sight of this rooms, I'd known it was meant to be mine. For a little while at least. Jules had handed me the long brass key and I'd fitted it into the lock of the door. I'd just succeeded in pushing it open an inch when suddenly the door flung itself wide open and landed with a thud on the opposite wall. Peeking into the room I saw that someone had left the window open and the ocean breeze was lifting the ivory curtains in a dance of their own. The room was bare except for a straight-backed wooden chair sitting beside a small desk, a quilt-covered bed pushed up against one wall and a long table of dark wood, scratched and worn in places, against the window.

Turning to Jules I said, "It's perfect. I don't know how to thank you."

"*De rien*," he said. "Besides," he smiled, "if Sister hadn't felt you were, er, suitable, you wouldn't be standing here now."

"Quite so," I said. I moved to the table before the window and asked, "Do you suppose it would be alright if we moved this back a bit so it doesn't block the window? The single window, facing north, was tall but narrow and I wanted a clear view to the ocean.

"I'm sure it would not be a problem," he said. "Let's do it now." He stepped briskly to the table. As I approached the other side, I frowned and said, "This looks massively heavy. We're not going to be able to move it very far."

"Nonsense," he said. "We can do it. Grab that end." I felt the strain of muscles all along my back and arms as we moved the heavy mahogany slab inch by inch until we had cleared the window. Sweat softened our clothing as we stood before the window and gazed out at the sea. For a moment we stood there in silence, and I became aware of a fullness between us. The pounding of the waves outside heightened the stillness inside. A bird cawed loudly as it swooped and dipped, riding the air currents. For a moment I closed my eyes and imagined how it would feel to let myself be carried along by the wind. To be able to trust enough to let go. To surrender completely to the air around me and let my entire body be carried, rising and falling, rising and falling.

"*Zut alors*, how I'd love to soar on the air currents like that!" Jules said. "Lucky fellow."

I smiled. "I was just thinking the same thing." Then I murmured. "How will I ever get any work done in this place?"

He turned to me and said, "You'll manage." He strode across the room and pulled the two chairs – a straight-backed wooden one belonging to the desk and the other, an overstuffed one with thick arms that curved around the body of the chair like an embrace – close to the fireplace. Jules took the wooden chair, turned it around and straddled it, kicking off his shoes. Something about his grin reminded me of an eager schoolboy as he leaned forward and said, "So, tell me more about this copper work you do."

I lifted myself up onto the table we'd just moved. "Working with copper is joy," I replied. "The most wonderful thing about copper – and why my heart soared when I first thought of using it for the *Opus Magnum* work – is its luminosity. First, you press your steel tools carefully along the gleaming surface to raise the design you want. Later, you brush paint over it. Until gradually you bring the form to life. Then, when you have finished and you hold it up to the light – *voilà* – there it is, reflecting its light onto you, the viewer. When the light shifts, you have something else. It's magical."

Jules nodded and said, "Impressive."

I continued, "Through sheer serendipity the year I entered my Master's in Fine Arts program, an artist by the name of Enrique Guadel was teaching a guest seminar on using metals. Thus, was my love of working with copper born." I found myself thinking back to my early art career and it took me a minute to return to what I was saying. Jules waited, his eyes never leaving my face, until I continued. "After a whole lot of miserable failures and experimentation I've finally arrived at my own system of treating the copper so it will receive the paint on its surface to reflect light as I desire it to do."

"Brava." Then he asked, "Do you remember when we walked in the Louvre?"

"Of course."

"I was deeply touched by how thrilled you were with what we were seeing. Your sense of joy."

"That was because of you," I told him without thinking.

He smiled, "I don't think those artists would appreciate that."

"Nontheless, it's true." I looked straight at him. He looked away and shoved his hands in his pockets as the shadows beneath his eyes darkened. When he remained silent, the pain of doubt filled me. I looked down at my hands. "Anyway," I said, "I know what you mean. Art conveys passion, of one type or another." He remained quiet so I swam on. "With every copper work I do, I keep with one medieval tradition: each piece of my copper work is engraved on the back with my personal artist's mark, a spider, and is numbered and signed."

"A spider?"

"My Granny told me a lot of folklore stories about them." I looked at him, challenging him not to make fun of her. Or me.

He said gently, "Folk stories are an art." I nodded, relieved. "And you're amazing."

"We'll see," I said, but I felt my cheeks flame. He started to say something more, but stopped himself. I wondered what he might be holding back, but I let it pass. He stood and said, "*Bon*, I must be off." He crossed the room, kissed my cheeks lightly three times – in the way of close friends! – and left. The carousel of my emotions today had tired me out. I crossed to the bed, lay down on it and rested. An hour or so later, I got up and squared my shoulders. I wasn't here to romance; it was time to begin my art piece.

Crossing back to the open window I made two promises to myself. One, I would go to the nuns some evenings and sew with them. It would be good to help others and get out of my own head. Two, I would not let my insecurities overwhelm me. I knew that before I could begin this new art composition, I needed to have both clarity and confidence. The former is not about having an exact image of the final 'product,' but rather having at least some insight into the tug that was pulling me toward this new creation. I closed my eyes and looked inside myself, resting my hands on the windowsill. The air caressing my face was pungent with salty brine. Slowly, I felt the pulse of inspiration arrive. The luminous image of a female form arose before me and I caught her in my hands.

For me, creating art was bi-rhythmal. Four parts joy and six parts damned hard work. I would push on and push on until I had success or die trying. I suppose that sounds dramatic, but that's how I was. And it was high time for a breakthrough. I was working against time and increasingly feeling the strain of the budget Thom had allowed me.

I had already decided – and of this I was certain – that for the *Opus Magnum* work I would use my stone hammer and anvil tools. This would be one way I would connect my Madonna rendering to ancient times, for artists had used stone tools on copper from as far back as 2000 B.C. It pleased me to think that this was a time even before the historical Miriam of Nazareth came into being. I would take my time and use painstaking care with each stroke, for copper hardens under continuous hammering. But copper could be forgiving, too. Once hardened, it could be softened again by annealing – that is, the process of heating an element and then slowly cooling it. The forgiveness of copper allows the piece to be reworked until the desired hammered effect is achieved. *Forgiveness, forgiveness* echoed in my head as I set to work.

I ran my hands over the smooth sheet of copper metal I had set up in the studio. I lit a candle before it and watched the flame send shivers of illumination over the ripples of metal. I pressed my hands together and let the warmth of the sunlight fall on them. As I rubbed them together creating more warmth it slowly dawned on me what I had unconsciously been doing; the warmth of my own hands would set this work in motion. Smiling, I placed them on the shining sheet of copper.

My thoughts drifted back to that first Madonna at *Cathédral Notre Dame de Paris*. Leaving my classmates behind, I'd entered the Cathedral by myself. Cavernous and dark, it was difficult to absorb everything within the flamboyant Gothic style: a throng of gilt statues, elaborate frescoes, and woodcarvings, as well as little antechambers each with it's own altar holding an array of lighted candles. The immense size of the place allowed for shadowy corners that somehow blurred the line between the sacred and the mundane. I moved halfway down a side aisle, too timid to go up close to the main altar, and knelt in a pew. Once my eyes had accommodated to the darkness, I lifted them up and found my gaze resting on the large statue of the Madonna standing near, but not on, the altar. At that moment I felt the thud of intense recognition. Unbidden, the thought came to me: *I, too, am holy. I, too, am made in the image of the Divine*. For the first time I wondered: why, in the central tenet of my Catholic faith, is there nothing of the *female* divine? For the first time I felt not so much the presence of God as the *absence* of the female face of God in my Church. I was eighteen years old and stunned that this had never occurred to me before.

I traced my hunger to know more of the Madonna back to that day. I was excited when I decided to explore and focus on the Madonna figure for the *Opus Magnum* art competition, to learn more about this other woman called the Black Madonna. But doubts lingered. In graduate school I'd studied and greatly admired the work of Frank Lloyd Wright. His astonishing work that joined nature – stone, light, sky, earth – all these were mingled in his remarkable architecture and touched something deep in me. Perhaps it was the connection to my love of nature. And Mumma's.

But lately in my mind I'd been hearing Wright's voice say with derision: "Mariology! Bah!" He had not thought much of this genre of Italian art. "People bowing down before statues. Where is the God in that?"

I sighed. I knew that I had to come to terms with the conflicting thoughts battering around inside my skull before I could begin. Then I thought, Bah, yourself! I'll tell you where the God is in that, Mr. Wright. It's in the connection that the artist has to the soul while shaping his or her unique art. I mean, can you honestly witness Michelangelo's magnificent Pietá without drinking in its beauty? You were moved by a different spirit, is all. *Stop dithering, Miriam,* I told myself. *This is my work and no one else's.*

Emboldened by my self-talk, I knew it was time to take my hands and begin revealing what I believed the Madonna archetype offers to the world. Slowly, I heard her. Woman. Woman fertile. Woman of grace. Woman of pain and sorrow. Woman of hope. I knew that the figure would be the shape of a woman. But I struggled with how to bring both the feminine and the masculine energies to it. My goal was to channel the former but not ignore the latter. How could I meaningfully convey how our culture has repressed the so-called feminine energy – intuitive, dynamic, flowing – and overvalued the so-called masculine ones – logical, analytic, linear.

I moved my hands again over the copper piece. Then I stumbled.

Bring all these meanings to my art? Aaaaaaarrrrghhhh! It's too hard. There are too many layers, too many complexities. An impossible challenge.

So, focus, I heard a voice say. *Focus!* The voice was stern; no frills, no lace, no silken robes attached. *Get up offa your ass and move!*

Startled, I reached across the table and picked up the tiny statuette of the underground Black Madonna, *Notre Dame Sous Terre*, that I had purchased in Chartres. Though I'd been disappointed when I'd opened the little white box and found her tucked inside, not looking much at all like the actual Black Madonna below the ground, I had come to accept the figure as she was. After all, how could a cheap replica ever approach the actual work of the artist? It was simply a souvenir. I rubbed the edges of the figure again and again across the palms of my hands. Like every artist, I had little control over the response of the viewer to my work. But I knew that in the process of making art I would uncover and reveal something of myself. Was I ready to take that leap? *Oh, just shut up and do it!* This time I laughed at the insistent inner voice and my laughter filled me with a surge of energy. I got up and strode across the room to the table where my tools awaited my touch.

I laid out my paints, pleased with the lapis blue I'd found. A learned teacher once told me that the human eye perceives the highest number of shadings in the color blue. I moved the Venetian red to the side; its insistent tone bothered me. I wanted the blues, the silvers, and the grays now. I knew that later I'd use the red with the deepest blue to make a luscious, rich plum. In this way I began my work, and a certainty came to me that at last I was moving ahead, my energy soaring straight from my soul to my hands.

At one point that day I was seized by an impulse to pass the copper sheet through the fire. Because the studio room was situated close to the ocean, the early mornings were cool. I had started a small fire after I'd awakened and felt the chill. Now, I started toward the fireplace. I walked quickly, for instinctively I knew that if I hesitated too long,

I would not do it. I grabbed my fire-resistant gloves and plunged the sheet into the flame, holding it there as long as I dared, then dropping it with a clang onto the stone hearth. Quickly, but with care, I pressed my glove-clad fingers into the melting copper causing long ridges to emerge. This would give the ripples of light on the copper added texture and depth. My own fingers in the work, a living piece of it, excited me.

I was taking hold of the Black Madonna mystery! Sitting back on my heels I thought about waiting for the copper to cool, but then I thought, no. Instead, I moved toward my paints. I chose a blue so deep it was almost black, for I wanted the darkest blue to be first upon the copper. From the first slash of blue I knew in my bones that this work would channel my passion.

As I continued to work, charged with energy, from time to time I felt an urge to hold the hot copper in my bare hands, to run the blue-black paint over my palms so alive with receptivity did my hands feel. Wisely, I resisted. Instead, I soaked up globs of paint on my brush and began smearing it thickly in the center of the warm copper watching it slither downward. Copper and paint merging as one to birth something completely new.

As I reached again for my precise steel tools, I slowed. The candle I'd lit and placed in front of me flickered as I began to discover the shape of a woman within the copper. I selected another brush, this one slim and light in my hand. I ran the soft tip of the bristles along the palms of my hand enjoying its tickle against my skin before I dipped it into a different color. What I did not do that day was bring my paint anywhere near the top area of the copper piece, for I sensed that I had not yet begun to uncover the terms of the woman's face. I became aware of the sun's heat on my back and I turned around to face the open window, breathing in the scent of the beach roses glistening with dew that I'd seen at dawn that morning. By this time the sun had risen high in the sky and the light spun over the water like golden ribbons. I turned back to face the copper sheet and laughed when I saw that the sun was playfully throwing ribbons of light upon it as well. I became aware of the sounds of tinkling bells, the Sisters singing in harmony, and further away, children's voices. I paused to enjoy the deepest contentment I had ever known.

After a time, I went back to work, and I did not stop until my hands cramped and I could not continue. When I stepped back and looked for the first time at my work from a distance, I saw that it resembled nothing more than a chaos of blue and black paint. Even now I am amazed that this evoked nothing in me of the disgust and frustration I once might have felt. I knew what I had to do. I put this work aside and placed a blank sheet of copper in its place. I drew in a deep breath and smiled as I let the breath out. I can do this, I thought. I can do this!

I lifted my brushes and rested them in the waiting tin filled with turpentine and water. Clouds were gathering low in the sky as I quickly changed into my bathing suit and headed outside. When I reached the beach, I tossed my shoes in the reeds and curled my toes in the warm sand. Then I ran to the water's edge and dove in.

CHAPTER 21

Miriam: Carcassonne

AUGUST 2001

July had turned to August and my work had begun in earnest. When I wasn't completely absorbed in my art, I tried to comprehend why I ever had agreed to Odile's wild plan. Several times I walked over to the main hall of the Convent to use the phone. I would tell her I had to break our agreement. Each time I chickened out. Granny had drilled into me: a deal is a deal. My stomach turned whenever I thought about my now-charged relationships with Odile and Dette, but most of the time I managed to push those unwelcome ruminations deep.

One morning a Sister came to my door to tell me I had a telephone call. Frowning, I washed my hands and ran down the stairs and over to the main hall.

"*Comment vas-tu, Mademoiselle l'Artiste?*" I was surprised to hear Jules's voice in my ear.

"I'm fine, thanks. And you?" I answered automatically.

He replied, "I'm calling with an offer."

My heart thumped so loudly I feared he could hear it. "And what might that be?"

"How would you like to fly with me to a work site in southern France?"

"Wait, really?" I pinched myself to make sure I wasn't dreaming.

"*Oui, vraiment*." He chuckled again.

"Well, um, when?" I was stalling for time. My mind was reeling, thinking about the work I had to do, knowing the timing was more fraught than ever since I'd made the agreement with Odile. But to be honest, I already knew I would move mountains to accept this offer.

"Tomorrow. I'm working at my site in Carcassonne," his deep voice replied. "I'll have the light plane pick you up in the late afternoon."

Carcassonne! "Oh my God," I said with genuine joy lighting my voice, "that city has been on my wish-list since my first visit to France! I accept!" A break from the intensity of working on art would bring a fresh perspective when I returned to it. As I've said, I was a pro at rationalization.

The following day in a borrowed car I drove from the Convent to the nearest airport where Jules, handsome in a dark navy blazer, pale rose shirt and cloud-gray slacks stood waiting for me. He'd let his wavy dark hair grow longer and it curled over the collar of his shirt. I was glad I'd worn my aubergine-shot-with-silver silk blouse and daubed my pulse points with *Fragonard* perfume. When he opened my car door, smiling, honest-to-God I nearly swooned. I slid out of the car and we exchanged light kisses on both cheeks. He took my hands and said, "*Comme tu es belle*." I'm not beautiful, my nose and chin too sharp, but still, it was wonderful to hear those words from him. He led me into the small airplane, nodded to the pilot and we lifted into the air. I stared out the tiny window as we flew, not wanting to miss a single detail. When we landed with a gentle thump, I was filled with an extraordinary lightness.

Stepping off the plane Jules took my arm and said, "*Le tour commence*."

"I want to see everything! And learn about everything! I already love this town!" I said as I gazed up at the walled city.

Shrugging, Jules said, "You have barely begun to see it. And unless you have several months, you cannot learn about it all at once. But, let's begin." As if telling a story, he said, "*Enfin*, I will be Lord *Jules le Grand* and you will be the *Lady Rose de Grace* –" he stopped when he saw the look on my face. "*Qu'est-ce que c'est*?"

"Nothing," I said, though my voice was tense. "But let's be just us, only us, Miriam and Jules." The way he looked at me made me wonder if the late afternoon sun had backlit my grey eyes to silver. "Please, Jules, just us, ok?" In a low voice I added, "Rose was my mother's name."

"Ah, Miriam." He took my hand, squeezed it. "*Pas de problème*. In fact, you're absolutely right. Just us."

And so, we began our tour of Carcassone, one of the largest surviving medieval walled cities in Europe. "The mountains you see in the distance,"– he gestured toward the south – "are the Pyrennées." I gazed at the distant range as the sky darkened from blue to a dusky plum.

"Come, I want you to see the two walls from above, so you get an idea of the enormity of what they built."

"On my way, Sir!" I rushed to catch up with him. Then I asked, "Who built?"

"The Romans. In their quest to conquer the world they leveled what had been here for centuries then built it into a mammoth fortification. They built it as a defensive strategy. It protected the travel route from Languedoc in the southeast over to the plains of Gascony in the west." He ran quickly up the stairs leading to the top of the ramparts taking them two at a time.

I removed my heels and walked barefoot after him. When we arrived at the top I stumbled and Jules held me steady. He caught my face in his hands and bent his face slowly to mine. When he kissed me, I felt both the leap in my groin and a sadness catch in my throat.

Why would this make me sad? I wondered before surrendering thought to feeling. I opened my mouth wider, moved closer to him and heard myself moan somewhere far back in my throat. Then I pulled away and rested my head against the warm expanse of his chest. Silently he ran his fingers through my hair. Swimming up from sensations so full I had trouble surfacing, I took in a deep breath, and, reaching for equilibrium, I said softly, "You've found one hell of a romantic place to kiss."

"Nor will I have difficulty finding more such places," Jules replied. "Given that we are in France," he added with a wink.

"No argument here."

We exchanged a smile and stood looking over the grand sweep of walls and buildings of golden stone, enjoying its invitation to pause. Then we moved apart and he said, "Shall we continue?"

"Let's."

He took my hand, waved at the scene around us and said, "Originally Carcassonne was the southernmost part of France, that is, until mighty France expanded her territory." He gazed proudly at the medieval architecture below. The pride on his face touched me more than any words could have. *How incredibly lucky I am to have met this man.*

"*Mademoiselle*, your thoughts wander? My impressive kiss?" Jules smiled as he put an arm around me.

"I'm listening. Quite intently, in fact," I replied. "I'm not a woman who lets one kiss distract her."

"You lie!" he retorted.

He continued, "This location formed the border between France and Aragon which today is modern Spain. Because of the town's defensive importance, it had to be fortified. Hence, one thick wall of stone was built, probably in the twelfth century. But you see two walls, *n'est-ce pas*?" I nodded. "You see the lower one and then the higher one, that one with the round towers inserted every so often? That one encircles the entire medieval town; it's approximately 3-1/2 kilometers around. That's roughly two miles in your world, *Mademoiselle*."

"Much obliged," I said, "Go on."

"Part of the walls date from the 1st century AD. Even back then they clearly served a defensive need. Beyond that, we know little about the history of the place during that time."

"You regret the lack of knowledge."

"I always regret lack of knowledge," he said looking at me intently.

I canted my head and said, "I meant because you're an architect and it would inform your work."

"I know what you meant." His eyes continued to search mine until I looked away. "Alright, then, back to the lecture." We began walking again. "For *centuries* the walls continued to be reinforced. To make would-be invaders think them impenetrable."

He stopped and I nearly bumped into him. Standing with his hands on his hips he said, "Speaking of borders, you do realize French men are skilled at charming their way across them, right?"

"You do mean charm and not lies, right?"

"Of course." He smiled. "Clever woman."

"And you're way off topic."

He laughed and continued, "Alright then." We resumed our walk. "Alas, time puts her mark on all places." I saw his shoulders straighten as he said, "The border of my country moved further south to the Pyrenées mountains. Carcassonne lost its military significance, and slowly began to crumble. Because of this, the French government proposed demolishing the fortress. However," Jules threw back his shoulders and shouted, "The mighty French people spoke!"

I smiled at his bravado.

"Yes, the people of France said, 'Forget about it, *gouvernement fou*! We will have our Carcassonne! Rebuild it! Heritage! Ancestry! This is who we are as French people! *Vive la France!*'"

"I see you're a man of many talents," I said wryly.

He raised an eyebrow and replied, "*Mais oui, bien sûr, Mademoiselle.*" With a grand flourish he bowed deeply and linked my arm with his and we fairly marched forth. Jules, fully into the grand storyteller role now, was continuing, "Thus, in the mid-19th century an architect and an historian rolled into one must be called for! Nothing but the best! We must find the man who restored *Notre Dame de Paris*! Aha! *Monsieur l'Architect et l'Historian, Eugene Viollet-le-Duc*! Come to Carcassonne, post haste, and restore our town, our castle, our church!"

I asked, "Was this architect plus historian really a Duke?"

"Yes, he was," he said. Then he added mischievously, "You American snob."

"No snob here," I said. We got rid of that in 1776."

"As you like," he said, smiling, "but don't forget the role Monsieur Lafayette played.

"Never would I forget that," I replied.

"Thank you," he bowed. "But we must move along. Because I'd like to fill you in on some controversy about the restoration here. That is, if *la très jolie Américaine* is interested?"

"She is."

Jules had moved back toward the wall. His visage grave, he said, "It's a very large challenge to do restoration work. There is a dualism inherent in the challenge: must one be absolutely faithful to the original? Or does one restore the work, given the present-day possibilities and the current vision of the artist-architect, to the *spirit* of the original? Viollet believed in the latter, that is, better to restore a building to a finished state, keeping it faithful to the spirit of what was intended. He worked with many stone masons, among the most well-known was Jean-Julien Poirier du Savonnet. *Enfin*, he is well known here, for he was born in Carcassonne."

"You mean Poirier, like your name. Any relation?" I said in jest.

To my surprise Jules said, "Actually, yes." I was astonished to see his face redden under his deep tan. "He was my ancestor. My great-great-grandfather."

"I see," I replied, slowly taking this in and thinking, *Holy shit*. "So that's why you've learned so much about it." Something about this new knowledge of him gave me pause. *He will enter my heart and leave me desolate.*

Jules nodded and was quiet for a moment. "It means a lot to me. I've traveled extensively to inform my work. For example," his face brightened, "There are the most amazing ancient monuments in Zimbabwe. They are made of granite but without the use of mortar!"

I enjoyed his excitement, wondering how exactly mortar fit into the picture.

"It's what later builders used to glue together huge stones," he smiled at the question on my face. "But in ancient Zimbabwe –which, by the way, means 'stone house' – they knew how to set the stones without 'glue'."

"You know a great deal," I said. "And building without mortar tells us a lot about the depth of *their* knowledge."

"I've been at it for a long time. And yes." He took a step away from me. "*Bon*, let's get back to our tour."

"Yes. As I'm guessing you know a lot more about this place – its history, the importance and meaning behind the architecture, the ties that link the past and present."

His face was serious as he explained, "That's what I do here, Miriam. I am working on the present-day, continuing restoration of *le Cathédral de Carcassonne*. I have traveled the world to learn more about architecture in various places to inform my current work in French architectural *restoration*," he said, emphasizing the last word. By that I don't mean reconstruction, but a more-involved process that honors the profound cultural importance of the structure." He paused. "I've also learned much of the stone masonry trade."

"A living connection to your ancestor."

"Yes." He put his hands in his pockets and shrugged. "Though nowadays, to be honest, much of the design planning is done with computers."

"Really? I had no idea."

"Well, most folks don't." He smiled and looked at the vast structure before us. "My role is to supervise and pull together all aspects of the work." He spread his arms wide, opened his hands out, palms up, "*Ce cité ici, je l'adore*." He glanced at me and shrugged as if embarrassed to reveal his deep sense of pride. He turned away from me and surveyed the town below us lost in his own thoughts. The soft glow of the gaslit lanterns offered their light to the early evening and cast our faces in a luminous shimmer. In silence we gazed at the valley below. The coppery golden hills seemed to spread like a Renaissance woman's skirts around the valley floor.

Jules began speaking again, his voice thoughtful. "Viollet was soundly criticized for the restoration work he did here. There were many who thought, and rightly so in the strictest sense, that he had not been faithful to the original. For example, they said the towers you see interspersed around the higher wall here were 'inauthentic' to the medieval style found in southern France. There are over fifty of them and each one, as you can see, are topped with the little black pointed cones."

"Yes, I see them. They look like 'witch hats'," I said. In the lengthening shadows they seemed threatening. I experienced an odd, fleeting sense of menace as I observed the long lines of black cones. I shivered.

"I thought you liked witches," he said with a grin.

"I said I'm interested in them," I replied evenly, "though I don't believe the myths that say they're menacing." We heard birds twittering overhead as they settled for the evening. The reassuring sound of normalcy.

Jules pointed to the nearest black conical structure. "This pointed-towers style roof was more typical of those in northern France. Of course, Viollet also worked there; for example, at Mount St. Michel."

My mind flashed to the splendid day Dette and I had enjoyed there a couple of weeks ago.

Jules was still speaking, "However, the castles of southern France at the time had flat, slate-topped roofs." He shrugged again, "I can see the critics' point. But I have to say that in my book we owe Viollet an enormous debt of gratitude for the work he did."

"Absolutely," I agreed. "It's magnificent."

"*Bon*," he said, apparently having decided something. "We must continue the tour later. It's eight-thirty and we have dinner reservations. Shall we?" he asked.

"*D'accord*," I said. I was glad I'd slipped my heels off so I could walk barefoot from the apex of the walls back down the winding stone stairs to the town. "What these stairs have seen!" I said softly. "Ancient stairs always make me think of the people who walked them before us."

"Because you're reflective," he said.

"If only they could talk," I mused.

Jules smiled and took my hand again. At the bottom of the stairs we paused so I could slip my heels on. He led us to a narrow side street, barely wide enough for the two of us to pass abreast, and stopped before a wooden door aged with time and caught with black iron hinges. "*Voilá*, he said, *Le Canard de Carcassonne*." The heady scent of fish mingled with basil, lemons, onions, and garlic greeted us as a man in dark suit and tie approached. He took Jules's extended right hand in both of his own.

"Monsieur Poirier, delighted to see you. I have your table ready," he said, a wide smile on his face revealing both his delight and his tobacco-stained teeth.

"*Également*." Jules replied, following him to a candlelit table draped in white linen. "*Mademoiselle*." He pulled out a chair and I sat down, taking in the scent of the pink roses in the low crystal vase on the table. The verdant green of the leaves and stems was visible through the glass. I made a mental note to sketch them later.

I looked at Jules and said, "What an enchanting restaurant!"

"I was certain you'd like it," he replied with his usual brio.

"The coalescence of your deep knowledge of the construction and engineering of this city and your appreciation for the multitude of stories it holds is impressive."

"Not really." He looked at me and shrugged. "It's in my blood. Not much I can do about it."

"What do you mean? Why would you want to do anything about it? You so clearly love it."

"*Oui*, I do now." He shoved a hand through his hair. "But not always," he said. His voice was quiet when he added, "I wanted to be a physician for the longest time. *Vraiment*, since I was a little boy." He looked at me, "However, *mon père* had other ideas. I was his only son. He told me he would disinherit me."

"For becoming a *physician*? I would think he would be terribly proud of you."

"It would have come in handy," he said cryptically as a shadow crossed his face. "But Miriam, this is France. You don't simply up and turn your back on your ancestors. If you do, you sacrifice a deep part of yourself. Something integral to who you are."

"Yes." I said. "I think I understand, at least a little." This was true; I was connecting to the deep sense of ancestry in the people of France as I traveled around, hearing stirring stories of the past that informed modern sensibilities. I was sure that they would invigorate my art, which made them even more important to me.

Jules said, "*Enfin*, I wasn't willing to turn my back. Along with my father's 'encouragement', of course." He looked steadily at me. "At least I think that's why I left medical school." He frowned, glanced away, The waiter approached, but backed away seeing the somber expressions our faces.

I said, "I believe you. That you left for an honorable reason."

"*Merci*." He paused and said, "But maybe you shouldn't. Believe I'm always honorable." he said.

"Ha!" I said. "Very funny." He was teasing me again.

He looked at me with an expression I couldn't decipher. Then he shrugged and said, "Well, anyway, my career has worked out."

"What an understatement," I said. "You work in the Louvre! As well as places that dazzle with their beauty and mystery!"

He smiled. "I don't take it for granted, Miriam. I have genuinely loved the restoration work. Perhaps it actually is in my ancestral bones." He shrugged and took a sip of water.

A waiter in black and white attire approached, bringing a bottle of red wine, "Monsieur?"

Jules lifted the wine glass to his nose, breathed in its scent, swirled the liquid around in his wineglass and tasted it, rolling it on his tongue. "*C'est éxcellent, merci bien, Richard.*" He gestured toward my glass. The waiter bowed formally and poured wine into my glass, then filled Jules's. I noted his use of the waiter's first name.

He's been here before. With other women.

"To our adventure together!" Jules had recovered some of his former ebullience.

I yearned to say, *It's alright. I want to know the deeper parts of you.* But the mood of sharing confidences had taken flight. I lifted my glass and said, "To our evening together." He smiled at me as the waiter returned with an appetizer of plump mussels swimming in butter.

"Julia Child, eat your heart out," I said, laughing.

"I believe that's exactly what she did," Jules retorted. "Though she's not thought of as well here as in America."

"Why not?"

"It's believed she and her husband were, shall we say, dining with the Nazis?"

"No!"

"Afraid so."

I swallowed and struggled to think of what to say next. I needn't have worried. Jules was ready. "But it's 2001. Let's stay in the present tonight, ok?" He winked at me and I relaxed. He reached for my hand

and squeezed it, then we ate in easy silence looking at one another from time to time. The buttery mussels slid across my lips and I noticed a trickle of butter sliding over his lower lip just before he caught it with his napkin. The waiter returned bringing plates of white bone china with a paisley pattern in gold. A few leaves of delicate greens sprinkled lightly with herbs and a pale dressing rested on each dish. The man returned with two parchment menus.

"I know what I want!" I said looking with excitement at Jules and placing my menu down.

"*Chérie*?" he asked, arching one eyebrow.

"The *cassoulet*, of course!"

Jules smiled and inclined his head slightly, "Well done, *Mademoiselle*. You know *la specialité de Carcassonne*."

"What, you thought I'd order a *croque-monsieur*?" I asked in mock indignation. "A ham and cheese sandwich?"

"*Non, non*, of course not." He grinned. "As for me, I will have another *specialité de la maison*, the beefsteak cut thicker than my hand!" He leaned back in his chair and placed one hand on the table. Then he gave the order in rapid French to the waiter who bowed and retreated. Grinning again he asked, "Shall I tell you a story about where the name, '*Carcassonne*', comes from?"

"Please do," I said, leaning forward with a smile.

"*Bon*," he said, "It begins with the legend of Madame Carcas. She was said to be a strong, beautiful and willful woman." He held out his hand. "Rather like you."

"Oh stop," I protested, laughing. "Just the story."

He shrugged and said, "Ok, fine. So, way back in the 8th century Charlemagne's army invaded the region. Madame Carcas, the widow of the deceased ruler at the time, was very clever. The town was nearly out of food which would have weakened its defenses to the extent that they would be forced to surrender to the invaders. But Madame had the servants feed a pig with the last of the city's bags of grain.

Jules paused briefly to take a sip of his wine, "She had the pig fed until he was good and fat." Jules puffed his cheeks out and I giggled.

"Then she had that fat pig thrown over the ramparts."

"*Mon Dieu!*" I gasped.

He leaned toward me and continued in a deep voice, "So, you see, *Mademoiselle*, Charlemagne had to believe that the city had an inexhaustible supply of food if that damn pig was so fat. And if that were true, that meant the town could not easily be defeated. Therefore, he and his army beat a hasty retreat."

"A captivating story!"

He murmured, "*Cochon*. That shall be my name for you."

The word meant 'pig', hardly flattering, though I had to admit it sounded lovely in French. "She was a very clever woman," I said, ignoring the pig comment.

"Yes, indeed!" Jules held up both arms. "Then this fine woman rang the bells of the city to celebrate the victory! Hence, '*Carcas – sonne*' which means 'bells ringing' or 'Dame Carcas rings'."

"Is this true?" I asked sipping my wine slowly. The waiter had been listening as he approached our table and rolled his eyes in answer.

Jules ignored the waiter, laughed heartily, and said, "*Mais oui, bien sûr!*" The waiter placed a glazed blue bowl in front of me and I floated a moment in the intoxicating aromas of dark duck meat, thyme, lavender, and bacon. Jules' face broke into a wide smile when his steak, oozing juices, was placed before him. We enjoyed the meal as if we hadn't eaten in weeks. When we were done Jules said, "*Et maintenant*, we must celebrate her victory!"

"Oh, wonderful, are we going to ring some bells? I'd love to do that!" I teased.

Jules laughed and signaled the waiter who approached immediately. He ordered, "Veuve Cliquôt, *s'il vous plait*." The waiter bowed and said, "*Bien sûr, Monsieur*."

Jules held one hand curled around his empty wine glass.

"You know," I said, "you are a gargoyle." He shot me a look of surprise.

"Well," he said, "that's original."

"What I mean is," I said choosing my words carefully, "You told me that gargoyles had a practical purpose – to keep the water away from the walls of the cathedral so they wouldn't disintegrate. You, too, Jules, are 'keeping the hounds at bay' as it were – fighting passionately for what you believe to be the physical needs of the structure – insisting on the best limestone, sending back the stone that might disintegrate too quickly under the harshness of this climate, ensuring that the funding be secured." He had explained all this to me during our flight to Carcassonne. He regarded me steadily as I continued, "But I have watched you today as we walked around. I think your deeper mission is to uphold the very soul of the city and its cathedral."

"Miriam," he said, his voice thickening, "*Merci*." His eyes, their golden depths sparkling in the candlelight, stared into mine and for a moment the temporal world retreated. It startled us both when the waiter returned. On a silver tray he carried a bottle and two champagne glasses whose intricately etched designs shimmered in the candlelight. Expertly, he twisted off the top of the bottle and our ears smiled at the celebratory 'pop!' followed by a delicate splash as the smooth golden liquid poured into the crystal goblets. The moment that had captivated us within its spell retreated.

"*À nous!*" I said.

He touched his glass to mine and said, "*À nous*."

"And now," I continued, the wine plus champagne taking effect, "*Le mousse au chocolât!*"

"*D'accord*," he said, smiling. The waiter, overhearing, bowed and retreated behind the swinging doors leading to the kitchen. I took a generous sip of champagne and it caught in my throat. I sputtered a few seconds before recovering myself.

"Perhaps *Mademoiselle* is truly becoming the little piggy? *Le cochon*," Jules said with a smile.

"Shall I huff and puff and blow your house down?" I said, returning his smile. "But Jules," I said, "That was not gentlemanly of you to call me that. Indeed, I think it is you who is *le cochon*.

"I'd far rather be the proud Charlemagne," he replied puffing his chest out.

"An excellent idea," I said with triumph in my voice, "as that would be make me, *Madame Carcas*, the woman you'd have to surrender to! Ha!"

He smiled, but there was a serious look in his eyes as he said, "Which would be *tout mon plaisir*."

I sure walked into that one. But I met his eyes while my cheeks flushed. At that moment the waiter appeared again. I was beginning to think he was our chaperone, there to remind us we were in a public place. With a flourish he placed our dessert on the table. I plucked the tiny raspberry off the top and ate it. "So," I said, looking at the dessert plate, its white dollop of cream a crowning counterpoint to the dark surface of the chocolate, "Is there more of the tour tonight?"

"*Oui absolument*." he said. "Carcassonne is a very different place at night. It's magical. As you will see. As soon as you stop shoveling that chocolate into your mouth, that is." He laughed out loud when I stopped and held my spoon mid-way to my mouth. He pushed his dessert toward me.

"No," I said. "I can't eat both."

"If you say so," he replied, shrugging, clearly not believing me.

"You really do think I'm a pig." I brushed my hair away from my warm face.

He took my hand from me and said, "On the contrary. I am delighted to see you enjoying this wholeheartedly. Spare me the dames who pick at their food." I settled back in my chair and finished my silk chocolate.

Once outside, Jules turned to me and said, "Miriam, I will never come here again without thinking of you." The sense of loss inherent in his words pierced me, even as they spilled exquisite sweetness through me. After a moment I said softly, "Well, I'm here now." He put his arm around me and we continued into the dark night, moonlight our only shepherd.

CHAPTER 22

Miriam: Couvent des Soeurs de Grace

AUGUST 2001

My time with Jules in Carcassonne sent both joy and inspiration soaring through me. *How grand the human mind*, I thought, *to conceive of such magnificence and make it happen!* The renewed energy helped me settle down. It was time to develop my *Opus Magnum* piece, to create – using a combination of intuition and logic – a work that would, hopefully, inspire others. And so, I set to work, alone.

I've long been one who enjoys her own company. I know the difference between being alone and being lonely. In my Washington, D. C. life despite my hectic teaching duties and my life with Seth, I'd carved out time to be by myself. Perhaps this served a need I barely knew I had, linking me to the time after my parents left when I spent hours alone in my room, daydreaming, drawing, and cutting out paper dolls and the clothes that came in the paper booklets with them. I never actually put clothes on the cardboard dolls. I cut and cut, but I never moved on to the next step of folding over the little white tabs to secure the clothes to the cardboard figures. I never seemed to want to complete the picture of those one-dimensional dolls. Without clothes they couldn't be perfect; somehow, I knew I needed them to be incomplete, like me. Only in this way could they be the companions I needed. To this day I don't know who all brought me those paper doll booklets. Probably Granny bought them first and then gradually the word that I liked them spread through our little town. Most folks will do anything to try and ease their own pain at seeing someone else's anguish, particularly a child's. Within a year of my mother's death I had naked dolls shoulder to shoulder outlining all four walls of my little bedroom. So, I don't mind being alone; on the contrary, stillness soothes me. There are times when the hush of a single petal unfolding is all I need.

I'd made my studio a refuge, as I always did wherever I worked. The space was now filled with bits and pieces I'd picked up either along the beach or in the fields or in town. Lavender flowers, reeds, pieces of a bird's nest. A shell, broken in the shape of a wing. A long rope of dried and salt-crusted seaweed. A lace handkerchief one of the Sisters had left by my door in a brown paper bag. A tin can I rinsed out and filled with water. Another smaller can where I rested several paintbrushes. Copper filaments. A long box of wooden matches. A deep blue bowl that held a collection of stones. Newspapers, some crumpled, others laid out flat on the carpet. A turquoise silk blouse Dette had given me. A butterfly brooch that I'd inherited from Granny. A poem Odile once sent me, written in her tiny perfect handwriting.

The day I began my art piece in earnest, these companions settled a deep part of me even as elation filled my heart. Truth be told, joy had blasted my heart wide open and I half-believed if I spread my arms out wide enough, I could fly. But the longer I worked, the deeper I went inside. I worked into the evenings and then fell into bed, drained. One night I slept for an hour or so before I heard a staccato rapping. Stumbling to the door, I asked, "Who is it?"

A low voice said, "*C'est moi.*" I recognized Jules's voice immediately.

He and I had arranged a time to speak on the phone every few evenings after I sewed with the Sisters. I lingered in the great hall ready to pick up the heavy black phone at the first ring. (I could have made the same arrangement with Seth, but I did not.) We knew it was a time the Sisters would be at prayer after sewing. I increasingly looked forward to those evenings because during our conversations we were unfolding more and more of ourselves to one another. Even so, the night I heard his voice at my door and saw him standing there, I hesitated. When he remained still, letting me decide, it didn't take me long. I opened the door wider and let him enter before me.

"I've been –" I began, looking around at the collections that had changed the space since he'd first shown it to me.

"Shush," he said placing his finger over my lips and tossing his cardigan on the chair. I smiled, my heart a hummingbird, as I took his hand and led him to the window. We stood side by side in front of the tall glass panes looking out at the water. Moonlight spilled like gossamer liquid over the sea. I pressed my hands to the window seeking its coolness. Jules took my hands and placed them on his face and his warmth rushed through me. He waited until I turned to him. I ran my hand over the muscles of his upper arms and I heard his quick intake of breath. He pulled me closer and traced the long curve of my spine up to my collar bone and on into the hollow of my neck.

"I've been walking along the seashore," he said quietly. I cupped one hand on his face and tasted the salt on his lips. "I can tell," I whispered. Trenchant light filled the room and spilled over us, across our faces, over our bodies as we moved towards one another. That night I learned that art was not the only way to the sublime.

CHAPTER 23

Miriam: Veneux D'eaux

AUGUST 2001

Part of me longed to spend more time with Jules, but I had to generate my entrant for the *Opus Magnum*. After he slipped out of my room at dawn, I spent a week wandering inside my art, working from sunup to late afternoon. After such intensity, I found being in the presence of the Sisters a balm, so I often attended evening Vespers. They sat together in the spartan Chapel, their prayers taking wing in the cool air. The simplicity of the surroundings accentuated the beauty of their voices. "Let my prayer rise like incense before you, O Lord," they sang. The words comforted me, although the rebel in me sometimes surfaced and substituted "Mary" for "O Lord". But always, I was calmed by the ritual. Every third night I wandered over to the room where the Sisters gathered to sew. Whenever I attended, the Sister in charge of the room for the evening handed me a piece of fabric, partially-completed, as they seemed to have correctly assessed that I was no expert at tailoring. I could do a simple slip stitch, that was pretty much it. I found it immensely soothing to pull the needle in and out through the fabric, over and over. It was after one of these evenings that I felt the pull to visit Dette again. I made my way to the phone, nodding here and there to a passing Sister. I picked up the phone and stopped. *Seth is the one I need to speak with.* I had to tell him that I'd fallen in love with another man. I stood there a moment then placed the call. When he didn't answer, I left a voicemail telling him we needed to talk and explaining how to call me at the Convent. Then I called Dette.

"Yes, do come!" she said excitedly. "I'm having *une grande soirée* and I want you to attend! My entire work team will be here and I want them to meet you! They will be thrilled that you're an artist. There's one man in particular I want you to meet, *chérie*," she said, with insinuation.

"Actually, I've met som –"

"Oh, and there will also be a local festival when you're here – complete with jesters, jugglers, minstrels and knights!" she said. I was happy to hear joy in her voice; I would tell her about Jules when I arrived.

Parking a rental car on Dette's narrow cobblestone street was dicey, so on a whim I rented a *Vespa* from the tiny garage in the village, thinking of my jest to Jules about doing just that. Dette was forever telling me I was too serious and she was right. Driving a *Vespa* would be fun! Besides, it was also a way to ensure I would have to focus on staying upright instead of dwelling on Odile. I'd become more, not less, troubled by our agreement as time went on. I took a short – too short! - lesson on how to drive the damn scooter and headed to Dette's. I was seriously debating whether to tell her the truth about the agreement with her daughter as I drove through villages and sweet-smelling fields. I suspected if I didn't tell her, my uneasiness would be evident, but then again, between the party and the festival she might be too busy to notice.

Dette greeted me with open arms and hustled me inside, keeping up a chatter that allowed me to wrap myself in quiet. This had always been the normal rhythm of our friendship. But this summer, I'd felt myself, and our relationship, growing in new ways. She'd listened for a long time while I talked at Mt. St. Michel about intellectual ideas. But now I needed to risk being vulnerable with her, to risk be honest about Odile.

The evening began well. We dined on her terrace in the soft green light of summer. Each time I was ready to tell her about Jules, she interrupted me to tell me more details about the people on her fabrics team whom I'd be meeting in two days. I did my best to pay attention as I knew that we'd be speaking French at the party and I wanted to remember names and the telling characteristics of each person to help orient myself.

Suddenly her deep brown eyes widened and she paused. I rushed in to tell her about Jules, but she stopped me short when she said, "Oh my God! How could I have forgotten? Odile is home! She arrived yesterday."

"What?" My mouth went dry. "Why now?" I asked, searching for clues while my mind scrambled. Had she lost the baby? Had she told her mother? What the hell was going on?

"She won't talk to me," Dette said. "She took a much-needed shower and went straight to bed." Her eyes filled. "Miriam, something is wrong. She was doing so well – and then everything changed."

"That is troubling," I replied. Dette looked at me and said, "I know how close you two are. Please tell me if you learn anything when she wakes up, ok?"

I hesitated, something I would regret for a long time afterwards.

Dette reached for a tissue to dry her eyes when the phone rang. "Be right back," she said before she went inside to answer it. I heard her speak in low tones before she returned to me. With a soft smile she announced, "That was Charles. He's arriving early, so I have to leave now to pick him up." She winked at me, "Don't wait up."

Surprised, I asked, "Is he someone special?"

"Yes." We exchanged kisses on both cheeks before she disappeared.

I finished the dishes and walked slowly to the guest room thinking I *may as well get some sleep before the shit hits the fan*. I knew there would be action, I just didn't know when it would start. Upstairs, I had trouble sinking into sleep. To relax myself, I thought about Jules. Maybe it's best I didn't tell Dette, I thought dreamily. I could still hold my joy inside, a private treasure box to open whenever I wanted to marvel at its sparkling jewels, rather than expose it to potential dragons. Then I wondered if I should wake up Odile. Remembering that Dette had described her as 'exhausted,' I decided to let her sleep. But I was frazzled with worry.

I knew from long experience that when I worried, sleep eluded me. So, after a restless hour or two I got out of bed. I opened the window, leaned out, and heard music. Dancing had always been a place I could let go of my troubles. So, I slipped on my new black leather pants and a sparkly violet tank top and ran down the stairs, slipping outside into the silky night air. I looked up at the sky and thought *Full moon, uh-oh. The wolves are out tonight*. The soft air seemed to calm my nerves and the lively music was sure to help me forget my worries and dance. I followed the pounding bass that was coming from a bar up the street. *Go!* an insistent voice encouraged me. As I moved closer to the bar, I was thankful that I'd put on the silver-beaded platform shoes that Dette had given me when we'd gone through her closet. "Take them, *chérie*, they'll bring out the sexy coquette in you!" she'd said. Arriving at the door of the bar I saw the wooden sign whose curled black letters spelled out its name, *Lune Azul*. Blue Moon. I hesitated until a slim young man in jeans so tight he must have poured himself into them, cigarette dangling out of his mouth, beckoned me in.

Inside it was dark and the smoke quickly filled my nose and eyes. *Damn, the French sure do love their cigarettes*, I thought. Moving to the wide wooden plank that served as the bar top, I said, "Blue Moon martini, please." The taste hit my mouth with the first sip. *Cut with curaçao, yum-mm, love it!* I gulped, hoping no one would notice my pathetic quest for quick liquid courage. Within minutes I ordered another one, hoping the intake of gin would obliterate the less pleasant smell of sweat. Bodies were pressed so close together in the shadowy darkness, writhing in spasms of energy it was like watching a giant organism move. Suddenly, I froze.

At the far corner of the organism, now distinctly separated into single bodies as my eyes focused, was Jules. He had rolled up the sleeves of his linen shirt, the white blinding against his tanned arms. It clung to his back, slicked with sweat. The same back, sinuous with muscle underneath his dark skin, that I had lain with recently. The man whom I'd convinced myself after knowing him only a few hours was opening a new door into the core of me. Dancing – his head thrown back in laughter – with Odile. Beautiful in a high-waisted coral mini-dress that clung to her bosom. But it was the way that they danced that stunned me. There was a level of intimacy in their movements that told me they knew each other well. Their faces moved before me like diabolical figures in a movie reel; his mock-grimaces echoed by hers, followed by shared laughter. Jules grabbed Odile's hand and drew her close to him then swung her around and they exploded with laughter again.

You goddamn fool, I chided myself. *You great big goddamn fool!*

Just then I saw Jules notice me. His face opened in surprise that quickly became a frown as he took in the expression on mine. He said something into Odile's ear, touched her shoulder, took a step away from her and began to move towards me. I turned and fled. Blindly, I ran back over the same cobblestones that only two drinks before had been jesters to my dancing feet. *Dammit, dammit, goddamn holy Jesus H Effing Feckking Christ*, I thought in the longest burst of profanity of my life. *This joke is totally on me*. I slid out of the silver platform shoes and threw one, then the other, with all the force of my anger onto the stones. *Who did I think I was wearing these slut-kickers? I can't change who I am and I never will*. I hated myself for crying. The blow to my pride was little compared to the loss of belief that I was on the right path, finally. To think that a charming Frenchman would fall in love with me. I continued chiding myself bitterly: *There is no goddamn Perfect Mary or Perfect Goddamn Goddess or perfect-any-female-solving-everything. What a bunch of crap!*

"Miriam! *Attends!*" I heard Jules calling me but I didn't stop. Instead, I ran faster, the damn shoes no longer holding me back. *Not interested in hearing it!* I burst into Dette's house, slammed the door, and turned the lock. As I rushed up the stairs the world tilted dangerously, but I was able to maintain balance by placing one hand on the wall as I moved. I stripped off my clothes and fell into bed, pulling the sheets and covers around me.

I heard pounding on the side door downstairs, then Dette's voice coming from the patio: "*Mon Dieu, qu'est-ce que ce passe ici*?" What's going on here?

I must have run so fast up the stairs that I hadn't realized Dette and Charles were back. Dazed, I heard Dette and Jules's voices ricocheting back in forth in French.

"Miriam?" I heard Dette calling me, but I didn't answer. I would explain my humiliation to her in the morning. And I would sit with her and Odile and have an honest conversation.

Within minutes I passed out, courtesy of the wine and the Blue Moon martinis.

CHAPTER 24

Miriam: Veneux D'eaux

AUGUST 2001

I awakened to a pale slant of light washing through a tear in the curtains. My head felt like it had been hit with an ax. As I came to fuller consciousness I groaned, remembering the martinis and the scene in the bar that had made me flee. And then, in a flash, I remembered the noises that had awakened me. When I got up and walked to Odile's room her bed was empty. Intuition told me I needed to find her. And quickly. I slipped out of Dette's house and ran through the village. *Oh, dear God,* I thought as I ran, *please let her slow down and talk to me.* I ignored the startled looks of the shopkeepers just rolling up the aluminum shades and opening their doors as I flew by. I knew Odile loved the waterfall and I assumed that was where she was headed, so I left the village and headed up the trail leading through the woods to its roar.

Suddenly, a terrible possibility came to me with such force I stumbled and nearly fell. An involuntary cry burst from my throat, the high-pitched yowling of a wounded animal. *Could Jules be the father of Odile's baby?* The image of the two of them dancing and laughing last night in the café-bar came to me. Nausea twisted my gut, but I steeled myself to keep going. *No, he can't be, that is not Jules.* I repeated it over and over like a mantra, as branches slapped at my face, sometimes scratching me, and drawing blood.

My gaze focused like headlights on the figure of the young woman running far ahead on the heavily wooded path that climbed up to the churning waterfall. There was something driven in her running, a feral force unleashed. For my part, I had moved outside the rational world and was running on sheer adrenalin. So narrowed was my focus that I lost the sense of myself as Miriam and her as Odile; I became a hyper-focused animal bent on its prey. I pursued her, not smelling the sap of the trees, nor hearing the crows that screeched overhead, nor feeling the pain in my foot when I tripped on a thick tree root that protruded like a macabre limb across the path. I didn't take in the spot where Dette, Odile and I had picnicked in an earlier summer, the field where Dette and I had rolled in the tall grasses and laughed until we ached, the river where Dette had warned Odile away from the rushing water.

My thoughts tumbled to a dark place where they roiled and circled madly: *Odile. Jules, Baby*. I began to recognize the danger inherent in my turbulent thoughts: unless I concentrated on running, I would not catch her. If I did not catch her: there, my thoughts met a wall I refused to go over. I realized that I was losing ground to Odile's youthful speed. "Odile," I shouted again, but the wind took my voice and flung it back at me. "*Odile*," a thin echo wailed through the pines. Odile continued to run; she either didn't hear me or chose to ignore me.

We had almost reached the crest of the steep hill and were gaining fast on its nexus: the waterfall. I pressed on, picking up speed. I tripped over another root I didn't see, and landed, hard, on the ground then started sliding down the bank of moss-slicked granite. I felt rather than saw myself spinning toward the edge of the rocky promontory that hung out over the water. Sprawled on my back I grabbed whatever vines I could grasp in my hands, silently praying that they were rooted deeply enough to hold me. I was able to slow my descent by slamming my feet against a huge stone jutting out from the side of the hill. I could feel the cool mist of the waterfall on my face but its sweetness passed me by quickly because I was desperate to regain the ground I'd lost. A moment later I captured Odile again in my sights. I drew nearer and then, like a slow-motion scene in a horror movie, I saw her begin to lose her footing on the slanting ledge of green-slicked rock. With stunned disbelief I saw her inexorable slide toward the maw of the waterfall, saw the terror on her face, saw her arms and hands clench in their frantic effort to stop what I could see – even as my stomach turned completely over and my mouth contorted in a silent scream – was inevitable. She fell into the open mouth of the water in a long arc that was at once awesomely beautiful and utterly terrifying. I lowered my head, hearing a steady voice that said, "Fall in with me." I felt rather than saw the dark wings that held me as I thrust my arms out, and leaped into the air to save Odile. I heard the fury of the water below and felt the slap of the wind as it hit my face when my feet left the ground. And then, as I soared, I felt a whoosh of elation as I abandoned every tether I'd ever had. Within the grand sweep of joy, I recognized a profound part of myself I hadn't known I'd been searching for: complete freedom. Only a few seconds in linear time passed, before, in a lightning-fast shift from exhilaration to fear, I saw my own mortality slamming toward me as the riverbed approached. I kept my head low to direct myself toward the deeper waters of the river. My hands, then my head, shoulders and limbs sliced through the surface of the water and shot through the inky depths. Despite the pain in my lungs, I managed to hold my breath until I broke through to the surface of the water. With a cry that pierced the still morning air, I saw that Odile's body was circling face down in the churning river. *Odile who could not swim.*

CHAPTER 25

Miriam: L'Hôpitale de Sainte-Marie,

AUGUST 2001

I opened my eyes, disoriented. *Where am I and why does my head hurt?* Slowly, I remembered my struggle to drag Odile's limp body out of the water, to turn her on her side, to watch her vomit. I recalled my beginning a frantic search for a pulse in her neck and finding none, shouting "Help!" again and again. Far downstream I could see two fishermen look up and wave, then start running towards us. I began forceful chest compressions, the muscle memory from a CPR course I'd taken long ago. The sound of panting breaths I took to be the fishermen arriving. Blessedly, one of them signaled to me that he would take over the chest compressions. Only after the medics arrived – an eternity – and continued the CPR before they placed a C-spine on Odile and moved her onto a back board, did I let myself collapse. All I remember after that is a prick in my arm when they must have started an I.V. Then strong arms lifted me up as my mind floated like waves and I was gently deposited onto a bed as hard as stone. I drifted away only to be interrupted by a male voice saying *Madame, Madame, comment vous appelez-vous? Savez-vous quel jour c'est?* Their asking me what day it was struck me as funny so I laughed. "Well, if she can laugh, I guess she'll be ok until we get to the hospital," the male voice said in French.

"*Odile*," I heard myself say.

"Great, that's great," the voice said. "She knows her name."

"No, no," I said. "Not my name," I mumbled.

"It's ok, Odile," the voice said. "You're ok." Then, "She's babbling, but at least she's still with us." Minutes, maybe hours later, I felt a hard bump, movement, voices shouting, and then, a tiny flashlight that shone into one of my eyes then the other. "Put this in her I.V. to subdue any pain," a different voice said. After that, I slept.

When I opened my eyes again, a very disheveled Dette was standing before me. Her hair stuck up in all directions and she was in her bathrobe.

Why are you and Odile in your night clothes? And that new hair style is not working for you flicked through my confused mind before the joy of seeing her poured through my body.

"Oh, Dette," I cried, reaching my arms out to her. She ignored them.

In a cold voice I'd never heard from her, she said, "I've just come from Odile's room."

"What? Wait, where am I?" The room was slowly coming into focus, though I had no idea why she was behaving so oddly.

"Don't you remember? You and Odile went swimming in the river. What the hell were you thinking?"

"Wait, what?" And then, slowly, it came back to me. Running through the town, the woods, and up to the waterfall. "No, no, we didn't go swimming." I had no idea how long I'd been asleep. I didn't recognize this strange room.

"Funny," her voice was tight with emotion, "because that's where the medics found you. Both of you drenched. You wearing clothes,

Odile in a nightdress."

"Oh, my God, Dette," I said with alarm, "How is she?" I rubbed my head and neck. Pain shot through me.

"She's alive. No thanks to you! You knew she couldn't swim!" I'd never heard Dette's voice twist with such fury. She burst into tears. It took her a minute to compose herself while dismay and disbelief tumbled through me.

It had dawned on me that I was in a hospital. "Wait a minute, Dette –" I struggled to sit up. She made no move to help me.

"Oh, I'm done waiting. You took her swimming for what reason I do not know."

"No, I didn't!" My own voice rose, "You have it completely wrong. Is she alright? Have you spoken to her?" I heard the alarm in my voice.

"Of course I have! I'm her mother, which you seem to have forgotten."

"Oh Dette. I *know* that."

"The doctor told me she was pregnant," Dette said. Her eyes filled. The use of the past tense made my throat clutch.

"So, she's ok? She's talking?" I said as my own eyes brimmed with tears.

"Oh, she's talking alright. And spare me your tears." Dette glared at me and said, "How could you? How COULD you? Not tell me my own daughter was pregnant? And promise to take her to the U.S. to have my grandchild? How dare you?"

Perhaps because my brain was so filled with fog, I had difficulty understanding the fabric of her words with their overlay of deep emotion. Odile and I were in the hospital and we were both alive after a spill down a roaring waterfall. And Dette was talking about our secret? Wasn't it enough that we were alive?

But increasingly I registered how shaken she was: her mussed hair, her clothes, this was not Dette. This was a woman at the most terrifying moment of her life. And I loved her. Stunned, I remained mute. She was right. I should have told her. And I'd known that all along down in the room where I kept uncomfortable truths from myself. I couldn't summon the words, though, before I heard her voice rasp on.

"You're so fucking good at hiding your true self, Miriam," Dette said, as if echoing my thoughts. "So 'caring', so 'compassionate'," her voice drenched in sarcasm, "yet all the while it's all about you. What you want. What you need. Walking on eggshells around you after your parents died. I am just so sick of protecting you!"

I gasped. Dette had never once intimated that the shelter she'd helped me build around my losses had cost her. I thought of the many times through the years she'd been intent on cheering me up, shopping with me, showering me with the joys of color – on clothing, on walls, in fabrics, in jewels. How could I not have realized that beneath the joyful friend was a woman with her own needs? She'd always seemed so strong, so resolute. What a terrible friend I'd been; I'd leaned way too hard on her and never even realized it. And then I'd kept a secret from her that was not mine to keep.

"Look, Dette, I know we need to talk," I said. "I'm sorry. But my head aches."

"The doctors say you'll be just fine in no time. Unlike my daughter."

Odile! I covered my mouth as the implication went through me.

I dried my eyes with the bed sheet and said, "Dette, I –"

She interrupted me, "You have problems with Seth so you come here and begin sneaking around with Jean."

I blinked and said, "What?" I was clearly too foggy-headed to follow her. But I kept trying. "Who's Jean?"

"Oh, don't pretend with me. That sneaky little game is over. Really, I had *no idea* you had it in you to be so fucking deceptive. Fucking every single one of us."

"What –" she cut me off again.

"You can't get pregnant so you steal my daughter's child." Her voice broke. "My grandchild. You've always been jealous of my having a child." I looked away. That part was true. "But, honestly, how dare you?

What a self-centered bitch you are. The mask has been ripped off – I see you now for who you really are."

I leaned back, stricken. I took a shaky breath and felt myself filling with a slow burn. In a low voice I said, "*Your* grandchild? What about *Odile*'s child? What about what she wants? Why didn't she tell *you* she's pregnant, Dette?" I waved my hands in the air. "I'll tell you why; she knew perfectly well you'd tell her what to do. And whether you like it or not, she *wants* this baby. Who are you to judge? Who made you God Almighty?" I closed my eyes, my energy spent.

Dette leaned over me and grabbed my arm, hard. I gasped as my eyes filled again, annoyed with myself for crying but helpless to stop. "No one made me God Almighty. Don't forget *you're* the one who betrayed our friendship." Her eyes circled the room wildly and her voice broke again as she moved away from me, "And the baby is gone. We're God-damned lucky *my daughter* is alive!" My mouth opened, but no words came out. And Dette had left the room.

I swallowed. She knew me better than anyone and she had trusted me. What darkness inside had blinded me to her needs and allowed me to betray her? Was I insufferably selfish? Did I always think of myself first? As these thoughts circled, I pushed them down as a more urgent need came to me. I rose slowly from the bed. The room was spinning so I rested my feet on the floor for a moment. *Lost the baby*? I had to get to Odile. She would be distraught. Standing, I carefully stepped, holding on to the bed or the chair, until I got to the storage cupboard. I pulled on my damp socks and gingerly, my head spinning, headed toward the door. As I moved my dizziness increased and I wasn't sure if it was from my fall or my churning thoughts. But then a light fluttered through the drifts of fog. The truth was I had dived in as soon as I'd seen Odile fall toward the water. I needed to explain that to Dette.

And yet, the image of the dinner I'd had with her the night before surfaced. Dette had confided in me her worry about Odile. I'd been silent. She'd told me Odile had been thriving and then, unexpectedly, everything had changed. Odile had become like a stranger to her and – Dette had wiped her hand over her eyes – she had no idea why. She'd trusted me to tell her whatever I knew and I'd said nothing. My very silence was a darkness. Shame filled me: Dette's words had struck home with the ring of truth: I had been completely selfish. Though Odile had begged me for the chance to come to America with me and raise her baby there, I'd done nothing to help her examine her motives. Nor had I examined my own. I'd not thought long about it because it was what I'd wanted. I hadn't done it for Odile, I'd done it for me. As the weight of this realization sank through me, I sat back down on the bed.

A shadow crossed into the room. Jules! My heart a bird taking wing, he crossed the room and took my hand. "Darling, I'm so glad you are alright! But what a confusing and amazing turn of events!"

"I'm glad to see you!" I said squeezing his hand and sinking more onto the bed. Then, frowning, I asked, "How did you find out so quickly?"

He smiled, "First, let me say again how relieved I am that you're alright." He hugged me closely. "And Odile will recover in time. *Mon Dieu!* What a coincidence you know her, too!"

"Wait, you know Odile?"

Ah yes, they danced together in the bar.

"Yes, of course. My friend Bernadette's child. She's like a daughter to me." I looked at him, dazed. I heard the fury in his voice as he added, "I'd like to kill the bastard who got her pregnant."

I dimly felt a rush of relief that he wasn't the father of Odile's baby, but it was quickly surpassed by confusion. "Wait, what?" I said. Maybe the physician who'd examined me had been wrong: maybe I had had a concussion and that would explain my bewilderment.

"Odile is as close to a daughter as I've got, *chérie*. I've known her all her life. I love her like she's my own."

"I don't understand." I clung to his hand like a life jacket.

"Yes, I know. Berne told me about you."

"Berne?" I asked. None of this was making any sense.

"You call her Dette. Bernadette has been a friend of mine for a long time. Though I don't see her often, when we do meet, we take up right where we left off. Honestly, we're like family." Dimly, I registered his words. Slowly the thoughts lined up: Odile was the daughter of his friend Berne. Was Odile the family member he'd been worried about on our train ride to Rouen?

"Wait a minute. You're Jean?" My headache was getting worse. *Maybe my friend Jean* Dette had said when she'd been thinking of French men to introduce me to. Then she'd changed her mind saying, *Non, pas lui.*

"The family calls me Jean. My name is Jean Jules. I've used Jules professionally ever since I went to Paris as a young man. But family and old friends still call me Jean." He gave me a smile that spilled over the borders of my heart. Then another emotion swelled.

"Jules," I said, taking his hand. "I would never hurt Odile," I whispered, suddenly fearful that Dette might have spoken to him negatively about me today.

He frowned briefly, caressed my cheek and said, "Of course not. What on earth are you talking about?" Pulling him closer to me, breathing in his familiar bergamo-spicy scent, I told him about the agreement I'd made with Odile. Like a series of separate vignettes, I saw first disbelief, then bewilderment, then understanding cross his handsome face before he released his hand from mine. Then he said, "Miri, I believe you've had a concussion. Let me fetch the physician."

"No, Jules." I said as my heart constricted. I caught his hand again. "The doctors say it's a miracle, barely a scratch on me. My headache is from the stress of the dive. My head didn't hit anything in the water. It seems I'm a good diver." I gave him a glimmer of a smile, but he did not return it.

"Miriam," he said, with mingled confusion and disappointment in his voice, "I just don't understand. Why would you do that?"

"But –"

"I mean, she's only 17 years old! And she – she – she was just beginning to pull herself together. At EPFL." He frowned and said, "It was so important to her. To succeed there. You can't know." His voice broke on the last word.

Ah, but I did know. Hadn't I spoken with Odile many times both before and after she'd been accepted to EPFL, cheered her on, told her how proud I was of what she'd accomplished, heard the joy in her voice, and the newfound confidence? These thoughts swirled like wind-blown confetti in my mind as I began to slink inside myself at the double punch of his words and Dette's. I tumbled back to my familiar shelter, hiding inside the cave of myself. So, I didn't tell him that it had been Odile's idea to carry the baby and come with me to America. That I had dived in to try and save her. That I'd cherished her since the moment I'd first touched the curve of her tiny face. All he saw was my gathering the folds of the hospital sheet in my hands, opening and closing them on the smooth fabric again and again as I realized how unable I was to convey the landscape of my feelings.

I saw in his eyes what he was thinking before he said the words, "I'm having difficulty processing this. Why not tell her mother?" He took a few steps away from my bed. "It's a lot to absorb," he added, looking as lost as I felt. He shook his head as if to clear it before he said, "This makes me wonder if you're the woman I thought you were."

"Maybe I'm not," I said. "And maybe I'm not who I thought I was, either. But for what it's worth, I'm sorry."

I watched a jumble of emotions coil through his body and his proud bearing begin to cant. He crossed both arms over his chest and sighed. He waited a moment longer before he leaned over me. I felt the soft touch of his lips on my cheek, not my lips. On only one cheek, not both. I wanted to touch him, to clutch at him, but I refrained. I would at the very least save my dignity.

So, when he said, "I need time to take this in," I nodded. I had made and kept a secret agreement with 17-year-old Odile. I was only beginning to learn what it was going to cost me.

Jules turned back to me and my heart flew open. "I just don't understand," he said and swept his hands over his face. "But Miriam," he paused. "I hope you heal well." He said the words kindly, but with the salt of politeness that brought me straight back to the day in the Louvre when we'd first met and he'd shifted from the ebullient art historian to the polite stranger. When he refused to meet my eyes, I saw that we had already moved to a new place.

"Thanks," I said quietly. I did not call him back. I closed my eyes and sought the refuge of sleep. When I awakened, I made my way to Odile's room.

CHAPTER 26

Miriam: L'Hopitale de Sainte-Marie

AUGUST 2001

As I walked to Odile's room, I turtled my feelings for Jules. Odile – sweet, brave, shattered Odile – was the girl I'd known and loved since her birth. When I'd agreed to her request, I'd broken the consecration of our relationship. It was up to me to mend it.

The door to her room was open. Her face appeared ghostly in the artificial lighting. Only in that moment did the enormity of what I'd done hit me. Again and again life had struck her down. And I was her latest betrayer.

"*Chérie*," I whispered. Her eyes fluttered, took me in, closed. "I am so, so sorry."

When she opened her eyes, they glistened with tears. "Gone. I'm empty now."

"Odile, listen to me." She closed her eyes. "You have such power. You're the smartest woman I know."

"Not a woman. Empty."

"A baby is not the only route to womanhood."

"There's no other path I can possibly take. I'm a complete failure at everything."

"Odile, that's just not true." I moved closer and lightly caressed her hair. "I've watched you grow your whole life. In D.C., just a year ago, I saw your tenacity. You didn't give a damn what anyone thought about the neon stripe in your hair or the way you hop-skipped down 'M' Avenue smack in the middle of Georgetown. Fuck the coeds, that's the verve you showed. 'I'm doing what I want. This is who I am. Fuck it if you don't like it. I like it and that's enough for me.' "

"So long ago."

"And EPFL. You applied and got accepted and triumphed all with your own bravado."

"Yeah, look how that worked out."

"You were succeeding brilliantly. You showed me your top grades in the hardest mathematics and engineering courses they offered!

"Done now."

"What happened later was not your fault! Please, darling girl, believe me."

Her eyes filled. Her voice came from a faraway place, "I worked so hard to believe that. But I couldn't stand the shame. Drinking was.... such a relief. I'd drink and feel better. Then ashamed of drinking so much, stumbling around, drank more." She closed her eyes again.

I said softly, "Remember the spider story I told you?" She gave a barely perceptible nod. "The spider uses the finest silk thread to spin her web. Its tensile weight is stronger than steel. The web holds through the strongest winds."

"I'm not strong."

"Listen, dear one. You are. The spider holds on through many a storm. But if, say, a human hand reaches up and grabs the web, it sticks to the skin of the hand and the web is destroyed. It's not the spider's fault. In your case, darling girl, a monster grabbed you. It wasn't your fault. That's why you lost your footing. Then your tensile strength sank under a morass of guilt and shame."

She opened her eyes, closed them.

I continued, "But the spider perseveres. Wherever she lands, she spins out new spinnerets. And they're still stronger than steel. You've been able to do that, Odile. And you can do that again. You will go back to EPFL and conquer that world. I know you will."

"Dancing with Jean always made me happy," she said in a faraway voice. "And I wanted to feel happy again. That's why I went to Maman's. I asked him to meet me at *Lune Azul*. But Miriam," her tired eyes met mine, "he left me in the middle of a dance."

She doesn't know her Jean is my Jules. I made a silent promise to tell her as soon as she felt stronger.

"I kept dancing."

"You see? You kept going."

"Later, I walked home and went to bed," she continued. She sighed deeply and said, "I promised Jean I would use birth control. That kept running through my mind all night. I'd failed him, too."

So, she ran to her healing place: the waterfall. Lightly I ran my fingers over her hair. "You went to your special place," I said softly. "That shows how wise you are, Odile. Even when you were so upset, you knew to go there. That's a strength, sweetie."

"I've always gone to the waterfall. She's been my friend for a long time. She knows all my secrets."

"How marvelous to have a mighty friend, *chérie*."

"But this time she failed me."

"But I was drawn there." That terrible memory of her fall filled my mind. But I couldn't focus now on how terrified I'd been. I took her hand and held it.

She looked at me. "I loved you so much, Miriam." The use of the past tense chilled me. " 'The goddess on a pedestal', that's what *Maman* always said."

"Oh, good heavens, I'm anything but that."

"I can't...I really can't stand losing you, too."

"You haven't lost me, Odile. I'm right here. You will never lose me."

Faintly I heard, "Why did you agree, Mirrie?" The use of her childhood name for me tore through my heart.

The nurse – bless nurses! – came in to check Odile's I.V. She signaled to me, 'Your time's about up', and went away.

"I was completely selfish, Odile. For a long time, I'd wanted to have a baby. But this was never my baby. And the truth is, I agreed for me, which disregarded what you needed most.

"I wanted my baby."

"I know, *chérie.* But as an adult who loves you, I owed you a talk about options, about thinking through the consequences of whatever decision you made. And most especially, I owed it to you to do whatever I could so you would have your mother by your side." Her shining eyes held mine. "A woman has many possible avenues to self-realization, Sweetie." *And other paths out of the anguish of renewed self-disgust.*

She remained silent under the white sheets and closed her eyes.

"Odile," I whispered, "I am truly sorry I didn't support you in the best way I could have." I moved closer, intending to again touch my fingers on her tangled hair.

"Get away from her!" Dette's voice cut through the room. I started to speak but her face stopped me. I made my way out of the room in silence.

CHAPTER 27

Miriam: Couvent des Soeurs de Grace

SEPTEMBER 2001

A day later I was released from the hospital. Thom called from Washington to check on me. He'd heard about my hospitalization, though I had no idea how. For billing purposes I'd given the hospital the address of the small hotel I'd be checking into after my discharge. I'd snuck back into Odile's room, kissed her sleeping face, and left the address on her table so she and Dette would also know where I was. Already Dette had sent my belongings there. Ouch.

"Miriam, how are you?" Thom began.

"I'm doing well, thanks."

"Great!" he said. He cleared his throat, then asked, "How's the work coming along?" Boom: the underlying reason for the call.

"Ah, well, it's taking a while," I admitted. I searched my mind for some positive news. "But, hey, in Paris I found just the right aquamarine blue paint. It will be gorgeous against the copper."

"So, you are using copper. Good, good," Thom sounded reassured.

"Oh, yes, for sure."

"Ok, then, keep at it. We're counting on you!"

"I will," I promised through the tension in my head.

I was learning first-hand how each new loss carries the weight of earlier ones. I had to allow myself time to re-integrate my body and spirit before returning to the Convent. Twice, three times I caught myself dialing Dette's number before I remembered our break. I did call Seth though I wavered on what I would tell him. Never mind, he didn't pick up. I did my best to press thoughts of Jules inside my armor. I began each day walking through fields of sweet-smelling wildflowers and along the burbling water of a brook, filling myself over and over again with the balm of nature.

Gradually, I felt sufficiently renewed to move ahead. I had a job to do for the Academy. And I knew that creating art could also help heal me. I borrowed a *Vespa* motor scooter, put the ugly helmet on my head, my meager belongings in my backpack, and headed to the Convent. I sped over the same roads Jules and I had traveled weeks earlier, although my ride was considerably less smooth. By the time I arrived at the Convent I was a shaken mess.

Sr. Agrippina took one look at me and burst out laughing. Recovering, she said, "*Brava, ma fille*, I wasn't sure you had it in you. Welcome back."

"Thanks," I said. I think it was hearing her laughter that emboldened me to embrace her.

Gracefully she released me and said, "I'm sorry about your accident. But I'm glad to see for myself you're alright. And we're praying for Odile." Of course. She knew Jules, so she would know Odile.

"I want to be sure it's alright if I continue working here," I said.

She frowned and said, "Of course. Why wouldn't it be?"

"Thank you." I felt the long exhale of relief move through my body. And a further lightening when I heard the distant sound of children's voices.

"*C'est rien*," she smiled. "We are all – how do you say in America? – 'rooting for you'."

My eyes glistened, "I appreciate that."

"Now," she said briskly, "do you want to eat or are you ready to go to your room?"

"My room, please."

She stood and regarded me sternly. "You're stronger than you think, Miriam."

"I know." My wobbly voice belied my words. "Thank you, again."

"You're quite welcome." She turned to go, "Don't forget to eat."

"I won't." I walked along the stone path up to my room and opened the door thinking, *I will finish this. I will.*

I began to work in earnest on my project for the *Opus Magnum*. I spent a whole day slathering a sheet of metal with black paint and then scraping it off when it had dried. I did it again. And again. The repetitive motion helped me, as each time I put more vigor into the scraping. There's nothing quite like exercise to relieve disappointment, confusion, anguish. When I'd had enough of scraping, I washed the paint off my hands and ran by the ocean until I couldn't breathe. Then I dropped onto the sand and let the tide come in until the water nearly covered me. Exhausted, I returned to my room and slept.

Some days I walked into the tiny village near the Convent. It had no more than two or three shops, plus a small brick building that appeared to be a school. I made my purchases and walked back to the Convent the long way, picking my path through the tall grasses by the marsh. The nuns, or maybe the same one, left food by my door. Delicious food seasoned well with herbs and spices: fish, greens, potatoes. Sometimes I sat in prayer with the Sisters, and sometimes I sewed, but other than a nod or two they kept a respectful distance. I was deeply touched by their kindness.

I reflected a long time on how to create the holy woman's face on my copper piece. What expression on her visage? What features? Could I create a composite of universal features, not one computer-generated, but Miriam-generated? Should it be a composite?

As each day passed, my vision of the project's design expanded. My knowledge about powerful women in history became entwined in the process. The legacy of whip-smart, powerful women was not, of course, invented by the feminist movement of the 1960's and 70's. Anne Morrow Lindberg, a fearless pilot herself, piloted the plane when Charles rested. Ada Byron Lovelace drew the first algorithm that described an analytical machine. Dovey Johnson Roundtree – a United States Army veteran, lawyer, and minister – fought tirelessly for justice for families being destroyed by unemployment.

While cleaning my paint brushes one day, my mind fingered through the virtual rolodex of ideas I knew regarding holy women. I knew that cathedrals in France were largely built in the 12th century and that they all honored Mary as the Blessed Mother. Since my time at Chartres, I could now clearly envision Her seated on a throne, the Divine Mother, ruling the world with Her compassion and showering divine energy on all. The paths I'd followed while in France and my energetic wrestling with what I wanted to communicate through my art, had combined to give me a deeper appreciation of the beauty of Her story. And yet, in the modern Christian tradition Mary Herself is not divine. She is the giver of life and the intercessor between the male God and the humans who pray to Her. "That's a damn problem," I said to myself, "because I don't get how She held a divine life in her body, yet She wasn't divine Herself."

I moved on to cleaning a third brush. "And, though I know it was a bow to ecumenicism, I don't understand why the men in Vatican II back in 1962 de-emphasized Her significance when they decided to move Her statue from a place near the altar to the back of the Church." I shut my eyes as a drop of carnelian paint flew off the brush splattering my smock with tiny blood-red dots. "Not to mention," I sighed, "that we're told in numerous parables and all-male sermons that a woman is either holy or sexual, but not both. Another damn problem right there," I added. "We are both! Besides, where do sexual needs go if repressed? Nowhere good, I'll tell you that." I was the performer and the audience in this tirade. "And yet, guys," I smiled, "Her roots claw so deep that Her power continues to prevail."

I stood up and walked over to the window to work through what I'd learned from other faiths. Jewish theology includes Shakhina who is interpreted symbolically as a feminine aspect of the divine presence. The Hindu faith includes four aspects of the feminine divine: Maheshwari who brings grace and light; Kali who destroys everything that is false; Lakshmi who creates beauty out of what is left; and Saraswatu who puts everything in its place. I liked the complexity of that view of the holy woman and I smiled playfully to think that perhaps Granny, with her love of order, had been influenced by the latter.

"Oh, how I'd love to talk with Granny about all this!" I mused. "Or Dette," I thought with sadness. I suddenly had a fantasy of walking through Cathedrals with Dette and going up to each statue of Mary to talk with Her.

"*Salût, Marie*," Dette would begin informally to set the tone.

"Why hello there," Mary would smile.

"We wonder," I imagined myself saying, "How're you doing in there?"

"I hate being inside this plaster!" She'd reply. "Can you help me get out?"

"Why, sure!" we'd reply together. And we'd take our magic wands and tell Mary to stand strong. Then we'd wave our wands and release Her. *Poof!*

"Alleluia!" She'd cry, stepping out. "Now, let's talk."

This fantasy made me laugh out loud and gave me the energy to continue my work. I remembered Dr. Baldwin's words about mothers Selu, Imanjii, and Guanyin. "Arrrrrgh," I groused, feeling overwhelmed. "I can't begin to synthesize all these ideas and hope to create anything but a muddle-puddle." I wiped my eyes, not realizing I left a rainbow of splatches on my face, "But I'll fight to the finish!" In my determination, I threw up my hands and the paintbrush flew across the room. As I bent to pick it up, my eyes landed on the scrapbook of sketches and clippings I'd brought with me to France. One of them had slipped out onto the Persian carpet. I picked it up and read the words of the 4th century Roman writer Symmachus who had argued against the Christians who sought to remove an altar to the pagan deity Victory: "*We cannot attain to so great a mystery by one way.*" These words calmed me. I deeply appreciated how his words widened the idea of the sacred.

But I knew the many ideas I'd gained since I'd begun to gather inspiration for my art had become tangled. *Clarity, Miriam, clarity* I said to myself. Which led to a lightbulb moment: my need to be honest. It was simple: She would be *my* art inspired by *my* own divine impulse. No more, no less. With that insight I put my brushes in the can, washed my hands, and removed my smock. I made my way to the ocean, allowing the sound of the waves to energize me. I sat down and drew pictures in the sand, thinking of Lakshmi. The possibilities inherent in creating beauty out of what is left behind seemed endless. And full of life-giving hope. There by the water as the sun went down in a burst of gold and orange, I understood in a deeper way that there is something so *primal* in what the Divine Woman calls forth that She cannot be obliterated. She will not be relegated to the shadows of any religious group. And She will be seen most clearly by those who can see in the dark.

I began working such long hours I barely took time to sleep. Night followed day and though I ate – the Sisters continued to leave food outside my door – food wasn't what nourished me when I entered this state.

One day while I was taking a walk outside to clear my mind, I came across Sister Agrippina and Coco in the courtyard of the Convent. "Miriam, may I have a minute?" she asked. I walked over to her and rubbed Coco's neck. I swear the dog purred. Then Sister said, "I've heard a bit more about your troubles and I'm sorry. My cousin has brought Odile here over the years." *Jules has been here again.* I bit my lower lip. "She's been a spark in our lives for a long time"

"Very nice," I said wanting to run. She looked so far into my eyes I swear she saw the roiling waters inside me.

"We all make decisions we later regret. That doesn't mean we're terrible people." She patted Coco who let out a happy yelp. "Just human." I heard the Sisters across the way beginning to sing Vespers.

"Yes. Thanks," I said.

She continued, "Forgiveness, like love, begins with the self. Whatever has happened, whatever you've done, Miriam, you start with that."

"Alright, Sister Agrippina, thank you."

She put one hand on my arm, "And unless you love, you serve not God."

I finally spoke. "I don't mean to serve God."

She straightened up an inch taller but kept her eyes steady, unjudging, on mine.

I added, "I serve only the divine, whatever it is, wherever it is."

"This Madonna you've been following, is She not of God?"

"She's of Herself!" I snapped, "And She's divine!" I would not yield. I would stand for all the women of the world who had yielded and who had suffered, bled, raw with pain, from yielding.

"Alright, my dear," she said. "Once you surrender, I trust you will find your truth." She spoke to Coco and they moved away.

In my confused state I conflated her words about surrender with my feelings of guilt at making an unwise agreement with Odile and my falling in love with Jules. I shouted after her: "I did surrender! And look where I ended up! Both betrayed and the betrayer." But she was gone. I soon heard her strong soprano join with the others.

I ran up the stairs to my room. Out of breath when I entered, inexplicably, I suddenly saw what I needed to do with my art figure's eyes. I sat back on my heels and sighed. "Thank you, Sister," I whispered.

"Or," I allowed, "whoever sent this inspiration."

I began painting with the blue I'd told Thom about on the phone. The color – ridiculously expensive – was originally ground from lapis lazuli stone from Afghanistan. I liked that it would connect my art piece to the day back in March when I'd first heard about the bombed Buddhas of Bamiyan. The same day I'd learned I would be the Academy's entrant in the *Opus Magnum.* My own small tribute to the importance of art in the world. To honor with art – be it music, dance, theater, or another form – that which we cannot in any other way see or touch: the divine.

My studio became a numinous space for me. More than ever I experienced it as a place of mystery and transformation. I slowly, incrementally, began to trust that if I held my heart wide open, I would be guided to create art that would touch people. I arose just before dawn so I could witness the light as it slowly transformed the space from shadowy darkness to full, rosy light.

As I worked, through the pregnant stillness I felt a connection, slowly, to the divine woman I sought.

CHAPTER 28

Miriam: Couvent des Soeurs de Grace

SEPTEMBER 2001

I needed a break. I ran down the stairs for a walk along the beach. I lay down on the packed sand and listened to the waves pounding their fury onto the shore. *Now* there's *an eternal power*, I thought as I squished mud through my fingers thinking of Dette. Missing her. The sun was warm on my face and I fell asleep. When I awakened the sun had slipped lower in the sky. The memory of a woman's voice came back to me.

"Woman, gather yourself!" Her voice had increased in volume and energy and split me like a knife slices flesh. "Close your eyes and gather yourself into the darkness. Surrender! There is no time to wallow at the edge of darkness. Get moving! Jump!" The strangest feeling come over me then. I felt my body begin to shake as though a powerful being had lifted me up and forcefully shaken me like a life-size rattle. She pulled me in with her powerful arms. I felt her thrashing through me, twisting me with enormous effort until I felt inside out.

When I came back to myself, I felt the ground supporting the weight of every bone in my body. I slowly pushed myself up to a seated position on the hard earth. Memories of the Black Madonnas I'd witnessed to here in France paddled one by one through my mind until the flash of illumination arrived: the Black Madonna is complete in Herself. She breathes energy to and from others, but She resolutely owns Her force.

I sat there a moment and heard the faint echo of the rattle-woman's voice saying, "Get moving!" But when I looked around, there was no sign that anyone had been here with me, no footprints, nothing. Yet I knew what I hadn't known before: my art piece would not emulate the gargantuan perpendicular structures I so admired of French cathedrals. Instead, I imagined an evocative figure swimming through the air like a bird. More akin to an epiphytic orchid who receives nutrients and moisture not from the ground but from the air. A woman, complete in herself.

I was heating my third piece of copper when I saw through the window a person approaching along the beach. As the figure drew nearer my heart began to pound: it was Jules. I had not seen him since the scene in the hospital and I could not imagine why he was here. Had Odile had gotten an infection and become ill?

By the time he'd climbed the stairs to my room I'd already opened the door and was waiting in fear.

"Is it Odile?" I blurted out.

"No, thank God. She's getting stronger every day." He looked increasingly uncomfortable. He said, "It's something in the U.S."

I frowned. How bad could it be? "Tell me."

He sighed and said, "Oh Miriam. Someone's intentionally flown airplanes into both towers of the World Trade Center. It's unimaginable horror." I saw him swallow.

"No. No, that can't be true. Where did you hear this?" It was too much to take in.

"It's on every radio and television station in the country. Probably the world." But not the Sisters', I thought, because they had only an ancient radio and they rarely listened to it.

He shifted and said, "There's more."

"Tell me."

"Another plane crashed into the Pentagon."

My hands flew to my face. "No!" the cry filled the space between us. Jules knew that Seth often worked in the Pentagon. He came closer and put his arms around me. I was too shocked to cry.

"I know so many people in D. C. I need to go back at once, Jules."

"Yes." He hesitated. "But not today."

"Yes, today!"

"Miriam, listen." He took a step back from me but couldn't meet my anguished gaze. "All flights are temporarily grounded. Until they figure out what's going on." I crossed to the bed and collapsed on it.

"I need to get to Paris to be at the airport as soon as planes fly." *Was that my voice?*

"Yes. I'll drive you there."

"No, Dette can take me." The moment I said it I realized she could not. Though I'd spoken with Odile, Dette had refused to take my calls. That's when I cried.

In the end, Sr. Agrippina drove me to Paris in her ancient Citroën. Neither she nor Jules told me that when the planes struck the World Trade Center, some 250 people chose to leap into the air rather than suffocate in the smoke and fire.

CHAPTER 29

Miriam: New York City

JANUARY 2002

Title: *Holy Woman: Emerging.*
Artist: Miriam Verger

The Opus Magnum flyer affirms my art. It's printed on linen paper of a lovely smoky-lavender hue and has the design of an equilinear spiral engraved in copper on it. Tiny letters below the design proclaim: *Every woman is equal in her divinity and dignity.*

The female figure hangs suspended in air below a circular skylight. There are no discernable lines attaching Her to anything of air or earth. She is complete in Herself. The burbling sound of water floats through the soft sound of women singing. A breath of air blows to turn Her body around slowly, magically, so the viewer is invited to witness all aspects of Her. In one hand She holds a tiny gold trumpet; the other hand holds a tiny prism that throws light around the alcove. Flickering candles on the wall shimmer light upon the woman's copper body. The wavering light invokes dawn, then fire, then dusk, then inky midnight.

Soaring from the woman's muscular body are huge spread wings, made of pressed copper with black and lapis lazuli paint feathering thickly through the ridges. A single teardrop of carnelian paint falls under one eye. But it's the woman's eyes that captivate: they peer into the viewer, and deeper still, until one is drawn into the ether with Her. Her eyes are fierce, searching. She will not be fooled, She will not be hidden, She will speak her truth.

On the tip of one wing crawls a tiny etched spider.

CHAPTER 30

Miriam: New York City

JANUARY 2002

My creation for the *Opus Magnum Internationale* was complete. I took the train from Washington to New York to attend the competition. My thoughts drifted to the numbing whirlwind of life since 9/11. Seth had called me before the planes flew again and I wept with relief that he was spared. But we grieved for those lost that day, most especially for the 28 children of Pentagon employees who'd been on the plane returning to Washington from a school trip. My understanding that both solace and light could come through forging art helped to drag me out of bed after those first surreal days.

The train ran terribly late, but fortunately I arrived at the *Opus Magnum* venue just in time to guide the last details on how my art would be displayed. Over the phone I'd directed my crew to paint the half-moon alcove a satiny midnight blue. I was thrilled to see the lit candles flickering off the walls, just as I'd imagined. I'd pressed a crystal into the palm of one hand and a golden trumpet in the other. I was filled with delight to see how She spun threads of light around the room as She moved. Just before the final touches of the installation were in place, the lights flicked on-off-on-off to indicate closing time. I wasn't worried. I strode out of the auditorium with exhilaration: I'd done it!

The next day I stood near but not in the alcove listening to comments and watching Her as She moved. When a stern voice over the loudspeaker announced the time for awards had arrived, and folks began streaming towards the auditorium, I moved towards Her. At Her feet I got the shock of my life. The brass nameplate had three names on it: mine, Rafe's and Jule's. What the *hell?!* They were in *no way* my co-creators, nor even my sponsors. I was nearly apoplectic with rage. I sped to the auditorium in search of them and heard the Master of Ceremonies call out: Second prize *Miriam Verger, Artist, with Co-creators Rafael Bartlemen and Jules Poirier.* When I spotted Rafe headed to the stage, I ran down the aisle and met him at the podium. Breathless, I took the prize in my hands, while shooting daggers at Rafe aka Judas. "Asshole," I said through gritted teeth. "Get the fuck away from me." I must have looked fierce, for though he continued to smile his practiced traitor smile he moved away. Jules was nowhere in sight.

How dare they take this moment from me? Feelings hurtled through me like water over Iguazu Falls – anger, disbelief, more rage. Finally, I let myself own what was mine to claim: joy. I saw Thom give me the thumbs up which confirmed my job was safe. I smiled at him in relief. A woman from Brazil won first prize. I was genuinely happy for her: she'd created a spectacular figure in glass and silver.

After the applause and congratulations, I walked backstage to collect my suitcase for the train trip back to D.C. I hadn't had a moment to look at the other entries, but as I passed the large bust of a woman's head it caught my eye. The title was in French: *Vièrge Noire*. My heart clutched. It was a sign of how completely in my own head I'd been that I hadn't noticed that there was another Black Madonna art entry. An orange tenth place ribbon hung on the woman. Then

I looked closer. The brass plate listed Véronique Tutenne, Jules Poirier and Raphael Bartlemen. *What?! Rafe knew Mini Skirt? That fucking bastard. And Jules? He'd introduced me to her in the Louvre as his 'assistant'. Assistant, indeed.* The bust was large, offensively so, as if size alone conveyed her power. *Very typical of Rafe. But Jules? Ouch!* Her blank eyes were huge pock mark craters in disturbingly large proportion to her face. I thought, *Why the hell did she even get a ribbon for this monstrosity?* Steaming, I continued my trek to the backstage room where I'd left my bag. I needed to check the time of my train and catch a cab. I reached into my satchel and frowned when I heard footsteps slowing near the door. For a few hopeful seconds I looked around to see if there was any where I could hide; there wasn't. I kept my head down hoping that whoever it was would look in and move on. No such luck; I saw the light widen as the door opened further. I heard my breath catch in my throat when I saw the man who moved from the shadows of the hall into the light of the room: Jules. He hesitated a millisecond before taking another step forward.

"Congratulations, Miriam," he said, formally extending his right hand. We hadn't spoken since I'd left France. A memory flicked to the surface: the day we met in the Louvre and our hands touched for the first time.

"Get. Out."

"I came to see –"

"Oh yes, Véronique. I saw her piece."

Something trembled across his face, a disturbance that might have gone unnoticed if I hadn't once known him so well. His eyes met mine for a split second before he looked away.

"Rather uncanny how she chose the same subject as I, isn't it?"

He had the grace to look pained and then I knew.

"You knew all that time!" I couldn't keep the note of shocked disbelief from my voice. "You knew and you didn't tell me. That's why you charmed me, showed up 'coincidentally' in Chartres. And," anguish filled the back of my throat, "flew me to Carcassonne and took me to dinner. So you could spy on me, pull ideas from my brain and make sure hers were more compelling. Or try, anyway," I added with a shudder I hoped he registered.

"Yours is, and always was, more compelling," he said quietly. "It wasn't like that," he added. "The Miriam I knew *knows* it wasn't." I heard pain in his voice. I ignored it. Bastard.

"Remember, I didn't know you at first," he went on. "I agreed to meet you as a favor to Thom. Yes, I was providing advice to Véronique. And later, yes, I was pretty sure you'd be heading to Chartres."

"Because I'd told you I was going there! And that's why you took me to the Convent – so I could get a room where you knew you'd have free access!" I said bitterly.

"No!" the growl sputtered from deep in his throat. "I did not have free access to your room. I would not trespass on an artist at work!"

He was right there, of course. I'd granted him access. I looked away.

"*Non*," he said again, moving closer to me. "At that point it had nothing to do with Véronique or the *Opus Magnum*. I resigned as an advisor to Véronique *before* I took you to the Convent and well before I came to you there or invited you to Carcassonne. I was drawn to you. I'd never met anyone like you – so cool, yet also so – fiery. I wanted to know more about you. About *you*."

There was a roaring inside my head so it took me a minute to reply. "You know," I said, "at the Blue Moon Bar when I thought that you and Odile," – my voice slipped and he put a hand out to me, but I held mine up to stop him – "I thought that was a sexual betrayal and I was deeply hurt. But this,"– my hand stabbed the air – "this is worse. My art is fundamentally *who I am*, Jules."

"I know that," he said quietly. "Don't I know that better than anyone?"

Even as I recognized the truth in his words, my indignation smothered it.

"But you are gone now. I see that," he said. "You run like your father did."

"You know nothing about my father!" I shouted, shocked at his cruelty. "He didn't leave my mother. She died before he left."

"I'm talking about *you*," he said. "He left you."

The weight of his words slammed against my chest. Grief and fury rushed out as the world tilted. I counted to ten, then twenty. Finally, I said, "He loved me, Jules. He really, really loved me." Saying the words righted my world. For the first time since he'd disappeared, I truly understood what my father had left inside me. I lifted my chin.

"It is not your right to judge my father, Jules. Who made you God? The same person who put your name and Rafe's on my work? So that both of you would get the credit for my work?"

"Miriam." He shoved one hand through his hair and looked into my eyes. "I didn't do that."

"So now you blame Rafe for that? What a coward you've turned out to be!"

"Look," he said, his shoulders slumping, "I came here to explain –"

"Forget it! Remember, I'm the selfish bitch who fooled you all."

"Bravo," he said. "There's the fiery woman back."

"It's not funny."

"I'm not joking. I'm relieved to see the blaze. By the way, Bernadette could use your energy now. And you clearly have it to spare."

"So you're her messenger?"

"Stop it, Miri!" his voice sharp now. "I came to see you because I *wanted* to see you. It's as simple as that."

"It's not simple! You're horrible! You betrayed me in the worst way possible."

"I did *not* touch your art!" He paused and said more softly, "It can be simple between us if you allow it to be. What happened to that woman I knew in France, her *joie de vivre*? Where'd that woman go?"

"I guess you could say she grew up! I'm an artist not a romantic."

"It's not dichotomous, Miri. Does no part of *Divine Woman, Emerging* stem from the passion you felt in France?"

"Of course She does! But She's not about you, you *bâtard*!" He winced at that, but I sailed on. "The passion has to do with my love for Odile, Dette, Granny, Mumma." I held myself together, I would not cry in front of this man, "And what I discovered about the meanings of the Black Madonna and my mother and the sound of seagulls at Mt. St. Michel and the bolt of blue when the sun shines through the windows at Chartres and the sound of the Convent Sisters singing in harmony and the church bells pealing their call at *Notre Dame de Paris* – all of these are in the *Holy Woman, Emerging*."

He put his arms across his chest and said, "Miriam, please look at me." I raised my eyes to his. "I wasn't saying that it's only about me. Clearly, She's about all those things. Not any one of them, but all of them together. I do see them – all of them – in the *Divine Woman, Emerging*. That's exactly what makes it an astonishing work."

"So you could take credit, you bastard."

"No, not that." He moved to me and brushed one hand butterfly-soft against the side of my face. "I wanted to be here when your talent was recognized."

"So you could reap the benefit. If you'll excuse me, I have a train to catch." I grabbed my bag and fled.

CHAPTER 31

Miriam: Partridge Island, Maine

JUNE 2004

After my tumultuous six months in France, the furor of 9/11, and the completion of the *Opus Magnum* competition in New York City, I was exhausted. The combination of shock, sorrow, and betrayals – mine and others' – had flattened me.

I decided to head back home to Maine. Seth and I had come to an amicable agreement to separate. I would miss him, his lovely manners, his kindness. But I needed time to be alone to try and sort things out. I had no wish to return to the D. C. Academy of Art. Rafe had played with my heart once and I was angry that this second time he'd managed to betray me with art. Bastard. I had no stomach for seeing him daily, but it was more than that. I needed solitude. Thom, dear Thom, offered to help me as I worked to eradicate any mention of Rafe's and Jule's names attached to my copper art piece; I thanked him, but accomplished it on my own. Thom also gave me a glowing referral to the Portland College of the Arts. He surprised me by saying I could return to the Academy at any time. I thanked him, gathered up my art tools and went to my condo to pack.

One sunny morning a week or two after I'd moved into my new place in Portland, I drove north to visit the graves of my mother and Granny, pausing to let my sorrow fill me. *I still miss you*, I whispered to each of them. *I'll always miss you*. I sat down on the grassy slope and said out loud, "Granny, I think you knew more about what troubled Mumma than you let on. You always did what you were raised to believe was best. We are all flowers that grow in the soil of our families and our cultures. You're the one who helped me learn that love is wide. You steadfastly ignored the serpents of judgment all around us after Mumma died and Daddy left. I always breathed in love when you moved over to make room for me on the shell chair on the front porch." The chattering chickadee on the tree above my mother's headstone was my only answer. When it continued to chatter insistently, I smiled. Satisfied, it flitted away.

Since I'd left Maine seventeen years before, Portland had become a place brimming with promise, especially in the arts. I was thrilled to accept the job at the Portland College of the Arts. The job allowed me plenty of time to do my own art and had me teaching again. I'd always been invigorated by my students' energies and this continued to be true. Their shining innocence, their passionate belief that the future held innumerable bounties. I needed that.

My heart thrummed to Portland's lively scene. The city was actively becoming a more diverse community, from the numerous signs – *all are welcome here* – to the strong community support around immigrants of color, to the museum's push to include a more diverse array of artists. I worked with Dr. Baldwin to bring Faith Ringgold's gorgeous art, and emerging artist Kehinde Wiley's portraiture on vividly-patterned backgrounds, to the Portland Museum of Art. During the winter I enjoyed the quiet, lulling vibe. But once ice melt arrived and Portland got markedly busier each day, I longed for quieter days again so I could more easily immerse myself in my art. Perusing the pages of the

Portland Herald one Sunday morning, an advertisement for a two-room cottage on Partridge Island, a 20-minute ferry ride across Portland's Casco Bay, caught my eye.

When I tuned up on the doorstep of the rental cottage, the unsmiling woman who met me at the door blurted out a question: "Why are you here?"

"To paint." I said.

"You here trying to change things?"

"No," I said. "I like things here just the way they are."

She took her time to gauge my words. Then she opened the door wider and said, "Well then, welcome to the neighborhood." After a quick tour of the cottage and my nod of approval, she handed me the keys. "No cars allowed on the island, but there's a bicycle out back. You can rent a kayak round the back of the general store. Get your groceries there, too." I barely had time to write her a check before she was out the door without another word.

I warmed to Gray Point, the tiny community on the northeast side of the island where my cottage was located. The cawing of seagulls and yelps of dogs greeted my mornings. I often awakened before dawn and gloried in watching the lemon and tangerine sun rise out of the ocean. Black coffee perking and munching Mrs. Casco's (my landlady having at last divulged her name) banana walnut muffins filled me with contentment. Some days I took the ferry into Portland for my classes at the College of Art and for my volunteer work teaching English to the tiny community of Somalian immigrants. With both of these efforts, I learned far more than I taught.

On other days I walked the few steps over to the north-facing shed where I'd set up my easels to paint. I'd shifted the current focus of my own art to large purple and blue seascapes with daubs of silver, gold, and copper. Occasionally I'd shift to painting faces, mostly my mother's. I thought I would one day also tackle my father's face. And Granny's. And Dr. Baldwin's. Occasionally I'd switch gears and work with a piece of driftwood snared by seaweed.

One September morning dawned unusually warm so I'd set up my easel on the beach as I liked to do when the light was right. I was finishing up a face shot with cinnamon when I noticed a figure far down the beach headed my way. I stilled, hoping the person would continue past me. As the figure neared, I saw it was a man wearing a loose cotton shirt and khaki slacks. For a second my heart leaped – *Jules.* But Jules never wore khakis. Slowly, he came close enough for me to see it was, unbelievably, Jules.

"What are you doing here?" I asked.

He took a step toward me then paused. "I came, ah, to apologize. As I tried to do in New York a while back."

"You tried." I put my paintbrush in the lip of the easel.

"I didn't try hard enough."

I crossed my arms over my chest. Jules was shading his eyes from the sun when he said, gesturing toward the canvas, "A metallic thread continues to find expression in your art." The woman's curly autumn brown hair was shot with gold.

"Yes."

"It's your talent shining through."

I didn't smile. I curled the toes of my bare feet in the sand.

He sighed. "I wasn't joking. The way you thread the metallic filaments through it is striking."

I remained silent. He added, "I was never making fun of you."

I kept my arms across my chest. "No, that wasn't the issue."

"Miriam, I am here to apologize." He stopped. "I did betray you in the worst way possible. As an artist. I didn't put my name on your work, but I did keep my initial work with Véronique's art a secret from you. You see," he hesitated then took a step toward me. I put my hand up and he stopped. "I was up for a big promotion. To become the Executive Director of the French Academy of Art and Architecture. It was something I'd wanted and worked toward for a very long time."

He took a deep breath. "And I needed to sponsor a female artist."

"Ah."

"But I never meant to hurt you." He paused while he seemed to sift through his thoughts. "After I ran into you in Chartres and spent more time with you, in all honesty much to my surprise, I began to reconsider the path I was on. I informed Véronique she needed to find a new sponsor. She wasn't happy, but she found one. At that point she hadn't begun her art, and I didn't know she eventually chose to work on a Black Madonna figure." He rubbed his sandal in the sand. "I guess you know by now it was Rafe who put our names on your art."

I nodded and thought back to that long-ago day in the Louvre and how long it had taken Véronique to bring our cafés. It was entirely possible she'd lingered and had overheard me tell Jules about my intended project. I said, "I did wonder about the piece she submitted for the *Opus Magnum*. When I saw you were her sponsor, I thought, well, he's not as talented as I thought he was."

He winced again and said, "She submitted the competition paperwork when I was still her sponsor. That's why my name was on it. She should have had it changed to her new sponsor's name."

I nodded. "Perhaps that person doesn't have the weight of your reputation," I said dryly. He looked away. I asked, "Does it matter now?"

"It matters to me that you know the truth. And I need you to know that I regret the hurt I've caused you."

I remained silent as I looked at his face, noticing the worry lines that had formed since I'd last seen him. "Is that all?" I was still wary, though the little bird was flapping its wings in my chest.

He swept his hand through his dark curls that were now dusted at the temples with silver. "*Non*, it isn't all. You see, I'm married. Or I was then."

"Oh, Christ," I swore and took a step away from him.

"Please, Miri, listen," he said, taking my arm. I pulled it away as he said, "My wife, Celeste, was injured in a car accident about a year before you arrived." He looked down at his feet then lifted his head and said, "It left her in a coma. I was driving. Suddenly, my life was no longer the one I'd imagined." As Jules spoke, I dimly heard the voices of two fishermen who tended to cast their lines nearby. I nodded at them and they moved on.

Jules said, "I visited her often." His face tightened and his voice was strained when he added, "Each time I visited I saw that my wife was disappearing. It was – wrenching. You can't imagine." Suddenly he stopped and looked at me. "Oh God, Miriam, I'm sorry. Your parents –"

I nodded but remained silent, closing my eyes while a shiver of compassion ran through me. What he'd suffered. And he'd never said a word. Why hadn't he told me? What kind of intimacy was that?

He said, "I apologize for that, too. For not trusting you, or us, I guess."

A relationship without trust makes love wretched.

"What I'm trying to explain," here his voice wavered before righting itself and continuing, "is that my work, and mentoring others, became my anchor."

"I see." I said. "Taking me to your work at Carcassonne provided some relief, I hope."

"I think you know it was more than that." He was trying to make eye contact.

"It's hard to trust what I thought I knew about you." I bent to stir the brushes in the pail of turpentine and water. "Has she recovered?"

Another pause and he stuck his hands in his pockets. "*Non.* She died last year."

"I'm sorry for your loss," I murmured, meaning it.

"Thank you." He added, "It's taken me a long time to sort through my feelings. To forgive myself. About her. The road was slick, she reached for the wheel..." He stopped. "We struck the guard rail. The car accordioned."

"How awful. I'm very sorry."

"Yes. It was horrific. She didn't deserve that."

"Clearly not. And how awful for you."

"Yes," again he shaded his eyes with his hand. "But what I'm trying to say is, I've been working hard to forgive myself for hurting you, Miriam. Honestly, I've never felt the kind of – abandoned joy – I felt when I was with you."

I stood, facing him, and said nothing. I wasn't sure what to say or what I felt. How quickly this bright morning had shifted course. I dug my bare toes deeper into the sand, reassured by their unchanging tactile comfort.

"Since you left, Miriam, you've filled my thoughts. I take a walk near *Notre Dame de Paris*, you're with me. I wake up early in the morning, I see your face. I visit the Convent, your presence lingers." He took a step closer. "Miriam," he added in a low voice, "you once told me you felt joy," I looked at him as he added, "because of me."

"That was then." I'd located my voice again.

"Alright," he said. He took a long pause and looked out over the bright blue water. "But I want you to know," he hesitated and looked down as if searching for the right words among the grains of sand, "that it was also true for me."

I looked at him with a question in my eyes.

"You gave me access to joy again."

My heart soared, though I said nothing. My mind was swinging wildly between memories of our times together in France and how becalmed I'd become here on this lovely island. And how sweet it was to recognize the feeling of my mother walking beside me here.

Jules's gaze had turned from my face to my painting. I said, "I like it here. I feel both energized and at peace."

"It shows on your face. And in your art."

I acknowledged the compliment with a nod to the canvas before us. "My mother."

"Such a tribute," he murmured quietly. Then he asked, turning again to face me, "Do you remember when we talked about forgiveness?"

"Yes. The cornerstone of the Catholic Church."

He nodded, not taking his gaze from mine.

"But only after repentance," I reminded him, "that's what non-Catholics don't get. No forgiveness comes without genuine contrition."

Slowly he reached for my hand and as our fingers twined, I felt the familiar pulse surge between us. I looked into his wet brown eyes and caught the deep, clear truth of him.

When I didn't move, he said quietly, "Do you understand how deeply I regret the wrong I've done to you?" I took a deep breath. I removed my hand from his and put them into the pockets of my smock. I moved my toes through the damp sand again.

I'd vented my anger over many cups of coffee with my Portland friend, Diane. I'd worked through my own sense of shame at how my selfishness had led me to betray both Odile and Dette. I'd called them, trying to convey my regret. I'd asked for their forgiveness. I wanted to feel worthy of their friendship again. I'd spoken with Odile many times and our closeness was renewed. But so far, Dette had not answered my calls. Her absence in my life had left a brokenness in me that I did my best to board up. But walking the ocean shores here I'd come to realize that I wouldn't truly be free until I took the nails out of my boards and let them fall.

And so, I made the choice to believe Jules. To unburden this man whom I'd loved since the moment I'd met him. Slowly, I lifted the smock over my head, dropped it to the ground and wiped the damp from my hands on my shorts. The silence of unspoken words hung between us while a seagull sailed overhead.

"I've crossed many a river since then. I've reclaimed the ocean inside me," I said, my voice steely. "You won't be able to deceive me in such a way again."

"I'm glad." He waited a beat before he added, "Nor do I intend to." He took a step closer to me. His eyes pleading, he said, "The question is, will you take a chance again?" I regarded him for a long moment while my heartbeat matched the pounding waves hitting the shore. "Let's walk near the water," I said.

We left our sandals by the easel and began walking at the edge of the chilly sea.

I took the ferry and then a local bus to the Muddy River café near the town of Freeport. When I entered the restaurant, I spotted them immediately, sitting side-by-side at a table on the veranda that overlooked the river. I removed my sunglasses and sat down across from them, my heart a pounding drum in my chest.

"What are *you* doing here?" Dette demanded. "I thought you were in D. C." She half-stood as if to leave.

"Sit down, *Maman.*" Odile's voice was strong. She looked like an angel, her hair cut short and golden waves framing her face. Her black bandeau top and jean shorts made her appear younger than her 19 years.

"You two planned this!" Dette accused. "Another secret. I'm leaving." She rose to her full diminutive height.

"Dette, please wait," I said as a waitress put three glasses on the table and moved away. "We did. But please hear me out." I took a sip of the icy water before I continued. Dette sat down as if in a trance. Odile ran one finger around the thick edge of her glass.

"I messed up. I really, really messed up," I said. Dette lifted her face. "I know you've been angry and you have a right to be angry. I should have convinced Odile to tell you the truth. It was selfish of me to not do that and I'm sorry. I'm *sorry*." She looked out at the river so I could not read her eyes. But she was sitting down.

"Dette, I'm not perfect." She looked back at me with a small gesture that said *you sure aren't.* Then she surprised me by saying, "Secrets are a burden, I know that." Her eyes bore into me. Odile, rapt, signaled to the waitress to leave the menus and give us a minute.

"What do you mean," I asked, fearful of what was coming without knowing why.

"My mother did tell me more about your parents. How they met. I just couldn't find the words to tell you." She paused. "Even when you asked."

"They met at a church social," I said.

"They first met in town, sure. But that's not where they were married."

"What?"

"Your mother got pregnant in high school."

"She was young, I knew that."

"Did you know your Granny sent her to a convent in New Orleans to give birth to you and then have you adopted by another family?" The words rushed out of Dette's mouth and I had trouble absorbing them.

"No way." My ears started ringing.

"It's true. She confessed the whole story to Anie, my mother."

"I'm aware that Anie was your mother," I said in a clipped voice.

"Edouard took a bus to New Orleans to fetch your mother back,' Dette continued.

"Rose?" I whispered, hardly believing my ears.

"Yes."

The spinning in my head was making me dizzy. This was not going the way I'd planned. I took a moment to let it sink in. "So, Daddy," I said softly, "did the right thing. He went there and brought Mumma and me back home. And he married her." I raised my tear-filled eyes to my friend.

"You've got half of that right," she said. "He took the bus to get her, but Edouard wasn't the high school kid who got your mother pregnant." Looking intently at me she asked, "Didn't you know how much older he was than your mother, a good ten years?"

My stomach twisted. This was more than a lie; this was my life completely re-imagined. "You lie!"

"I don't." It was the calm way she said this that told me it was true. Ed had loved my mother, after all. It had never occurred to me they might have a hidden story. But don't we all?

My mind rattled around some more before it settled on the little black figurine I'd taken from my mother's bedroom night stand.

"She got the dark figurine there," I said slowly.

"Most likely," Dette agreed. Odile was glancing between the two of us with her mother's wide brown eyes.

"Rose told Anie that right after you were born, she'd touched your skin and looked into your eyes; in that moment she decided to run from the convent. She wrapped you in a shawl early in the morning the day you were to be adopted and took you to the bus station. Granny had given her a round-trip ticket so she could return home. So, Rose had the return ticket and just enough cash to buy herself some sandwiches."

Granny! I felt stunned. *We are all flowers that grow in the soil of our families and our cultures.*

Dette's voice continued while Odile's eyes now stayed on my face. "When Rose was paying for a sandwich at the bus station, Eddie appeared. He'd heard about the baby – a small town has no secrets – and, unasked, had come to bring Rose home. He didn't blink when he saw the baby in her arms." Dette paused. She looked at me and said, "Rose told Anie he never pressured her. He mumbled that he wanted to accompany her on the ride home. As they bumped along on the bus, one night he said, 'I'll take care of you both. If you'll have me.' Rose said she looked at this bear of a man, an exceptionally kind man, and replied, 'I'll have you'."

"Mumma kept me." That's what was expanding my mind like a drug. "She fought for me." I looked at Dette and Odile and said slowly. "No wonder she often looked like she was faraway. She was keeping so much inside."

"Now, who's that like?"

"I'm like my mother." The thought both disturbed and pleased me. I heard a white roaring in my head as I took in Dette's words.

"So, Eddie wasn't my father?" The words came out in slow motion.

"He was your father in all the ways that count." This was a gift Dette hadn't needed to offer me and I gathered it in my arms.

"It's really, really hard to believe all this."

"I get that," Dette said, a bitter note in her voice now. "I know how much a secret can hurt. Especially when it's kept by someone you never expected. Someone you loved." Odile put her hand on Dette's arm and a bolt of pure envy shot through me.

I said, "I'm not sure why you waited so long to tell me this. Remember when I asked you that moonlit night on your patio?"

"Yes. But it was so loaded. And I saw how tired you were – and finding the right words – it was too hard." The reflection of the water turned her eyes a muddy shade of green, though I could see there were tears in them.

Hadn't I lacked the courage to tell her about my agreement with Odile? I said at last, "I need time to take this in."

"It is a lot to absorb," Odile offered, reaching across the table to touch my arm.

"I don't know how long you two will be in Maine," I said quietly. "So, I want to say this." I looked straight at Dette, my firefly friend, my mud-pie friend, my artist-woman friend. *She's been my friend for a thousand years.* "I did keep a secret and that was wrong of me. But I dove into that river in France to try and save Odile."

"She knows that. I told her," Odile said glancing between her mother and me.

"She could have died, Miriam!" I wasn't surprised to see tears well again in Dette's eyes.

"I know that. But I jumped into a waterfall to save her!" Dette's fingers gripped Odile's. "And do you know why?"

"No." Her voice was small.

"Because I love your daughter. I know she's your daughter, not mine. I know that. But the truth is," I wiped my own eyes quickly, "I've always been part of her family." No protest from either of them, which sent a surge of relief through me. I went on, "You know, while I was following the path of the Black Madonna in France, I learned something fundamental: the sacred mother blesses creation in all its formulations. She tends to it in all its myriad forms. She cares for her family wherever she finds them, however she finds them. If they mess up, she doesn't let go of them."

Odile's eyes were shining and she nodded.

"Dette," I paused. "You're my sister in all the ways that count." Dette was staring at her plate as if the secret of all mysteries was written there. "And I will keep trying for as long as I live to crawl back to you if that's what I have to do to get you to trust me again. I will. Because you and Odile are my family." I stopped. I would fight for our friendship. I would wait as long as it took. I batted away a fly, dismayed that Dette made no reply. The only sound was the rushing of the river.

I saw Dette look up and Odile's eyes widen. Dette said, "Crawling seems over the top." Odile snickered and rested her head on her mother's shoulder. A corner of Dette's mouth lifted.

My tense body rested back against the chair. "All right, then," I said. "Maybe we should leave it there for today and meet again in a day or two."

"Well, we're here," Dette said. "We may as well eat." She picked up her menu.

"Alright, then," I agreed. I knew Her sustenance was already with us.

ACKNOWLEDGMENTS

To Jean L. and Jeanne C. who joined hands and led me to the Black Madonna.

To Max Regan (hollowdeckpress.com), amazing writer, teacher, and editor for his effervescent support, keen eye, and deep insight as he reviewed the final version of the book.

To Mark Gelotte (markgelotte.com), who designed the beautiful cover and the inside pages, for his talent, patience, and ability to stay mellow throughout the process.

To Lynn Schwartz and Laura Oliver, teachers at the Writer's Center, who were astute content development editors as they individually reviewed early versions of the book.

To Jennifer Fisher, a serious line editor.

To my first writing group in Concord, MA, led by Pamela C. Wight – thanks for the sunshine and support as we shared each other's writing.

To my writing group from the Bethesda Writer's Center – Andrew Hamilton, Kathryn Masterson, Nicole Pascua and Vinod Jain – thanks for the happy café times where we shared our writing and you cheered me on as you read the earliest drafts of this novel.

To the Firedrake Writers – being within your circle feels like the moon and the stars shining on me. I'm sending light back to each one of you – talented artists, all.

To Tina Rosenberg of the Maine Writers and Publishers Alliance – your writing talent and joy are ever-inspiring.

To the 30 college students who went with me to 4, Rue de Chevreuse, Paris on our year's adventure – I am deeply grateful for our continuing friendship.

To my nursing colleagues – you are my real-life heroines.

To my friends – you know who you are – you brighten my life with wisdom and laughter.

To Mary Lyons and James Boyle, deeply missed, who taught me

that the essence of love endures.

To Carol, Elaine, Jim and Cliff – we walked together early on and I am ever grateful for you.

To Gil Brown, here it is, finally; I see you applauding from beyond. To Adrian Brown Kuzel, thank you for sharing the importance of the written word just as your mother did.

To Gerry Brown, my love, for your unending patience, love of cooking, zany good humor, and brilliance (at more than choosing me).

To our amazing children, Natalia Brown Baum and Evan Boyle Brown, and their talented spouses, Lawrence Baum and Stephanie Latocha Brown – you make every day shine.

To our littles – Eliana, Alexis, Susannah, and the one(s) to come – ever grateful for the miracles of you.

Deborah E. Boyle is a nurse practitioner and a writer of fiction, poetry and memoir. She is a member of the Bethesda, Maryland Writers Center, the Maine Writers and Publishers Association and the East Coast Hollow-deck Press Writers. This is her first novel. She is working on her second novel, *Aubrey's Light*, and her third book, *Maine Inside Me*, a memoir about her Maine parents – one who served in an important U. S. military post following W.W. II and the other who landed in federal prison after fiercely defending her beliefs. When Boyle is not visiting her amazing children in New York, she lives with her husband in Maryland and Maine. For more information go to DeborahEBoyle.com and follow Deborah on:

Made in the USA
Coppell, TX
12 October 2020

39726630R00142